FORBIDDEN MILES

THE MILES FAMILY BOOK TWO

CLAIRE KINGSLEY

Always Have LLC

Published by Always Have LLC

Edited by Elayne Morgan of Serenity Editing Services

Cover by Lori Jackson

ISBN: 9781710080353

www.clairekingsleybooks.com

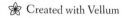 Created with Vellum

For all my readers who were shipping these two from the beginning.

ABOUT THIS BOOK

"You're not supposed to fall for your brother's best friend."

Brynn Miles thought moving back to her family's winery was a good idea. But when you're the baby of the family, life can get complicated. Dating? Forget about it. Not with her three older brothers acting like human chastity belts.

To Chase Reilly, his best friend's little sister has always been invisible. She's so forbidden, he doesn't let himself see her. Besides, she's totally girlfriend material, and he doesn't do the relationship thing.

Until the night Chase sees her. Really, truly sees her. And nothing will ever be the same.

Looking for love isn't Brynn's focus, and Chase is the one guy in the world she can't fall for. He's T-R-O-U-B-L-E. Untouchable. And just as forbidden as she is.

But once Chase set his sights on Brynn, there isn't anything—or anyone—who'll stop him.

Author's note: A childhood crush. An irresistible attraction. The cutest scavenger hunt ever. And a surprisingly sweet hero who puts it all on the line when he falls head over heels for the one girl he can't have.

ONE

CHASE

I WAS SO SCREWED.

Shelly was all the way across the parking lot, but any second she'd look up and see me. I pulled my baseball cap down—like that was going to matter. She knew what my truck looked like.

The heat blasted against my legs and I had the window rolled down to let in the cool October air. It was late afternoon, but the temperature had already dropped. Fall was like that in Echo Creek, the town I lived in on the east side of the Cascade Mountains. The change of seasons stole its way into the air, turning hot summer days into cold fall nights without warning.

My stomach growled, and I checked my rear-view mirror again. How long could a girl stand outside her car before she finally got in? Wasn't she cold? I'd worked through lunch and I was fucking hungry. If this went on much longer, I'd have to suck it up and walk by her.

I wished I didn't feel the need to hide from her like a dumbass. But I'd screwed this up pretty badly and I was determined to stay out of Shelly's web of crazy.

Was I an asshole for calling her crazy? No, I assure you, I was not.

The cab of my truck was getting too hot, so I turned down the heat. Another car pulled into a spot and a couple of guys got out. Went inside Ray's Diner. Lucky bastards. Shelly was still standing outside her car, and even though she was busy texting, I wasn't fooled. She had a Chase-radar that would zero in on me the second I tried to walk by. It had been a long fucking day and the last thing I wanted was to deal with a Shelly episode. I just wanted some dinner.

I'd had a thing with Shelly earlier this year. She'd seemed like a nice enough girl. Pretty. Blond hair, blue eyes. We'd hooked up a few times, but I'd broken things off pretty quickly. I usually did. Relationships were complicated, and I liked my life the way it was. Simple.

I made a good living as a heavy machinery mechanic. Lived with my best friend, Cooper. Coop was never going to settle down, and I probably wouldn't either. We worked hard, played hard. It was a good fucking life and I had no interest in changing anything.

Shelly? She'd wanted to change everything.

It was my fault for breaking the rules. Shelly had started texting me again after I'd broken up with her, and Coop had warned me. Crazy girls are fun sometimes, but you don't date them. Ever. It's rule number one.

And Shelly had turned out to be the queen of crazy.

What had started with a few texts had quickly become me dating her. It had felt like whiplash; I wasn't even sure how it had happened. One day I was answering her text, and next thing I knew, she was asking me to clear space in my closet for her shit.

She'd wanted me to text her before I left for work in the morning and call her on my way home at night. If I didn't let her know where I was and what I was doing, she'd flip out. I'd gone out for a few beers with Cooper one night and she'd accused me of cheating on her. The next day, she'd started talking about me meeting her parents, like she hadn't gone all psycho on me the night before.

And meet her fucking parents? Hell no.

My tolerance for her kind of drama was very low, so I'd put an end to it. And she hadn't taken it well. The angry phone calls and texts were one thing—not entirely unexpected. But I'd caught her driving by my apartment twice, and she'd tried to corner me at work. That was getting into psycho stalker territory. I wasn't much for confrontation, but I'd had to tell her, in no uncertain terms, that she needed to back off.

So far, she had. It had been a few weeks since I'd heard from her. But the last thing I needed was to run into her in a parking lot and have her try to suck me into her vortex of insanity again.

So here I sat, my empty stomach gnawing at me, watching her in my rear-view mirror, hoping to god she was going to get in her car and leave.

This was why I kept things simple. Casual. No strings.

Finally, she put her phone away and got in her car. My stomach rumbled again, as if to express its displeasure over the delay. I waited until her car disappeared from sight, then went into Ray's.

Ray's Diner had been here for as long as I could remember. And Jo, the fifties-something waitress, had probably worked here since it had opened. She had bleached hair with gray roots and a warm smile that deepened the wrinkles around her eyes. Cooper flirted with her, hardcore—of course, Cooper flirted with anyone who had a vagina—but she'd always felt like more of a mom-type to me.

"Hi there, cutie," Jo said with a smile when I walked in. "Just you, or is your twin joining you?"

Jo knew Cooper and I weren't related, let alone twins. But a lot of people assumed we were brothers. I had mixed feelings about that. On the one hand, we did look alike. We were both tall, kept in shape. Dark hair. Cooper had blue eyes, whereas mine were gray. But I could see why people thought there was a resemblance. The fact that we were together more often than not, and had been since we were five, added to the brothers thing.

"Nope, just me," I said.

On the other hand, how many times had I wished I really was Coop's brother? That I was a Miles? I felt like an idiot for admitting it, even to myself, but it was the truth. I'd grown up wishing I was one of them. Sometimes the *twins* remark was a gut-punch reminder that I wasn't.

Jo seated me at a booth near the door. I glanced at the menu, more out of habit than anything.

"You need a second, or do you want the usual?" Jo asked.

"The usual." I handed the menu back to her. My usual was a cranberry walnut salad with grilled chicken. Cooper loved to give me shit about what I ate, but I figured I needed to balance out all the beer. He could eat anything and stay toned, but he also never stopped moving. He probably burned a few thousand calories a day just fidgeting.

Jo brought me some water and I flipped through shit on my phone while I waited for my dinner. The diner was quiet. Just a few other tables were full. I had a view all the way to the back of the restaurant and I noticed a couple sitting in a booth tucked around near the restrooms. They were both on one side of the bench seat, snuggled up close. No food on their table—just drinks. But what caught my eye was the fact that they were totally making out back there.

Not that I was judging. Hell, I'd made out with girls in that back booth plenty of times. It was a good place for it. Hidden enough that you probably wouldn't get in trouble, as long as you quit when Jo or one of the other waitresses walked by. But out in the open enough to make it fun.

The guy was leaning over the girl, so I couldn't see much. Not that I was staring. But it was hard not to glance up a few times. That dude was definitely getting a blowjob later. Kinda wished I was getting a blowjob later, but I was still pretty gun-shy after Shelly. Wasn't up for jumping into something with a girl right now—no matter how casual I kept it.

Jo brought two plates to their table. I couldn't see the couple, but I assumed they'd quit the make-out session to get their dinner. My phone buzzed in my hand.

Cooper: Where u at?

Me: Ray's

Cooper: Done for the day?

Me: Yeah, u?

Cooper: Yep. Mom fed me. Leftovers?

Me: Always yes.

Cooper: Cool bro. See u at home.

Dinner at Ray's or not, I never said no to leftovers from Mrs. Miles. Cooper's mom was an amazing cook.

Jo brought my salad, but before I could start eating, the couple at the back table caught my eye again. They were no longer sucking face—they were eating—but now I *was* staring. My fork hung over my plate, dangling from limp fingers. I didn't know the guy, but the girl? That was Brynn Miles.

Brynn was Cooper's younger sister—the baby of the family. She was almost six years younger than me and Cooper; I'd known her since she was born. She'd recently turned twenty-one, and she'd been off at college for the last couple of years. In fact, I'd thought she was still going to college, so I had no idea what she was doing here.

Of course, I didn't pay much attention to Brynn, so for all I knew, she was moving back. Or here for the weekend. Except, what day was it? It was a Tuesday, so shouldn't she have been in class? Or going to class tomorrow? Who the fuck was that guy she was with?

And why the hell did I care?

Brynn wasn't just the baby. She was Cooper's baby. Weird as it sounded, it was how he saw it. She had three older brothers, but Cooper was the alpha-brother when it came to Brynn. He'd made it his personal mission in life to take care of her. If I thought about it—which I didn't— Brynn probably didn't appreciate Cooper's interference in her life as much as Coop thought she should.

But that was the thing, I didn't think about it. I didn't think about Brynn. She was around, I knew she existed. But it was like there'd always been this barrier around her that I couldn't see through. Brynn was so forbidden, I'd subconsciously ignored her.

When we were kids, she'd just been an annoying little girl. As she grew up, it was like she'd faded from my vision. Like she was translucent—insubstantial. I didn't let myself see her because deep down, I knew she was the one girl on the planet I could never, ever touch. I'd instinctively created a shield around her that I couldn't penetrate—couldn't see through. Even the temptation of her wasn't worth the risk.

But looking at her now, with some dude in the back of Ray's Diner, that shield shattered to pieces.

TWO

CHASE

BRYNN'S thick dark hair hung around her shoulders. She smiled at the asshole she was sitting with and tucked a strand behind her ear. Had her hair always looked so shiny and soft? Had that smile always been so sweet, her lips so full? She was twenty-one, she'd probably been hot for like five years now. How had I never noticed it before? Brynn was a fucking knockout.

What the hell was I thinking? This wasn't some sexy little thing I'd spotted across the room. I couldn't saunter over and feel her out, see what it would take to make her smile. Tease her, find reasons to touch her. Get her in my lap and put my hand on her thigh. Talk close to her ear.

I wondered what Brynn smelled like. I bet she smelled amazing.

Jesus, what was my problem? That was Cooper's Brynncess. I couldn't sit here and wonder what she smelled like. If Cooper knew I was thinking about how his sister smelled, he'd kick my ass.

I tried to focus on my food and quit thinking about Brynn. So what if she was in the make-out booth—that was definitely what I was calling it now—with some college prick. What a douche that guy was, with his patchy facial hair and knit hat. I rubbed my jaw, feeling the even stubble. If a dude couldn't grow proper facial hair, he should just freaking shave.

Who was he? Brynn's boyfriend? She'd been dating some guy at school last year, but he'd cheated on her. Cooper and their other brother, Leo, had put the guy's face on a bunch of STD awareness posters. Then Cooper and I had blanketed the campus with them. The poor sucker had been the face of herpes. I wondered if he'd transferred to a different school. That wasn't the kind of thing you could come back from.

But this wasn't the same guy. After hanging hundreds of posters with his picture, I'd remember his face. Was Brynn dating again?

I asked myself—again—what the hell I was thinking. It didn't matter why Brynn was here, or who she was with. It wasn't any of my business. I'd never paid attention to her before. Why start now?

But I hated seeing her cuddled up with that guy. Was it a protective thing? Maybe I was just channeling Cooper's vibe. He wasn't here, so I felt like I needed to defend her in his place. That made sense.

I glanced down at my plate. I'd eaten some of my salad, but it didn't taste like anything. And for reasons I didn't understand, I couldn't sit here anymore. Not when I might have to watch Brynn make out with that guy again. I dropped some cash on the table and walked out.

The drive home went by in a blur. I had a sick feeling in the pit of my stomach and what felt like a hole in my chest. What the hell was wrong with me? If Brynn wanted to date some douchecanoe college boy, who was I to give a shit?

And why the fuck was I imagining what her hair would feel like sliding through my fingers?

I really needed to get myself together.

Cooper was home when I got there. His work boots, caked with dirt, stood next to the door, and he'd taken off his jeans on the way to his room. They lay in a crumpled heap on the floor.

He came out of the bathroom with wet hair and a towel wrapped around his waist. "Hey, bro."

I blinked at him. I knew I should answer, but my brain was all kinds of fucked up.

Coop didn't seem to notice. He went into his room and shut the door. When he came out a few minutes later—half-dressed in a t-shirt, boxer briefs, and socks—I was still standing in the middle of the room.

"Dude, what happened to you?" Cooper asked. "You have a shit day at work? You broke something, didn't you? You were supposed to fix it and you made it worse?"

"No." Something about Cooper's comment snapped me out of my stupor. "I didn't break anything. Jesus."

"Did you call Shelly? Do I need to take your phone privileges away? Because I'm telling you right now, if you called Shelly, or texted her, or even thought about her today, I'm taking your phone forever."

I took my coat off and tossed it over a chair. "No, but I saw her outside Ray's."

"Oh, fuck. Tell me you didn't talk to her. Chase, buddy, we've been over this. You can't get caught in the web of crazy again. Every time you do, it's harder to get yourself out. You get all tangled up in her drama, it's going to be surgical level shit to get you out again."

Seeing Shelly wasn't why I felt like I could barely speak. It certainly wasn't her face burned into my mind. But

I was smart enough to see an out when one was handed to me. If Coop thought I was freaked out over seeing Shelly, he wouldn't suspect it had anything to do with Brynn.

"No, man, I didn't talk to her. I waited in my truck, but I was fucking panicking."

Cooper patted me on the shoulder. "Brutal, bro. Glad you got out of there in one piece."

"Yeah."

I didn't feel like I was in one piece. I felt like someone had hit me upside the head with a two-by-four.

Coop started talking again, but I went into the kitchen, only half listening. I'd hardly eaten anything at the restaurant, and I was still starving. I pulled out the leftovers he'd brought home from his mom.

Part of my brain listened to Cooper—just enough to make sure I didn't miss anything important. He talked a lot, but I was used to it. The trick was to listen for phrases that meant I needed to pay closer attention. Otherwise, I let it flow past me.

I started shoveling food onto a plate—chicken and vegetables with sauce that smelled spicy—but stopped dead when I heard him say *Brynn*. I whipped around to look at him. "What?"

Cooper blinked, his mouth half open, like he'd been about to say something else. "Brynn's moving home, so we need to go help with her shit when she gets here tomorrow."

"She's already here."

"How do you know?"

I shrugged and turned back to the counter. I was still all tangled up and I didn't want him to see my face. "She was at Ray's."

"You had dinner with my sister and you didn't tell me? That's low, Chase. I didn't even know she was in town yet.

Mom said she was coming tomorrow. What the hell? You should have texted me. I would have come down."

"I didn't have dinner with her."

"So you let her eat alone? Where's your manners? I thought I taught you better than that."

I shook my head, wishing we could stop talking about this. The more I thought about Brynn sitting in that back booth—her pretty smile, her shiny hair, her soft lips—the more confused I got. Especially because I couldn't stop thinking about the guy she was with. That stupid little prick with his stupid beard and stupid hat. I hated the fact that he'd been touching her. Kissing her. Fuck that guy.

"She wasn't alone." I closed the plastic container with the rest of the leftovers and stuck it in the fridge with more force than strictly necessary. "She was making out with some douchey college kid in the back booth."

Cooper stopped moving. It was always eerie when he did that. A still Cooper was never a good sign. "What?"

"Some guy was with her."

"Did you say *making out*?"

I shrugged again, not wanting to relive the awfulness that was seeing Brynn kiss another man.

"You're telling me some guy was making out with my Brynncess in the middle of Ray's Diner?"

"Not in the middle of the diner. They were in the back."

His blue eyes were focused, his body tense. When he spoke again, his tone was different. Flat. "Do you think they're still there?"

"How should I know? Maybe."

"Let's go." He grabbed his keys.

"Cooper, you're not wearing any pants."

He was already out the door. "I don't have time for pants."

Leaving my plate of food—damn it, I was still fucking hungry—I grabbed my coat and followed him outside. "Coop, what the fuck, man?"

He wasn't wearing shoes, either, but he didn't seem to care. He got into his truck, so I climbed in the passenger's side.

"Dude, you need to calm down," I said as he pulled out of the parking lot. "What are you going to do? Roll up into Ray's in your underwear?"

Coop didn't answer.

And that's when I realized what I'd done. I'd just ratted out Brynn for making out with a guy that was probably her boyfriend to the most overprotective brother in the universe.

This was not going to be pretty.

THREE
BRYNN

KIERAN PROPPED his arm along the back of the booth behind me while I picked at the last of my fries. Ray's Diner had the best food. There were lots of greasy spoon diners in Tilikum, the college town where I'd been living for the past two years. But I always missed Ray's. It was near my family's winery, and I'd grown up coming here. Kieran had never been, so I'd insisted we come after we'd dropped my stuff off at home.

I'd started my third year of college and decided to move back to Salishan. After my boyfriend cheated with my roommate last year, I'd moved to a studio apartment. Living alone wasn't bad, but it was expensive. And a little bit lonely. I'd grown up in a busy house with three older brothers, plus a bunch of winery employees who'd always been like family.

So I'd decided to move home. I could still go to school; Tilikum College was only about thirty minutes away. This way I'd save money on living expenses. With the financial mess the winery was in thanks to my asshole father, it would take some of the pressure off my mom.

Plus, I wanted to be closer to my family. Mom had kicked my dad out after discovering he was having an affair. As if that wasn't bad enough, that hadn't been the first time he'd cheated. He'd been hiding an entire family from us since before I was born. I had an older half-sister named Grace and a little half-brother named Elijah. I'd met Grace once, when she'd come looking for Dad after he'd gone deadbeat on them. Roland had been in touch with her—her mom had needed help with Elijah's medical bills. But we hadn't gotten together with Grace again, nor had we met Elijah.

I wasn't sure how to feel about the whole thing. It hadn't been very surprising to find out my dad had been cheating on Mom. Seemed pretty obvious... which was sad. But a secret family? Who the hell does that?

I popped another fry in my mouth and licked the salt off my fingers. Kieran pulled out his phone to text someone. He was what my sister-in-law Zoe would call a *fuck buddy*. We weren't really dating, and there was no expectation of commitment. It had been Zoe's idea, really. After Austin had cheated on me, she'd suggested a fling to get over my broken heart. I hadn't done it right away—the thing with Austin was months ago. But I'd met Kieran at a bar a few days after I'd turned twenty-one and had my first ever one-night stand.

Afterward, we'd exchanged numbers. We'd hooked up a few more times, and we had fun. He was hot, in a hipster kind of way. And he loved giving oral even more than he liked receiving—or having sex—which made him kind of a unicorn. I figured we could mess around a little until one of us wanted to move on.

I'd been with him a few nights ago, and mentioned I was moving home. He had a truck, so he'd offered to drive my stuff out to my family's property. I didn't have a lot, but it would save my brother Cooper the trouble of coming out with his truck.

I was buying dinner to thank Kieran for helping me move—and planning to thank him in other ways when we went back to the guest cottage my mom had offered to let me live in.

The front door flew open, sending a rush of cold air into the diner. I blinked a few times. Either I was seeing things, or Cooper was stalking down the aisle between the booths. In his underwear.

Nope, I wasn't seeing things. It was my nightmare come true.

Kieran was on the outside seat of the booth, still looking at his phone, oblivious to the insanity about to descend on our table. I heard Jo say something to Cooper—and was that Chase behind him?—but Cooper kept walking, his eyes fixed on Kieran. I had the weirdest sense of relief that super-powers weren't real, and Cooper didn't have laser vision or something. Kieran would already be dead.

I reached my arm across Kieran to block whatever Cooper was about to do. "Cooper, what are you doing?"

He stopped next to our booth and kept his hard stare fixed on Kieran. "Stay out of it, Brynncess."

God, I hated it when he called me that. It had been cute when I was little, but he still treated me like I was ten. "Stay out of what? Where are your pants?"

"Who the fuck are you?" Cooper asked, effectively ignoring me.

Kieran looked up, his brow furrowed with confusion. "Um, I'm Kieran."

"Outside," Cooper said.

"Cooper, stop." I kept my arm straight across Kieran's

chest.

My arm was as useless as my protests. Cooper grabbed Kieran by the shirt collar and hauled him out of the booth.

"Whoa, what the fuck." Kieran tried to get free of Cooper's grip, but my brother was unnaturally strong.

"Cooper," I whisper-yelled, trying not to cause a scene. Or trying not to make the scene Cooper was causing worse.

Cooper paid no attention to me. Just forced Kieran to walk in front of him down the aisle of booths toward the door. Chase cast a glance my direction—why did he look so guilty?—and quickly followed Cooper.

There was nothing else for me to do but go outside. I didn't want to make this worse in front of the other patrons. But as soon as I was in the parking lot, I was going to lose my shit. I took my purse off the seat and rushed outside after my psycho brother and his dumbass roommate.

"I'll be back in a second to pay," I said over my shoulder to Jo.

Cooper had Kieran backed up against his truck. Chase stood off to the side. Something about his expression struck me as odd, but I didn't have time to contemplate what was going on with him.

"This is what you need to know." Cooper got right in Kieran's face. "Brynn Miles is precious and no jack-monkey like you is going to defile her in public."

"Defile me? Cooper, what the hell?"

He ignored me. "Have some fucking respect. You don't make out with a girl like her in a goddamn diner."

Kieran held up his hands. "Hey, man, I don't even know who you are."

"I'm her brother," Cooper said. "And a skinny prick like you doesn't deserve someone even half as special as my sister. You think you can treat her like that? Fuck no."

"He treats me fine," I said, although I knew it was useless.

Kieran looked past Cooper at me. "Sorry, Brynn. I'm out."

Cooper stepped back and crossed his arms. If I weren't so angry, I probably would have been able to see the humor in the situation. My ridiculous brother standing in a parking lot in a t-shirt and underwear—he wasn't even wearing shoes—staring down the guy he apparently thought was defiling his little sister.

But I *was* angry, and I did *not* see the humor.

Kieran slipped away and practically jogged over to his truck. Without looking back at me, he got in and peeled out of the parking lot.

My heart raced, and my cheeks felt hot. I was going to kill him. Kill him dead.

"What the fuck was that?" I asked, enunciating each word slowly.

Cooper turned, and his mouth hooked in a grin. "Hey, Brynncess."

If I could have shot fire out of my eyes—or better yet, out of my fingers so I could burn my brother to ash—I would have. "*Hey?* That's what you're going to say to me after running off my... my..." What the hell was I supposed to call him? "After running Kieran off?"

"I was protecting you from that dickhead." Cooper crossed his arms. "You're not very appreciative, Brynncess. I came all the way down here to make sure your virtue remained intact."

"In your underwear," Chase said.

"Exactly." Cooper nodded to him.

"My virtue? What the hell does that even mean? Kieran helped me move."

Cooper's confident smirk faded, and he glanced between me and Chase a few times. "Wait. You mean you weren't making out with him in there?"

"What does that have to do with anything?"

"Chase said he saw that asshole defiling you in Ray's Diner," Cooper said.

My eyes moved to Chase. He looked like he wanted to disappear. "*You* told him?"

"I just mentioned that you were here," Chase said.

"No, you distinctly said some guy was making out with her in Ray's Diner," Cooper said.

"Oh my god. Cooper, you can't do that," I said. "You can't pick a guy up by his shirt and drag him outside and lecture him about my virtue. My virtue was gone freshman year of college, buddy. And you just screwed me out of an orgasm tonight. Maybe two. I hope you're happy."

Why did Chase suddenly look like he wanted to kill someone? And Cooper? God, you'd think I'd just told him I was a serial killer.

"Brynncess, don't talk like that," Cooper said. "You're too young."

"What?" I was practically shrieking, but I didn't care. "Too young? Cooper, I'm twenty-one years old, and probably more mature than you and your jackass sidekick put together. How can you stand there—in your underwear, I might add—and judge me? How many girls have you slept with? Don't give me that sexist bullshit about it being different for guys. That's a load of crap. You can fuck anything with a vagina and people think you're awesome. I have a fling with a guy who likes to go down on me and you have to step in with some hypocritical moral code? Kiss my ass."

I turned around and stalked toward the street. Salishan

was a long walk, but my car wasn't here. I still owed Jo for dinner, but I'd call her after I got home and give her my debit card number. I had to get out of here or I was going to wind up saying something I'd regret.

"Brynncess, don't," Cooper said. "I was just trying to help. At least let me take you home."

"Nope. You've done enough helping for one day."

"Brynn, wait."

I paused, because that wasn't Cooper's voice; it was Chase. I whipped around, glaring at him. "What?"

"I'm sorry, I didn't mean..."

I stared at him for a few seconds. It felt weird to make sustained eye contact. Usually it felt like Chase looked right through me—like I didn't exist.

"Go home, Chase."

There was no reason for Chase to look so stricken, so I must have been imagining it. I turned back around and started up the road. These shoes were terrible for walking, but barefoot would be worse. I'd just have to deal with the blisters. Maybe I'd make Cooper go to the store for bandages. It was the least he could do after the shit he just pulled.

I was well down the road before I looked back. I could see the big red Ray's Diner sign casting a warm glow over the street, but no Cooper or Chase. Knowing Cooper, I wouldn't have been surprised to see him following behind me in his truck at two miles an hour. Maybe he'd circle and pass me a few times until I gave in and let him drive me home. The raw spot already forming on the back of my foot made that a tempting possibility.

God, my brother. He was insane. He always had been. I figured he'd gotten the majority of the fun-genes out of the Miles boys, leaving Roland and Leo without their share. But fun as Cooper was—and he really was a blast—his protective thing was killing me. It had only gotten worse since Dad had left. I guess it made sense. Cooper had always watched out for me and now he seemed to think he needed to be my father.

I wished he'd let me be a grown-up. Although none of my family did. Yes, I was still young. But I was putting myself through school with only a little bit of help from my mom. I was on track to finish my business degree early. While Cooper was out drinking and banging random chicks, I was home studying. I'd worked for everything I had, took care of myself, helped my mom. I didn't act like a child, so I didn't understand why they still treated me like one.

Okay, walking home in very cute, but very uncomfortable, heels was not my most mature moment. But Cooper made me crazy.

"Hey, sweets." A black sedan slowed to a stop on the empty street. Zoe, my oldest brother Roland's wife, leaned out her window. "Need a ride?"

"Oh, thank god." I adjusted my purse and hurried around to the passenger's side.

"A little far from home for a walk," Zoe said. "Cute shoes, though."

I set my purse in my lap and fastened my seatbelt as the car started moving again. "Thanks. I had a little Cooper incident. Were you just driving by?"

Zoe glanced at me. "Not exactly. I was in the car, but a certain goofball boy texted me a few minutes ago, so I detoured over here."

"I should have known Cooper wouldn't let me walk all the way home alone. God forbid I not have an escort."

"It wasn't Cooper," Zoe said.

I raised my eyebrows. "Chase?"

Zoe nodded.

"That's weird. Maybe Coop didn't have his phone on him."

She shrugged. "I don't know. But Chase texted that you were walking home from Ray's, and he was worried about you because your shoes looked like they'd give you blisters."

"Chase said that?"

"That he did."

I tilted my feet to look at my shoes. I hadn't worn them to move, of course. They'd been sticking out the top of one of my bags, and after Kieran and I had unloaded his truck, I'd changed into them. Felt like wearing something sassy. It was weird that Chase had noticed what I was wearing. Chase never noticed anything. Not about me, at least.

I'd known Chase my entire life. He'd been best friends with Cooper since before I was born. He was like another brother to me.

Except... he really wasn't. He'd never been very brotherly. He'd always ignored me. Chase wasn't a brother; he was just Cooper's best friend.

Granted, for most of my childhood and adolescence, I'd harbored a mountain-sized crush on him. It wasn't until I'd gone away to college that I got my head on straight. I'd been such a dumb little girl. Sure, Chase was finger-licking sexy, but who carries around an unrequited crush on her brother's best friend for years with zero encouragement from the guy?

This girl, apparently.

It would have been next to impossible for me to date in high school anyway, so it wasn't like I'd missed out on much. Every guy in town had been scared of my brothers—especially of Cooper. There hadn't been a bad boy bad enough to risk going after Brynn Miles. Not with my psycho brothers around.

So I'd daydreamed about Chase Reilly, imagining that one day he'd notice me. I'd written our names in little hearts in my journal. Pretended I was destined to be Brynn Reilly. I'd even practiced my signature with his last name, over and over. How embarrassing.

Thankfully, Chase had never found out. And I'd grown up enough in the last couple of years that I was so over it.

"Well, thanks for picking me up. Chase was right—these shoes were already killing me."

"No problem," Zoe said. "I was running to the store, so I'll drop you off and then go."

"Thanks."

By the time we got to Salishan, I had three texts from Cooper. The first was an apology and the second and third were to make sure I was home safe. I thought about waiting a few hours to reply—make him sweat a little. But he'd probably just come over and bang on my door until he could see I hadn't been hit by a car or kidnapped by an ax murderer.

I said goodbye to Zoe and went inside my cottage. I replied to Cooper's text to let him know I was home. He sent back a series of gifs—dancing kittens, a unicorn farting rainbows, a little girl hugging a teddy bear, a cat in a taco costume.

He made it really hard to stay mad at him.

But what was with Chase? Why the hell had he tattled on me to Cooper? He knew Cooper better than anyone. He had to have known Cooper would do something crazy if he found out I was with a guy.

The more I thought about it, the more I was angry at Chase, rather than Cooper. Chase needed to mind his own business.

FOUR
CHASE

COUNTRY MUSIC with a surprising amount of bass bumped through the speakers. Mountainside Tavern was busy tonight. I held my pool cue, the end resting on my shoe, while Cooper took his shot. He sank the three in the corner pocket and smiled.

"I rock at this."

"Yeah." I eyed the table, but I was having a hard time concentrating on our game.

"We should road trip and hustle at pool bars again," Cooper said. "We cleaned up that one time. Remember that? Fuck, I think we made a couple grand that weekend."

"Mm hmm." I walked around the other side to study the table from a different angle.

"Of course, there's always the danger of getting our asses kicked. But I think we learned some valuable lessons. College bars near private schools are better than dive bars with biker dudes. It seems like that would be common sense, but it took us a while to catch on. Go figure." He missed, then nodded to me to take my turn.

"Yeah, go figure." I lined up a shot and took it. Missed.

"Shit."

Cooper grabbed the cue out of my hand. "Okay, buddy. Enough of this crap. You're acting weird. You gotta talk to me, man. Get it off your chest. I know that's kind of a chick thing, but I'm telling you, there's a reason men die of heart attacks more than women. We bottle shit up." He put a hand on his chest. "We keep it all in here where it slowly kills us. Let it out. Tell me what's going on."

That was a hard no. There was no chance in hell I was going to open up to Cooper. First off, I didn't know what the fuck was wrong. It was like I'd suffered a head injury—one of those that permanently alters your state of mind. I couldn't even think about Brynn without getting all twisted up inside.

Second, this was Cooper, and Brynn was... Brynn. She was so off limits, I'd be facing the death penalty just for thinking about her. And the amount of time I'd spent thinking about her over the last few days was ridiculous.

Don't even get me started on the fantasizing. I'd whacked it to Brynn fantasies way more than was healthy. I just hoped the whole going blind thing really was an old wives' tale. Because if it wasn't, I could kiss my vision goodbye.

"There's nothing going on," I said. "Just a long week at work."

Cooper narrowed his eyes. He wasn't buying it. "Work? You never stress about work."

"How would you know if I stress about work? I leave it at the shop."

"Whatever is stressing you out, you're not leaving it anywhere. It's like you're walking around with your own personal raincloud. It's bumming me out, man."

I ran my fingers through my hair. "Nothing bums you

out."

"That is *not* true. Lots of things bum me out. I can name at least five right now." He started ticking them off on one hand. "Shitty things on the news, especially involving children or puppies. Hangovers. Anything that makes Zoe sad. Droughts. And you acting all broody. All those things bum me out."

"Yeah, well, I can't be responsible for your state of mind. If I'm bumming you out, go do something else."

"See? This is what I'm talking about. You're holding it all in and it's going to eat at you until you get it out. Should I call Zoe? Do you need a woman's perspective?"

I paused for second because that was actually tempting. Zoe might help me sort this out, and she was less likely to freak out on me. But if she let it slip that I was having dirty thoughts about Baby Brynn Miles—even if it was an accident—I'd be screwed. Roland would tell Cooper, and once Cooper knew, I'd be dead.

"No, I don't need a woman's perspective. You know what I need? For you to shut the hell up and leave me alone about it."

"Fine, Jesus. I'm just trying to help, asshole."

Good, he was calling me asshole. That meant he was about to get pouty, and pouty Cooper would probably stop talking for five or ten minutes.

"I'm getting another beer. Want one?"

He tipped his beer bottle and looked at the contents—or lack thereof. "Yeah."

I went to the bar and ordered two more beers. Cooper stayed at the pool table and took a shot. He must have missed because he grabbed my cue and played my turn.

When I came back, two ice cold beers in hand, Cooper was wearing an enormous shit-eating grin.

I handed him his beer. "What?"

"I'm such an idiot. I know exactly what's wrong with you. I can't believe I didn't realize it earlier. It's so obvious. And so simple to fix."

I leaned against the pool table and took a drink, waiting for him to drop his revelation on me.

"You need to get laid."

I almost spit my beer all over him. I made a quick recovery, but it left me coughing.

"Good thing we came out tonight," Cooper continued. "This place is crawling with hot girls. I've seen six in the last ten minutes who need some Cooper in their life. Who do you have your eye on? Let's get this show on the road."

Shit. Picking up girls was standard procedure for me and Coop. Usually it was great. We had a system, and as long as we stuck to our rules, things worked beautifully. Ordinarily, he'd have been right. Sex was a great way to get rid of a bad mood.

I scanned the bar, picking out the single girls. It was easy. Girls getting fucked on the regular had an air about them—made them look closed off. Coop and I could practically smell the other dude on them. Single girls gave off a vibe that they were available. And he was right, there were a ton of them in here tonight.

But the thought of bringing one of these random girls home with me made my stomach turn. This had never happened to me before. I didn't understand what the fuck was wrong. Girl in the red top and tight jeans over there? Completely fuckable, and I'd bet any amount of money that she was single and looking to hook up. I could tell Coop she was the one, and chances were good I'd be fucking her before the night was over.

"Having trouble?" Cooper asked. "I know, I've got three

I like and I can't decide. Things are so much harder now that I have to put them through the dad test."

That made me chuckle. Ever since Cooper found out his dad had been hiding a second family—including a half-sister he'd hit on before he found out who she was— he'd been crazy paranoid that he'd accidentally fuck a girl who was related to him. Now he asked every girl he met if she knew her father, and what his name was. The weird thing was, it was an awesome ice-breaker. Of course, Cooper could probably win a girl over with anything.

I took another swig of beer. "I don't know if I'm feeling it tonight."

"Are you kidding me? I'm not buying it, buddy. I bet you're into..." He rubbed his chin while he scanned the bar. "Her. Blond hair. Red top. Ass-hugging jeans."

She was hot, no doubt about it. Pretty hair. A little curvy. Nice tits. So why was the thought of getting her naked making me want to vomit?

Maybe I'd contracted some sort of disease. I wondered if I should Google my symptoms. Although it would probably tell me I had three months to live. Could you die from a sudden aversion to meaningless sex?

What was wrong with me? I loved sex. And I was fucking awesome at it. I wasn't necessarily boyfriend mater-ial, but I took my sexual exploits seriously. Women never left my bed unsatisfied. It wasn't my fault if I ruined them for other men. Everyone had talents. Multiple orgasms happened to be one of mine.

It was the mechanic in me. Once I understood how something worked, I was a genius at getting it to do what I wanted. And I understood how the female body worked very well.

But for reasons I did not understand, I knew I wasn't

bringing Hot Red Top home with me. No fucking way.

"Nah. She's hot or whatever, but I don't think so."

"I like where you're going with this," Cooper said, poking me in the arm. "The disinterested thing works like fucking magic. Let's do good cop, bad cop, except I'll be eager fun guy, and you be disinterested aloof man. Hot Red Top has a friend who definitely needs me. I bet we can lock this shit down in half an hour."

"Jesus, Cooper, I said I wasn't into her."

I took my beer over to an empty table and slid onto a stool. I knew I was acting weird, but I couldn't help it. I was so fucking confused. Hot Red Top was perfect. What else did I want?

I wanted Brynn.

Fuck. No. I had to quit thinking like that. God, what the hell? I'd seen Brynn kissing a guy and suddenly I wanted her? What kind of asshole did that make me? I was acting like a damn toddler, throwing a temper tantrum over a toy. Just because some other kid had it didn't mean I needed it.

Was that all it was? Some weird jealousy thing? If that was the case, maybe Cooper was right. Maybe I just needed a good fuck. Thanks to crazy Shelly, it had been a while.

"You know chicks totally dig the angry asshole." Cooper slid onto the other stool. "I don't think you're doing this on purpose, and clearly you aren't going to tell me what's wrong. I'm just saying that in the last ninety seconds, since you stomped your way over here and sat down, you've attracted the interested attention of half the girls in here. I can definitely work with this, if this is what we're doing tonight."

I gave him a non-committal grunt and took another drink. The beer buzz was starting to help—relaxing me at least.

"But go take a piss already," Cooper said. "You're driving me nuts with your fidgeting."

It wasn't until I stopped moving that I realized I'd been shaking my leg. "*My* fidgeting is bothering you? You realize what a hypocrite you are, right?"

He shrugged. "I am who I am, buddy. You're the one being a fucking lunatic tonight. Go take a piss."

I was about to argue, but I did have to pee. And maybe a few minutes in the bathroom would help clear my head a little. I left my beer and headed for the restrooms in the back.

The men's room was empty. I did my thing and washed up. Felt better, physically at least. I looked in the mirror and ran my hand through my hair. Took a deep breath.

Get your act together, Chase.

I wondered what Brynn was doing tonight. Was she out in Tilikum at the college bars? I didn't know what she usually did on a Friday night. I doubted she'd be with the guy from the diner. Cooper had scared him off pretty good. That whole scene would have been hilarious, if not for the fact that Brynn had been so mad. The way she'd looked at me... fuck, I'd been gutted. I'd hated myself—hated that I'd done that to her. Hated that her anger had been directed at me. I didn't want Brynn to be mad at me. I wanted her to like me.

Which was, once again, stupid and ridiculous. But there was something going on inside me that didn't give two shits about whether it made any sense. It wasn't toddler jealousy over another guy's toy that was making me feel this way. I wasn't sure what it was, but it was deeper than that. Not once in my life had I been jealous over a girl. There were always more—always someone else if one was taken.

There was only one Brynn.

Something had awoken inside of me. Something primal. I couldn't name it, let alone explain it. But it was there. Maybe if I saw her again, it would help me figure it out. I could see if I reacted to her the same way. It could be some weird head trip and she wouldn't do anything for me. She'd be back to the little girl I'd always ignored, and I could go on with my life like nothing had happened.

Or maybe this was irreversible.

Either way, I needed to see her, at least to apologize for the other night. Cooper swore she was fine, but it wasn't like I'd talked to her. She was probably still mad at me. I needed to find a way to make it up to her, without doing anything that would make Cooper suspicious.

I'd do something nice for her, like change the oil in her car. Who knew when she'd had it serviced last, and I could do that with my eyes closed. Just a little favor to show her I was sorry—and an excuse to get close to her again.

Having a plan made me feel better. Chances were, I'd see Brynn and wonder why I'd gone all loco over her.

I walked out of the restroom and stopped dead in my tracks. Cooper was sitting with Hot Red Top and her friend, and the sick feeling in my gut was back with a vengeance.

Fuck. How was I going to get out of this?

Because until I figured out what was wrong with me— and whether this infatuation with Brynn was just me being temporarily insane—I couldn't bring home some random. It just wasn't going to happen.

I ignored the pseudo-coy looks the girls gave me as I walked up to the table. "Sorry, Coop, I'm gonna head home. Headache."

Cooper's mouth dropped open and his eyes widened.

You'd have thought I'd just told him my dick fell off. "You're going home because of a *headache*?"

"Yeah." I pulled my keys out of my pocket.

"Dude, you know the best cure for a headache is sex, right?" He turned to the girls. "Forgive my impertinence, ladies."

Hot Red Top glanced at her friend. "I don't think I know what that means."

Cooper gave her a crooked grin. "Impertinence means boldness coupled with a lack of manners, in this case accompanied by an assumption of something that has yet to be established."

"He means that he said *sex* and we all just met," Hot Red Top's friend said. She leaned closer to Cooper.

"See, she gets it," Cooper said, smiling at her.

Yep, he was getting laid tonight.

"Yeah, that's not... My head hurts, I'm just going to go."

I turned before Cooper could change my mind. He was unnaturally good at getting his way. If I didn't bail now, I'd end up hurting Hot Red Top's feelings. I wasn't taking her home with me, and there was no doubt those girls were looking for just that. I'd done this enough; I could tell. My reasons had nothing to do with her, but girls always thought it was about them. This way she'd assume I was sick or something, not that I was abandoning the hook-up mission before I'd closed the deal because I'd changed my mind about her.

Cooper called my name a few times as I walked away, but I pretended I couldn't hear him over the music. I had to get out of here before I really screwed up and let slip what was on my mind.

That was the one thing I couldn't do. Cooper could *not* know.

FIVE

BRYNN

THE BLACKBERRY COTTAGE was a mess of boxes and bags. I'd been trying to organize, but there wasn't anywhere to put things. The kitchenette was already fully stocked, so my kitchen stuff wasn't needed. Neither was the bean bag chair I'd been using for a couch. My bed was newer than the one that had been here, so my mom had arranged for the old one to be taken out before I'd moved in. But there were still things I either needed to get rid of or put into storage so I could actually function in here.

Once I got settled, it would be perfect. It was next to the Hummingbird Cottage, which no one was using at the moment. My mom's house was a short walk across the property—far enough that I felt like I had a bit of space, but close enough I could pop in whenever I wanted. The blackberry-themed decor was a little dated, but I loved the charm. It reminded me of my grandma.

Other than Cooper's obnoxious interference with Kieran the other night, I hadn't seen much of my family. I'd been busy commuting back and forth to school for classes every day. I'd be working in the tasting room here on weekends and going to school during the week. It would be busy, but I was used to it. I'd been working part-time at a café near campus before I'd moved home, so the biggest change was the hour or so of driving I had to do every day to get to and from classes. It cut into my study time, but I'd make do. It wasn't like I had anything else going on.

Kieran hadn't replied to my calls or texts. I'd tried to apologize, but I didn't really blame him for ignoring me. I probably wouldn't put up with my family if I was a guy—especially not for a short-term fling—so I didn't expect him to. The fact that I wasn't too disappointed was telling. It probably meant it was best that whatever had been going on between us had run its course.

Although I was still mad at Cooper and Chase.

I wasn't starting work until next weekend, so I wanted to take advantage of the day and get some things put away. Plus I needed more food if I was going to quit relying on my mom's fridge for sustenance. I knew she didn't mind, but I wasn't here to mooch off her.

But that was going to have to start tomorrow, since I didn't have anything here.

I walked the short distance to my mom's house. It was a huge, beautiful home, built by my grandparents. They'd meant for it to be a bed and breakfast, so it had seven bedrooms. The kitchen was enormous, it had a big fireplace, and it looked incredible decked out in Christmas lights.

My parents had raised us here. We'd lived here with my grandparents until they'd both passed away. Then it was just us. Mostly Mom and us kids, really. My dad had always been gone a lot.

It was strange, but I'd barely noticed Dad's absence since Mom had kicked him out. You'd think my father having totally disappeared from my life would hurt more. I guess that was the upside to growing up with an absentee father. I'd never been close to him. I was angry for what he'd done to my mom, but it wouldn't be the end of the world if I never saw him again.

I paused on the front porch, feeling a twinge of guilt. Maybe it was wrong for me to be so apathetic about him. But he'd never given me a lot of reasons to care. Between my brothers and Ben, Salishan's groundskeeper, I'd had plenty of positive men in my life. Mostly I felt sorry for my dad. He'd had this great family and he'd thrown it away.

The hum of conversation greeted me as I walked in. Apparently I wasn't the only one who'd descended on Mom's place for Saturday breakfast.

Roland and Zoe sat at the big farmhouse dining table. They both had coffee and were picking at a huge cinnamon roll. I was so glad Roland had gotten his head out of his ass and found a way to work things out with Zoe. With the two of them married again, living close by, Roland running the winery, and Zoe still working events, it felt like so many things were as they should be.

Leo sat across from them, his long hair obscuring part of his face. My heart always hurt when I looked at Leo. His scars weren't as bad as he seemed to think. They'd taken some getting used to, because he did look different, but the damage ran far deeper than the burns on his skin. *He* was different. He'd never been wild like Cooper, but Leo had been outgoing and fun. Now he was so reclusive. Sometimes even angry. I wished there was something I could do to help him, but I wasn't sure what he needed. I figured the best thing was to treat him the same—not make a big deal of his injuries—and maybe coax him out of hiding to spend more time with the family.

"Hi, sweetheart," Mom said. She stood at the kitchen

sink, rinsing a plate. Her dark hair had little streaks of silver that I liked to call her pixie dust, and she had it pulled back in a ponytail. "There's cinnamon rolls and scrambled eggs if you're hungry."

"Thanks, I'm starving."

The cinnamon rolls were the size of my head, so I cut a piece off and dished up some eggs. After pouring myself a cup of coffee, I sat at the table with everyone else.

"How was your first week back?" Zoe asked.

"It wasn't bad." I poured some cream into my coffee and stirred. "It'll be nice when I get more of my stuff put away. But at least my old apartment is all cleaned out."

Mom sat down at the table next to me just as Cooper burst in the front door.

"I knew it." He beelined for the cinnamon rolls and grabbed a whole one, not bothering with a plate. He peeled off a huge chunk and stuffed it in his mouth. "You assholes are lucky there are some left."

"Really, Cooper?" Mom said.

"Sorry," he said through a mouthful of food and winked at her. "Oh my god, these are so good. Mom, you have a talent. If you ever stop making wine, you could become a baker. But don't stop making wine because you're even better at that than you are at making cinnamon rolls. And I don't think I want to share your baking. It's bad enough I have to share with these guys."

Cooper walked over to the table, still shoving cinnamon roll into his mouth, but didn't sit down. He paced around the room as he ate.

"You're very chipper this morning," Roland said.

"I'm always chipper." Cooper finished the cinnamon roll and went straight for another one. "Brynncess, how's my baby sister? You aren't still mad at me, are you?"

"No, Cooper, you're fine."

"What happened?" Mom asked.

Oh god, Cooper, don't tell her. "Nothing. Just Cooper being Cooper. It's fine."

Cooper met my eyes and winked. At least he wasn't going to make a big deal out of it.

"Since we're all here..." Zoe fidgeted in her chair and smoothed down her hair. "We have some news."

The room went silent. Even Cooper stopped moving.

"Roland and I are having a baby."

Mom shrieked and stood, grabbing Zoe in a hug. Roland looked happier than I'd ever seen him. He beamed at Zoe, his eyes shining. Cooper got in on the hug, wrapping his arms around both Zoe and Mom. Even Leo cracked a smile.

"This is so exciting," Mom said, wiping a few tears from the corners of her eyes. "I'm so happy for you."

"Uncle Cooper," he said. "That sounds awesome. What do you think, Auntie Brynn?"

"I think it's the best news ever."

Zoe smiled. "Thanks, everyone. It's still really early, but we couldn't wait to tell you."

"When is the baby due?" Mom asked.

"July first," Zoe said. "So he or she will probably come sometime in late June or early July."

Mom launched into questions about Zoe's health, how she was feeling, and whether they'd started thinking about names.

I finished my eggs and picked at my cinnamon roll. Roland and Zoe having a baby was such amazing news. I knew they'd wanted kids, and their new house was perfect for a family. It was like things just kept clicking into place.

"Where's your laptop?" Leo asked me out of the blue.

His question caught me by surprise. "It's at home, why?"

"Bring it by later. I should take a look to make sure everything is up to date and you don't have any viruses."

I picked apart a piece of cinnamon roll. "Okay, but I don't have any viruses on my laptop."

He raised his eyebrows, like he didn't believe me.

Before I could answer—I was trying very hard not to let this irritate me—Roland turned to me.

"Brynn, we should go over your budget when you have a few minutes."

I blinked at him. "My budget? Why?"

"Just to make sure everything is on track," Roland said. "When is tuition due?"

"I already paid it."

"What about next semester?" He shifted in his seat. "Plus, books cost a fortune. And you need to factor in the increased gas cost from commuting."

I took a deep breath, telling myself Roland was only trying to help. I wasn't going to be a jerk and throw it in his face that not long ago he wouldn't have given a crap about me or my budget. This was my brother's way of caring.

"Yeah, I know about the gas. And books. I've got it under control, but thanks."

"You should take him up on that, Brynncess," Cooper said. He leaned against the table and licked frosting off his fingers. "Roland is really good at this stuff."

"I know. I appreciate the offer, but my budget is fine. My scholarships cover tuition this year, so that's not a problem. You have enough going on with a baby coming. You don't need to worry about me."

"Scholarships?" Roland asked. "Wow, I'm impressed."

I knew Roland meant that as a compliment, but it was

hard not to prickle at the surprise in his tone. I'd spent countless hours applying for scholarships since my senior year in high school. It had always been important to me to be as self-sufficient as possible. Was that so shocking?

"Thanks."

"Of course we're going to worry about you." Cooper pulled out the chair next to me and started eating off my plate. "We're your brothers. It's what we do."

"I'm good, really."

Mom paused her pregnancy interrogation. "Honey, I meant to ask, have you met with a student advisor lately?"

"Not recently," I said. "Why?"

"I just want to make sure you're on track to finish all your requirements for your degree," she said.

Deep breaths, Brynn. Deep breaths. "I don't actually need to because I have it all mapped out."

"Maybe you should make an appointment anyway," Mom said. "Just to be sure. You wouldn't want any last-minute surprises. That can mean the difference between graduating on time and having to go another semester."

"That's a good point," Roland said.

I shoved down the desire to snap at everyone. I didn't need to meet with an advisor because I knew more about the requirements for my degree than they did. I'd figured it all out, made sure I had my prerequisites done, and planned all my classes until graduation. I was double majoring in business administration and accounting, so I'd gone to school over the summer to get more of the requirements out of the way. I had a plan, down to the last class.

"Okay, well, I have a lot to do today, so I'm going to bounce." I went around the table and hugged Zoe from behind. "I'm so happy for you guys. This is the best news ever."

"Thanks, Brynn," Zoe said.

It was a good thing they let me out of there. Happy as I was for Roland and Zoe, I was ready to blow up at everyone —tell them to leave me alone and quit babying me. But throwing a tantrum would make me look like I was exactly what they thought—a child.

Did every girl with older brothers feel this way? I'd been home less than a week, and I was already starting to wonder if being this close to my family was such a good idea. Cooper had always been overprotective, but what was with Leo and Roland? And my mom jumping in on it?

Was it all about my dad? I wanted to tell them that I was fine without Dad around. But I didn't want to hurt Mom's feelings or dredge up stuff she was trying to move past. But seriously? I wasn't an idiot. I knew how to take care of myself. I'd been doing it for a long time. What did Roland and Leo think I'd done when they'd been away? I'd handled things. Being young didn't make me stupid.

When I got back to the cottage, I stopped. The hood of my car was up, and brown boots stuck out from underneath.

What the hell?

I tilted my head to try to see more, but all I could see was a pair of jeans. "Um, hello?"

The legs moved, rolling out from under my car, revealing a muscular body in a black t-shirt. Thick arms with defined biceps pushed him the rest of the way out, and a familiar face grinned up at me.

Chase had a smudge of grease on his cheek, mingling with the stubble on his jaw. He stood up and brushed his hands together. "Hey."

It was irritating that the sight of Chase made my heart beat faster. Not that I still had a crush on him—that was pointless—but he hadn't stopped being gorgeous. He still had that adorable grin and those sweet gray eyes. That body that made girls want to climb him like a tree.

But I couldn't dwell on that. Little girl Brynn would have. I was totally over it.

"What are you doing to my car?"

He took a rag off the edge of the car and wiped his hands. "Changing your oil, checking your spark plugs, that kind of thing."

"Um... why?"

He shrugged and put down the rag. "I kind of owe you after the other day. And I figured you could use a hand."

I stared at him. "But... how did you get the hood open?"

"I found your keys."

"My keys?"

"Well, yeah. I needed your keys to pop the hood."

I blinked at him a few times. "You went inside while I wasn't here and took my keys?"

His easygoing smile faded a little. "Yeah, they were right inside. And the door wasn't locked, so..."

I was so confused, I hardly knew how to respond. Since when did Chase do me favors? Had Cooper put him up to this? "But... why?"

"I didn't know how long it had been since you had any maintenance done," he said. "And since you're driving back and forth to school, I figured someone should make sure your car is in good shape."

"Someone should make sure?" My racing heart no longer had anything to do with Chase being stupidly sexy. My self-control was about to run out. "I know how cars work. They need oil changes."

"Yeah, and tune-ups. You have a lot of miles on this thing."

I took a deep breath. "Yes, I know it has a lot of miles. It's old, but it's what I could afford."

"Which is why it's especially important to keep up with regular maintenance."

I was about to lose it. I did *not* need another older-brother type stepping in to take care of me. Especially Chase. Clenching my hands into fists, I bit back the snotty remark on the tip of my tongue and stormed into the cottage.

And then Chase made the mistake of following me.

SIX

CHASE

BRYNN LOOKED MAD, which was the opposite of what I'd been trying to accomplish here. Why was she mad? Did I need to apologize again for ratting her out to Cooper? Because at this point, I'd get down on my knees and beg her not to look at me like that anymore.

Seeing her was not making me less insane, apparently.

In fact, seeing her standing there had only made the coal burning inside my chest flare hotter. Her hair was in a ponytail and she was wearing this cute little pink t-shirt and a pair of distressed jeans. God, she was gorgeous. Those curves. Those eyes. That mouth. Even glaring at me, she was adorable.

But I didn't want her to glare at me. So when she went inside, I followed. I just wanted to explain.

"Brynn, I was just trying to help." I shut her door behind me.

She whirled around, her hands on her hips. "Breaking and entering isn't helping."

"I didn't break in. The door was unlocked. And you

should be more careful about that, especially on weekends. There are a lot of guests wandering around the property."

Her cheeks flushed—damn, that was sexy—and the heat in her expression beat at me like the sun on a scorching summer day.

"Do I look like I'm stupid?"

"No, I—"

"Because I'm not. I grew up here, I know there are guests around. I wasn't gone very long, and I don't need you lecturing me about locking my doors. And I don't need you changing the oil on my car. I'm perfectly capable of doing things for myself."

"Yeah, I know."

"Then why did you assume my car needed an oil change or a tune-up? I'm an adult, Chase. I can take care of myself."

No shit, she was an adult. It was like she'd grown up when I wasn't looking. I wasn't sure what else to say, but she saved me the trouble. She kept talking, getting madder by the second. This was going off the rails so fast, I didn't know what to do. If she'd just shut her mouth for two seconds, maybe I could get a word in. Then again, as soon as I started talking, I'd say something stupid. Because I was an idiot like that, and I always said something stupid. Apparently it was my thing.

But I still needed to make her stop. This verbal assault was killing me.

"Brynn—"

"Don't *Brynn* me, Chase. I don't know what your problem is, but—"

Before she could finish, I grabbed her wrists, pushed her up against the wall, and covered her mouth with mine.

There, now she couldn't yell at me anymore.

Except, oh... oh shit. What had I done? This was bad—so very, very bad. I was kissing Brynn Miles. Saying something stupid would have been much better than this. What was I supposed to do now?

But instead of doing the smart thing and letting go—removing my lips from hers and releasing her wrists—I did the idiot thing. The Chase thing.

I kept kissing her.

She wasn't quite kissing me back, but she wasn't stopping me either—and she wasn't talking. So despite the fact that this was the single stupidest thing I'd ever done in my entire life, it seemed like a good change.

I could feel the pulse beating through the delicate skin of her wrists. Her body was rigid, but she didn't struggle. And her lips. Oh god, her lips were soft. I tilted my head and slanted my mouth over hers to capture more of those delicious lips.

This was shaky ground, but our tongues weren't involved. Without tongues, it was barely a kiss at all. I just needed to keep her quiet long enough that I could fucking think.

And then her body softened, her arms going slack. I loosened my grip on her wrists and lowered them. Let go. She stayed pressed against the wall, but her mouth moved, her lips exerting gentle pressure against mine.

Okay, now she was kissing me back.

I was going to stop—I really was—but her lips parted. My tongue swept out and brushed the tip of hers. It was instinct, I didn't even mean to. She gasped and shivered. It was like being hit with a shower of sparks. I'd never felt anything like it.

My fingers had found a little spot of skin at her waist, where her shirt didn't quite touch her jeans. When had that happened? I caressed her smooth skin while I sucked her lower lip into my mouth. She made a little noise, a half-gasp, half-whimper. It was the sexiest thing I'd ever heard in my life. I knew I was supposed to be thinking about something —I'd started kissing her for a reason—but I couldn't remember anything. I was too busy *feeling*.

Her silky mouth. Her warm skin. Her velvety tongue and how it brushed against mine. She tasted sweet. Not like I thought she'd taste. Better. So much better. I loved how she tasted, and I wanted to keep tasting her. Touching her. Kissing her. I did *not* want to stop.

At this point, I was already dead, so I figured I might as well enjoy my last moments on earth. Because when I finally pulled away from this kiss that was blowing my fucking mind, she was going to murder me. And if she didn't, Cooper would.

But even thoughts of my certain death at the hands of my—probably now former—best friend couldn't pull me away from the sweetness that was kissing Brynn Miles.

The sharp knock on the door, however, did.

We both gasped. I pulled away, jumping off her like she'd burned me. Her lips were red and swollen, her eyes glassy. For a second, we stared at each other. I waited for her to get angry. For her to smack me. I deserved it, and I'd have taken it gladly. I'd pay the price for that kiss.

But she didn't hit me. She didn't yell at me, either. She just looked at me like she wasn't sure who I was.

There was another knock and a thread of fear uncurled in the pit of my stomach. Oh shit. I was half-drunk from that kiss, but reality sobered me up quick. What if it was Cooper? Or Zoe? She'd know something was going on. So would Leo. That guy didn't miss a thing.

Brynn smoothed down her shirt and opened the door. It was Roland.

Probably the best option if it had to be another Miles, but Roland wasn't exactly good news either. Since he'd moved back, he'd taken up the mantle of protective big brother just like the others. And he had money for lawyers.

I needed to get out while I still could.

"Hey kiddo. You weren't answering your phone." Roland glanced over and noticed me. "Oh, hey Chase."

"So, do you want me to close the hood?" I asked, gesturing outside toward her car. Thank god my voice sounded mostly normal. "Your car should be good to go for a while."

"Sure. Thanks."

I nodded to them both and slipped past. When I got outside, I let out the breath I'd been holding. Holy shit, that was close. I closed the hood, making sure it latched, and glanced back. She was standing in her doorway, talking to Roland. Her eyes flicked to me for a second and I thought about waiting until Roland left.

But then he went inside, and she closed the door. I couldn't very well loiter outside her cottage. That would be suspicious. And I needed to process what had just happened. I hadn't come here intending to kiss her. I'd only wanted to see her, maybe figure out what was wrong with me.

Fuck. What the hell had I just done?

My shop was closed on weekends, but I went there anyway. I needed to think.

I worked out of an industrial building on the east edge of town. My shop was flanked by an auto body repair guy and general contractor. I worked in the field pretty often, since a lot of the machinery I worked on was too big to move

—like the bottling equipment at Salishan. But about half the time, I worked here.

I went inside and flipped the switch for the lights. They flickered and buzzed as they came on. The familiar smells of oil and rubber hung in the air. It was cold, but I wasn't going to bother with the heat.

My boots echoed on the concrete floor, the sound filling the cavernous space. I went back to the office and rifled through the papers on my desk. Nothing I wanted to deal with now. What I needed was to get my hands busy.

Back in the shop, I had an orchard tractor in for some repairs. It was a great piece of machinery—low emissions and quieter than standard tractors. There were a lot of pear orchards and vineyards in the area, so I worked on these all the time. I could fix them in my sleep, so I grabbed some tools and let my mind wander while I worked.

I'd kissed Brynn. Really kissed her. I could claim it had been an accident. That I hadn't meant to do it. Which was true. I hadn't. Cooper would still be pissed, but I knew how to calm him down.

But that would mean calling the kiss a mistake. I'd have to tell Brynn I hadn't meant anything by it. That it wouldn't happen again.

Seeing her had helped clear my head, but it hadn't gotten her out of it. She was there, and I knew now she wasn't going anywhere. Kissing her had only confirmed what I'd already known, deep down. I wanted her.

I wanted Brynn more than I'd ever wanted anything in my entire life. I didn't understand how it had happened, but now that it had, I couldn't deny it. Something inside her called to something deep inside of me. She'd awoken a need I hadn't realized existed.

Now that I was seeing her clearly, everything was

coming into focus. Brynn was smart, funny, and loyal. She was sweet, but still sassy. She always had been; I'd just never allowed myself to see it.

Most of the girls I'd hooked up with over the years had been in it for a good time, and not much else. Looking for the same thing I was. I'd always steered clear of girls like Brynn—the ones who'd actually make good girlfriends. Cooper did too. It was the real rule number one—and we both knew it—but it had always gone unspoken.

I didn't want to hook up with her. It wasn't about getting in her pants. Wanting her body would have been easy to shrug off. That was nothing. I loved women, and there were always more.

Brynn wasn't just *a* woman. She was *the* woman. And fuck, she was changing everything.

I tightened a bolt and wiped away some excess grease with a rag. If I did this, I'd have to do it for real. Take her out. Get to know her better. Date her and let things unfold. Granted, I didn't exactly know how. I'd never been a relationship guy, so this opened up a world of unknowns. But I had pretty good instincts when it came to women, and I could figure it out.

Cooper was another matter. He didn't want anyone to date his sister. He was going to be tricky. But if I could explain to him how I felt, and that I was serious about her, I was pretty sure he'd listen.

I put the wrench down. Ran my thumb over the cool metal of the tractor. It was like Brynn had flipped a switch. I'd had a taste of her, and there was no going back.

SEVEN

BRYNN

I WAS ready to burst by the time Roland left. He'd stopped by to tell me our half-sister Grace was coming over later, which added a whole new layer to the chaos in my brain. I nodded and gave short answers so he wouldn't catch on to the fact that I was about to lose my mind.

After he left, I leaned against the door and breathed out a long sigh, trying to calm my racing heart. Thankfully he hadn't asked any awkward questions about Chase.

Chase. Holy shit. What had just happened?

He'd pushed me up against the wall and kissed me. The shock of it was so acute, I could barely think. I touched my swollen lips, amazed Roland hadn't been able to tell. Shouldn't it have been written all over my face? Wouldn't anyone be able to take one look at me and *know*? I felt like I'd been marked. It had to show. But Roland hadn't said anything.

I pushed aside the curtain and looked out the window. The hood of my car was down, and Chase was gone. I wasn't sure whether to be disappointed, or relieved.

Mostly, I was confused.

Why had he done that? I'd been yelling at him for messing with my car. Damn it, that had been a pretty crappy thing to do. I'd been angry at my family, and he'd been the unfortunate recipient of my frustration. He'd been trying to do something nice for me.

But that kiss. God, that kiss. It still blazed across my sensitive skin—warmth and tenderness and surprise. I could feel the scratch of his jaw, the firmness of his lips. It had felt good. *Really* good.

I had no idea what to think. I'd daydreamed about Chase kissing me like that a thousand times when I was younger. Now that it had actually happened, it left me reeling.

Times like this, I missed my friend Carrie. Maybe not her specifically—she'd been sleeping with my boyfriend—but I missed having a best friend to turn to. I'd made friends at school, but no one I'd feel comfortable confiding in.

I had a hard time relating to the people I met at school. It seemed like half of them were only there because their parents expected it, not because it was what they wanted. And so many were living off their parents' money. They had no idea how lucky they were. I worked my ass off so I could be there. Working part time—because I needed money—and studying kept me busy, so I didn't go out partying a lot. I'd had some fun, but so often I felt like the only serious one in every group.

Although in some ways that had been a nice change. At least people at school took me seriously. Unlike my family.

I loved my family, but sometimes they were a lot to handle. And tonight I had to go meet my half-sister. I wasn't sure how to feel about Grace. I didn't have anything against her personally. It wasn't her fault our father was a cheating asshole. He'd screwed her over just as much as he'd screwed us.

But it also meant a change in our family dynamic. I didn't want to be a brat about it, but I was used to being the only girl. I liked the idea of a sister; I just wasn't sure how it was going to work. Did she want to be a part of our family? Did she want to get to know us?

She was probably struggling with it as much as we were. And she and her mom had been through a lot with her little brother. Our little brother.

God, this was weird.

I distracted myself with unpacking and cleaning until it was time to meet Grace. It was good to get my mind on something else. I turned up the music and before I knew it, the afternoon had passed.

After a quick shower and dabbing on a little makeup, I went over to the Big House. No one had said so aloud, but I knew we were meeting her here so Leo would come. He hadn't been off Salishan land since he'd come home after his medical discharge.

There were guests in the tasting room, but I found my family in the event space upstairs. It was normally used for small groups—lunches or private tastings. Roland and Zoe were already here, so I helped them set up chairs around one of the tables. Leo and Cooper came in shortly after me.

"I found him," Leo said.

"You mean Dad?" I asked.

My dad had gone missing not long after my mom had kicked him out. From what we knew, he'd moved in with his most recent mistress. But soon after, he'd dropped off the map. Disconnected his cell. Deleted his social media accounts. Emails we'd sent all went unanswered.

"Yep," Leo said. "He obviously disappeared on purpose.

Back in June, his mistress liquidated a bunch of assets. They've been using cash ever since."

"Let me guess," Zoe said. "He's down in Mexico living it up on the beach."

"No, he didn't go far," Leo said. "Or if he did, he's back. He's living in Seattle."

I was insanely curious as to how Leo knew that, but he kept his secrets close. I didn't bother to ask because I already knew he wouldn't tell me.

"Does this mean Mom can file for divorce?" I asked.

"That's exactly what this means," Roland said. "We have the paperwork ready to go. We just needed to be able to serve him. This will make the whole process a lot easier."

It bothered me that he was still so close, yet trying to stay hidden. Granted, I wanted my mom to be able to get her divorce, so finding him in Seattle was good news. But what was he doing there? Why go to all the trouble to avoid contact with us? He was with another woman; he couldn't possibly be avoiding the divorce.

"What do you think he's doing?" I asked. "Why try to disappear in the first place?"

"I don't know," Roland said.

Cooper snorted. "Because he's a dick."

Roland shrugged, like that was as good an answer as any. He was probably right.

There was a soft knock on the open door and we turned to see Grace, clutching her purse. I felt sudden surge of sympathy for her. Here we were, on our home turf, and she had to come to us. This couldn't be easy.

"Hey," I said, pulling out a chair. "Come on in."

"Thanks." She smiled and came in, taking a seat at the table.

We went through introductions, although she remembered our names. While we talked, Zoe brought out wine and poured us each a glass. She filled hers with water.

Grace was beautiful. She had pretty blue eyes, and blond hair pulled back in a ponytail. She bore a slight resemblance to both Leo—or at least the way Leo used to look—and Roland. They looked more like Dad, whereas Cooper and I took after Mom. I had a feeling Grace looked more like her mother, though. There was a bit of Dad in her, but not much.

"I'm sorry it's taken a while for me to come back," Grace said. "This has all been a little overwhelming."

Roland shrugged. "It's fine."

Cooper didn't sit, nor did he reach for his wine. He held onto the back of a chair and leaned on it. "Nice ring, Gracie. Are you engaged? Married? Aren't you kind of young for that? It's weird that I didn't notice it the first time. Did you have it then? Because normally I can smell a ring without even seeing it."

Roland glanced at him. "Jesus, Cooper."

Grace smiled and looked down at her hand. "Yes, I had it then. I'm engaged, but we're not married yet."

"You better invite us to the wedding. Do you have a venue picked out? You should have it here."

"Um, no. We haven't set a date." She glanced at her hand again and there was something in her expression I couldn't quite place. Like she was hesitant to talk about her engagement.

"That's fair," Cooper said, clearly oblivious to the hint of sadness in Grace's expression. "These things take time. Just make sure he's not dragging his feet because he isn't serious. If he gave you that ring, he should be ready to step up and marry you."

"Are you giving her relationship advice?" Leo asked.

"Why not?" Cooper asked. "I'm awesome at giving advice. And she's my sister now, so I have responsibilities."

"When was the last time you had an actual girlfriend?" Leo asked.

Cooper's brow furrowed. "What does that have to do with anything? Gracie's our sister, Leo. She can't be my girl-friend. Fucking gross."

Leo shook his head. "That's not what I... Never mind."

"I'd say they're not always like this, but they're always like this," Roland said.

Grace smiled. "It's fine."

I figured she might appreciate a change of subject. "How's your little brother?"

"*Our* little brother," Cooper said, pointing at me.

"Cooper, chill," I said.

"He's doing great," Grace said. "He's still susceptible to complications if he gets sick, so we'll have to be careful this winter. But right now, he's running around like a little kid should."

"What's up with your mom?" Cooper asked. "Did she know about our mom, or—"

Zoe reached over and smacked his arm. "Coop!"

"What?" he asked. "It's a reasonable question."

"It's really okay," Grace said. "This is why I'm here. No, my mom didn't know he was married. She was only nine-teen when she met him. She got pregnant with me and I think he helped her out a lot in the beginning. But after a while, she got tired of him only being around part time. She wanted to get married, but he didn't. His reasons are obvious now, but she didn't know at the time. She broke up with him when I was about five, and after that I didn't see him much."

"But he's Elijah's dad, too?" I asked.

Grace nodded. "About eight years ago, he started coming back around. At first my mom didn't want to have anything to do with him. After a while, he wore her down, I guess. He swooped in with money. Fixed a bunch of things on our house. Bought us new furniture. Then he took us on a cruise, and nine months later, I had a brother. But Dad didn't stick around, and Mom broke things off with him for good not long after Elijah was born."

He took them on a cruise? God, he'd never taken us anywhere. I guess we'd gone to Disneyland once. But Leo had gotten sick and we'd had to go home early. I'd been about four; I barely remembered it.

"Some of Mom and Dad's financial problems were due to him supporting two households," Roland said. "It looks like he was paying your mom child support until about eighteen months ago."

"Exactly," Grace said. "He was pretty good about helping her financially, even though he wasn't around. But then he just stopped. We all appreciate what you did for her. Things are so much better now that she's not drowning in all that debt."

"I'm glad we could help," Roland said.

Grace had a lot of questions for us. We told her about Salishan. How we'd all grown up here, and now we all worked for the winery. She and I laughed over the fact that I was going to college in the town where she lived. Roland and Zoe told her about getting married twice, and once Cooper started talking about himself, it seemed like he'd never stop. Leo didn't say much. To Grace's credit, when he did talk, she always looked him in the eyes, and never once flinched at his appearance.

The door opened, and my mom appeared, dressed in a Salishan Cellars t-shirt, her hair in a messy bun. The tension in the room heightened. Mom had known Grace was coming; Cooper had told her. We didn't want to hide anything from her. Dad had done enough of that already, and we'd all agreed that wasn't how we were going to handle this. But none of us wanted to cause her more pain. Grace was a living, breathing reminder of her husband's infidelity. If she wanted to keep her distance, we didn't blame her.

"Mind if I come in?" Mom asked.

Grace shifted in her seat. "Hi, Mrs. Miles."

"Please, call me Shannon."

Cooper pulled out a chair next to Grace. Mom smiled at him and sat. He stood behind her, keeping a hand on her shoulder.

"Grace, I think the best thing for me to do is be honest with you," Mom said. "I spent a lot of years holding things in, and it didn't do me a lot of good. So I want you to know, I don't blame you for anything. Your father made those choices, and now we all have to deal with the results. But you didn't ask for it any more than your brothers and sister did."

"Thank you," Grace said. "And since we're being honest, my mom didn't know about you. She feels terrible."

"I know," Mom said. "But hopefully she feels a bit better now. We had a very nice talk earlier today."

We all stared at her. She'd talked to Grace's mother?

"Mom, you spoke with Naomi?" Roland asked.

She nodded. "I reached out to her. She's as much a victim in all this as I am."

"Thank you for that," Grace said. "She's been sick over it since I told her about all of you."

"Don't go thinking I'm a saint," Mom said. "A few months ago, I wasn't exactly in the same frame of mind. But

I've had time to work through it. And I decided I wasn't going to let him cause any more pain."

Cooper squeezed Mom's shoulders and kissed the top of her head.

"Thank you so much," Grace said.

We all relaxed as we talked. Even Leo opened up a little more. By the time Grace said she had to go, she no longer seemed like a stranger. She and I made plans to meet for coffee during the week when I'd be at school. I wasn't sure if we felt like sisters—whatever that was supposed to mean—but I did feel like we could at least be friends.

After we all said our goodbyes, Cooper followed me outside. He grabbed my arm and pulled me aside. "Hey, are we cool?"

I sighed. "You shouldn't have done that to Kieran. You know that, right?"

"Okay, I might have gotten a little bit carried away." He pinched his fingers together to show a small amount. "A tiny bit."

"You got a lot carried away."

He widened his fingers to about an inch apart. "This much?"

"Why are you such a child?"

He grabbed me in a bear hug and crushed me against his chest. "You love me. You know you do. Don't even try to deny it."

I laughed, then coughed when he squeezed me tighter. "Cooper!"

"Say it," he said, still squeezing. "Say you love your brother."

"Okay, okay. I love my brother."

"Which one?" *Squeeze.* "Say I'm your favorite."

I was laughing so hard through compressed lungs I could hardly talk. "You're my favorite."

"Who is?"

"You are, you brat. Now let go. You're smothering me."

Cooper finally let go of his death grip on me. God, he was strong.

He was also right, if I was being honest. Maybe it wasn't cool to admit to having a favorite brother. I loved Roland and Leo. But I'd always been closest to Cooper.

"Come on." He put his arm around my shoulders and squeezed—gently this time. "I'll walk you back."

The gravel crunched beneath our feet as we walked from the Big House toward the guest cottages.

"Gracie's pretty cool, don't you think?"

Leave it to Coop to give her a nickname in the first two minutes. "Yeah, she is."

"Is it weird for you? Obviously it's weird in general. I don't know how the fuck a guy hides a family for so long. But is it weird to suddenly have a sister?"

"Yeah, a little bit. But it's kind of cool, too. I don't know if I could handle more older brothers."

"And how could anyone compete with me? Let's be real."

I laughed, then stopped in my tracks. There were plants in front of the cottage that hadn't been there when I left earlier. Some were freshly planted in the dirt beneath the front window. Others were in large ceramic pots on either side of the door.

"What on earth?"

Cooper stopped next to me, a mischievous half-smile on his face.

"Did you do this?"

"Yeah. We put some *Agastache* over there. They bloom

all summer and smell amazing, plus they attract humming-birds. I added some *Dalea purpureum*, too. They'll produce purple blooms, but the best part is the way they add nitrogen to the soil. It'll help keep everything over here healthy. The pots have tuberous begonias. Those flowers are legit. They'll bloom like crazy starting in the spring. Really bright colors."

"Oh my god, Cooper."

He dug his toe in the dirt, looking a little sheepish—which was pretty endearing, coming from him.

I held out my arms and he wrapped me in a big hug. That was Cooper for you. He didn't bring flowers, he planted gardens. When he loved, he loved big.

"Thanks, Coop, they're beautiful. But when did you do all this?"

"A magician never reveals his secrets." He winked.

For a second, I thought about telling Cooper what had happened with Chase this morning. But I decided against it. I had absolutely no idea what it meant, if anything. It would only get Cooper all riled up.

I was riled up enough. All I could think about was Chase kissing me. His lips. The scratch of his stubble against my skin. The way he'd pinned me against the wall. If Roland hadn't interrupted us, what would have happened?

Kissing my brother's best friend was not a good idea. But I couldn't help but wonder—and imagine—what it would be like if he did it again.

EIGHT
CHASE

THE TEXT from my mom was unexpected. It just asked if I could stop by, but I wondered what was going on. I didn't talk to my parents very often. Weird, because they lived about a mile from me, in the house I'd grown up in. But we'd never been a close family. In fact, it had been at least a few months since I'd seen them.

But she had texted. And as I drove to their house, a sense of dread formed in the pit of my stomach. I hoped they didn't have bad news. Maybe we weren't close, but I didn't want anything to be wrong. The whole thing felt ominous, like life was about to pull the rug out from under me.

I pulled up in front of their house and got out of my truck. There was a *For Sale* sign with *Sold* in bold letters across the front of it. Were they moving? What the hell?

My mom answered the door dressed in a blouse and slacks. She'd never been much for casual clothes, even on weekends. Her eyes flicked up and down, and I could feel her irritation at my t-shirt and worn jeans. "Were you at work?"

"No, it's Sunday."

She glanced at my hands. She always did that. Looking to see whether they were dirty, like I was still three years old and likely to get smudges on her furniture. Without saying anything else, she stepped aside so I could come in.

"What's with the sign?" I gestured outside, then closed the door behind me.

Mom kept walking back to the kitchen. Their house was about forty years old, but they'd done two extensive remodels, so the finishes were all modern. She liked things bright, so everything was light-colored. Off-white walls, white kitchen cabinets, beige floors. After I'd moved out, she'd bought all new furniture—all the white and pale pastel things she'd wanted but couldn't have with a kid living in her house.

"We sold the house." Her voice was matter-of-fact, like the sign out front should have given me all the information I needed.

"Yeah, I can see that." I stopped at the entrance to the kitchen. "When?"

"It sold a few days ago."

I leaned against the door frame. "Did you find a new house? I had no idea you were thinking of moving."

My dad walked in and gave me the same once-over that Mom had at the front door. "Chase."

"Hey, Dad. You guys are moving?"

He opened the fridge and took out a bottle of Perrier. "Yeah. The house took about a month to sell, but we finally found the right buyers."

Their house had been for sale for a month? "Um, that's good I guess. But what made you decide to sell?"

"We're relocating to Nevada," he said.

I stared at both of them while they went about their

business in the kitchen, like nothing had happened. "You're what?"

"Relocating to Nevada," Dad said, a hint of annoyance in his voice.

"When did you decide this?"

Dad screwed the cap back on his bottle of sparkling water and glanced at Mom. "Six months ago? I'm retiring and turning over my practice to Dr. Yong."

I was so stunned, I just gaped at him. My dad was a dentist; he'd owned his dental practice in town for over thirty years. They'd never once told me they were planning to leave Echo Creek. I'd always figured they'd retire here. They'd lived in this house since before I was born.

"Close your mouth, Chase," Mom said.

"Sorry if I'm freaking out a little bit, but you just told me you're moving to Nevada, and I had no idea that was something you were thinking about."

They glanced at each other, like they were confused.

"I didn't think I needed to run it by you," Dad said.

"That's not what I meant. Were you going to tell me?"

Mom gave me that same look, like she had no idea why I was upset. "We just did."

"But you put the house up for sale a month ago, and you didn't bother to mention it?"

"Chase, I have no idea why you're reacting this way," Mom said. "It isn't as if you live here."

"No, but you're moving out of state. That's a big deal."

Dad laughed. "It's Nevada. That's what, a two-hour flight? You're acting like we just told you we're moving to South America."

"Chase, you're an adult with your own life," Mom said. "You haven't lived with us for years."

"That's not my point."

Mom sighed. "Then what is your point?"

I glanced around at the pristine white kitchen. The marble counters, shiny appliances. The perfectly placed décor. Their house looked like something out of a magazine, or a home design show. Not a place where real people lived. There weren't any photos on the walls, not even of them. Never had been. Certainly none of me.

I *was* an adult with my own life. Why *did* I care? "Never mind."

"We're downsizing to a condo, so we'll need you to clear out the rest of your things," Mom said.

"My things?" I'd moved out literally the day after high school graduation. Really, I hadn't lived here for months before that. It had never been official, but I'd crashed at Cooper's so often, I'd basically stopped coming home. But after we'd graduated, Mrs. Miles had let me live in one of their guest cottages for a while.

"There are a few boxes in the back room," Mom said, gesturing down the hall. "If you don't want them, just take them to the thrift store, or the dump. But we don't have room for it."

I didn't know what stuff they would have kept—maybe it was just some random junk I'd left behind. I'd haul it back to my place and figure it out.

"Okay, whatever. What's your new place like?"

A glimmer of impatience flickered across Mom's face. It was subtle—a tightening of the skin around her eyes. But I knew it well. "It's beautiful. New construction."

"Sounds nice."

"It is," she said.

"How soon do you leave?"

Dad put his sparkling water back in the fridge. "The

movers will be here to do all the packing tomorrow. Then on the road by Wednesday."

Holy fuck. They really were leaving. And they hadn't told me.

I took a deep breath, trying to bury the ache that wanted to reach up and grab me by the throat. "Sounds like you have a lot to do. Where's my stuff?"

"In the spare room," Dad said.

Neither of them asked if I needed a hand, so I just went to the back bedroom. It had once been mine, but not long after I'd moved out, they'd converted it into an exercise room. Mom had a TV, a treadmill, and a bunch of yoga stuff. They'd put in big mirrors along one wall and wispy lavender curtains in front of the window.

Two moving boxes sat in the center of the room. They looked odd in the tidy space. I opened them and poked around the contents. It was mostly trophies and medals, stuck in the boxes in a haphazard heap. There were a few bent certificates, the corners creased or torn. The second box had a folded blanket that I didn't remember—blue and green stripes—and set of sheets that might have been mine.

I didn't really want any of it. The trophies and medals were meaningless. Who cared if I'd been a sports star in high school—what had it mattered? It wasn't like my parents had cared. They'd mostly just gotten on my case about my grades. But they hadn't been big on going to my games or matches. They were always too busy with work. Their careers had been their priority. Me, not so much.

I thought about leaving the boxes here, but decided to take them. I didn't have much use for a bunch of old stuff, but they obviously didn't want to take it with them.

After I loaded up my truck, I said goodbye to my parents. It was the weirdest feeling. I had no idea when I'd see them again. They were leaving in just a few days, and neither of them mentioned coming to visit, or inviting me down to see them.

I wondered if they'd bother.

Seeing my parents never left me in the best mood, but today was worse than usual. I felt like shit. I kept trying to move past the feeling of inadequacy—to give up caring—but it wasn't easy. Sure, I had other people in my life. I had Cooper, and his mom treated me like another son. I had friends, and plenty of people who had my back when I needed them.

But a guy should be able to count on his parents. And I'd never had that.

Our apartment was quiet when I got home. I hauled the boxes upstairs and shoved them in a corner. A trip down memory lane didn't sound so great. I'd figure out if there was anything in them worth keeping later.

We had beer in the fridge, but I didn't bother with one —wasn't in the mood. I rifled around, looking for something to eat, but I wasn't hungry. I was bored. Restless.

Cooper was gone for the next week and a half. He was out at another vineyard in Walla Walla where Salishan sourced some of their grapes, helping with a late harvest. Shitty timing. He had a way of making it easy to forget when I felt like this. He'd come up with something crazy for us to do. Like the time we brought five hundred dollars in quarters to the arcade and spent them playing every video game imaginable with a bunch of kids. Or when we wanted a beach party, so we hauled truckloads of sand to an empty field over at Salishan. That had practically turned into a luau.

Although, truthfully, it wasn't Cooper's company I was craving. I was thinking about Brynn.

I hadn't talked to her yet. I needed to. The longer I waited, the more awkward our next conversation was going to be. I'd kissed her, then bolted at the first sign of a Miles brother. Not that anyone would blame me. I'd grown up with those guys, and they were fucking scary when they wanted to be.

But I wasn't going to let that deter me. What I was feeling for Brynn was too big.

I needed to wait to make a move with her—talk to Cooper first. Anything else was a dick move, and I wasn't going to play it like that. But I should probably still talk to her. I'd kissed her, and I needed to address it.

Plus, after the shitty visit with my parents, I wanted to see her. Even being in the same room with her would feel good.

At the very least, I wanted to make sure she and I were okay. I hated the idea of her being mad at me. And I'd probably confused the hell out of her with that kiss. I'd bring a movie—see if she wanted to hang out. No hidden agenda. I'd keep my hands to myself, hard as it was going to be. Nothing that would get me in trouble with Cooper.

When he got back, I was going to sit him down and have a little chat. But in the meantime, I was craving Brynn so badly, I could practically taste her.

NINE

BRYNN

IT HAD BEEN a long day and I was exhausted. I flopped down onto the couch, pointedly ignoring all the boxes I still needed to unpack or move into storage.

I'd been working in the tasting room today while an event was going on in another part of the Big House. Zoe had been there, but had needed to leave. Poor thing had started throwing up, so we'd sent her home. Jamie, one of the winery employees, had come in, and I'd offered to help as well, so the event had gone fine. But it had made for a long day and my feet were killing me.

There was a knock on my door and I glanced up. It was probably my mom. She was more likely to come over than text or call, now that I lived here.

"Just a second." I sat up and quickly fixed my ponytail before answering the door.

But it wasn't my mom. It was Chase.

"Oh, hey."

My breath felt trapped in my throat. I hadn't seen him since he'd kissed the hell out of me, just a few feet from where I was standing. My heart started to pound at the memory of that kiss. God, it had felt good.

"Hey." He glanced down, and if I didn't know better, I'd have said he looked shy. But this was Chase. He wasn't shy. "Are you doing anything tonight?"

"Um, no."

He held up a movie case. "Want to watch a movie?"

I took the movie out of his hand. *Ten Things I Hate About You*. I raised my eyebrows.

He took the movie and looked at it. "Maybe it's dumb, but I like it. I had kind of a shit day and it always makes me feel better. Puts me in a good mood, you know?"

I laughed. "Yeah, I can just imagine you and Coop hanging out to watch this together."

He grinned, that crooked smile that was so damn cute. "Yeah, right. Actually, I probably should have sworn you to secrecy before I showed you the movie. If Coop finds out I have this, he'll never let me live it down. I'm still paying for giving Zoe my copy of *Beauty and the Beast*."

"*Beauty and the Beast*?"

"What? It's a good movie."

I laughed and stepped aside so he could come in. For a second, I wished I was wearing something cuter than a t-shirt and pair of leggings. But somehow, it didn't seem weird with Chase. I had no idea what was happening between us—if anything—but I didn't feel like I had to try too hard. Like I could just be me, and that was enough.

I'd never felt like that with either of the guys I'd dated at school.

He set a grocery bag down on the kitchen counter and pulled out a few things.

"What did you bring?"

"Snacks." He held up a package of microwave popcorn. "Movie night, so, you know."

"Perfect."

He took out a bag of M&Ms, but put them back in the bag. "Sorry, these are for Zoe."

"Zoe?"

"Yeah, I owe her chocolate from a while ago." He put the popcorn in the microwave and turned it on. "Want to get the movie ready?"

"Sure."

I put the movie in and turned on the TV. Chase finished up with the popcorn and brought it to the couch.

"Why did you have a bad day?" I asked.

He took a deep breath and his brow furrowed. "I went over to visit my parents. I guess they're moving. They sold their house already."

"You didn't know?"

"Nope."

"Where are they moving?"

"Nevada."

"Wait, *Nevada*? I thought you were going to say they're moving across town. They're moving out of state, and they didn't tell you?"

He shrugged. "Nope. They said I'm an adult with my own life, so they didn't understand why I was upset."

"I'm stunned that they didn't tell you."

"Well, I don't see them very often."

"Really? But don't they live here in town?"

He shifted and propped his arm up on the back of the couch. "Yeah, they do. But we're not really close."

There was something in his eyes. It was like he was scrutinizing me, trying to decide if he wanted to keep talking. If he was going to trust me with something important. I desperately hoped he would. I wanted to understand the pain I saw behind his easy smile. And I could feel him on the brink of sharing it with me.

I had an urge to push—to ask him about it. But I didn't. Instead, I held his gaze, and hoped. Hoped what I was feeling between us was really happening, and not just a childish fantasy bubbling to the surface.

"I don't think they wanted kids," he said, finally. His words hung in the air for a second and there was a look of relief on his face, as if he'd needed to say it.

I had no idea how to reply. I wanted to grab him and pull him to my chest and stroke his hair. But I had a feeling he didn't want me to baby him like that, any more than I wanted people babying me over my father leaving. "What makes you think that?"

"I'm pretty sure I was an accident," he said. "And just... things they said over the years. I overheard them talk about how things would be different when I grew up, wishing time would go by faster. Plus, my dad had a vasectomy when my mom was pregnant with me, and she had her tubes tied immediately after I was born. They wanted to make sure it didn't happen again."

"Oh my god. Did they tell you that?"

"Yeah, well..." He shifted on the couch, seeming to relax. "When you were born, Cooper came to school every day going on and on about how great it was to have a baby sister. So one day I went home and asked my parents if I was going to get a baby sister, too. And they said no, they'd decided not to have more children. I think I asked more questions. I was too young to know the biology of it, but they said they'd both had procedures so they wouldn't have more kids."

"Way to crush your little boy dreams."

The corner of his mouth turned up in a grin. "Right? I was pretty jealous of Cooper."

"Well, who wouldn't be, with me as a baby sister."

His smile widened, tugging hard at my heart.

"Exactly. It was tough. I tried everything to get them to notice me. My dad liked watching sports, so I played sports. And I won shit all the time. I had shelves of trophies and medals. But he only came to a handful of my games. We were state football champions senior year of high school, and I was the only kid on the team who didn't have parents in the crowd."

"Oh god, Chase."

"I tried doing the opposite, too. I went through phases where I raised hell. I figured out how many times you had to get in trouble to get the principal to call your parents in for a meeting. And they'd come, but just ground me forever and make me stay in my room all the time. Sophomore year I even tried hard drugs for a while."

"Holy shit."

He shook his head and laughed. "Only until Cooper found out. He put a stop to that shit. He was madder at me than my parents were. They just said I better quit or they'd send me away to rehab. I'd gotten high a few times, I didn't need rehab. But Cooper stuck to me like glue for months. Hardly let me out of his sight. I'd been skipping school, too, so he started coming to my house to pick me up in the morning to make sure I went. And most afternoons, I went home with him. Had dinner at your house. I'm still surprised your mom tolerated me."

"I remember that." It had seemed like Chase was always at our house. At the time, I certainly hadn't complained. I'd been able to look at him all through dinner every day. "Mom never minded, though."

"I guess not," he said. "After that, I quit trying with my parents. I just stuck with Cooper and tried not to care what they did."

My heart broke into a million pieces for him. How could his parents not care? How could they not see how great he was? They were like my dad, throwing away something amazing. I wondered if they had any idea what they were losing out on by alienating their son. No wonder he and Cooper were such good friends.

"I'm really glad you had Cooper."

His easygoing grin was back. "Me too. I mean, Coop's crazy, but he's a good guy."

"He is."

"How are you doing?" he asked. "You had all that shit with your dad, and your half-siblings and stuff. How are you handling all that?"

It was the first time anyone had asked me a direct question about my father and his affairs. Everyone else tiptoed around the topic, as if I was too fragile to talk about it.

"I'm... I don't know. I'm torn. On the one hand, I wasn't close to my dad. And he was gone all the time anyway, so it doesn't seem all that different. But..."

I paused and scrutinized Chase like he'd scrutinized me before he'd shared. I hadn't talked to anyone about this, but as I looked at his gentle expression, I knew I could trust him. I knew it was safe to talk.

"He was cheating. I don't want to make it sound like I know what my mom is going through because my boyfriend of less than a year cheated on me. But... that was awful. I've never felt so betrayed. It wasn't just that we'd been dating and the expectation was that we wouldn't date other people. I trusted him with my body, you know? And I know sex can just be sex or whatever, but it meant something to me. I thought it meant something to him, too.

"When I realized how wrong I'd been, I felt so stupid. He'd been sleeping with my roommate for months. How could I not have known? But then I think about my mom. Chase, my sister is older than me. My dad hid an entire family from her for over twenty years. He had children with another woman. He saw them on weekends and took them on vacations. And all the while, my mom was here, raising four kids mostly on her own. And then to find out that her husband had been betraying her for more than two decades? God, how do you cope with that?"

"I don't know. I can't even imagine."

"My mom is doing really well, but this whole thing is so crazy."

"Sorry, but your dad's an idiot," he said.

"He really is."

He smiled, his expression so sweet and genuine it sent a cascade of butterflies through my tummy. "It sucks being stuck with a shitty parent. But it's not all bad, right?"

"No, definitely not all bad." I grabbed a handful of popcorn to distract myself from the urge to jump in his lap. "So, movie?"

"Yep. Let's do it."

We settled onto the couch and I turned off the lamp. The tension between us was palpable, and I wondered if he felt it, too. It was hard to tell. He hadn't said anything about yesterday, and at this point, I wondered if he was going to.

He was certainly keeping things friendly. As the movie went on, my disappointment grew. He didn't move closer. Didn't brush my hand when I reached for popcorn. In fact, he put the bowl between us, effectively eliminating any possibility of touching.

Why did he have to be so delicious? He always had been. It just wasn't fair. He was athletic and toned, with bulges in all the right places. A perfect mix of rugged and pretty boy, with a square jaw, a bit of stubble, that sweet smile, and stormy gray eyes.

It was no wonder I'd had such a crush on him. Spending any amount of time with him seemed to turn me to mush. And now that I knew what his lips tasted like? Kill me.

After the movie ended, he took the bowl into the kitchen. He cleaned up, even washing the bowl and drying it with a dish towel.

"You don't have to do that," I said.

"It's okay, I've got it." He put the bowl in the cupboard and grabbed his grocery bag with Zoe's M&Ms. "I should get going. It's late, and I'm sure you have class tomorrow."

"Yeah, I do." I followed him to the front door.

He opened it and paused in the doorway. "Thanks for hanging out with me tonight. And thanks for listening."

"You too."

"I'm not sure how to bring this up, exactly, but... I'm sorry about yesterday."

My stomach dropped straight through the floor. He was sorry. Did that mean he thought it had been a mistake? Had tonight been all about establishing he was just another brother to me?

"It's okay."

"Good, because I'm hoping I'll get a do-over."

"A do-over?"

He tucked my hair behind my ear, the brush of his fingers against my skin making my breath catch. "Yeah, but not yet."

I laughed a little to cover the nervousness making my

stomach tingle. The way he was looking at me was not the least bit brotherly. "Chase, what are you talking about?"

He took a deep breath. "I like you. A lot. That kiss was... I shouldn't have done it the way I did. But despite that, it was kind of amazing, right?"

"Um... yeah."

He grinned again, and god, that smile. He was going to kill me with that thing. "So, I'm hoping you'll give me another chance. Except this time after a date instead of after I break into your house, steal your keys, and change your oil."

"So you admit you broke in?"

"I'll do just about anything for attention. You know this about me already."

I laughed again, but oh my god, he'd said *date*. "Are you asking me out?"

The hint of pink in his cheeks was so cute, I wanted to eat him up. "Almost. I'm asking if I *can* ask you out. I want to give your brother a heads-up before I make a move."

My brother. Who knew how Cooper would react to this. "You're brave if you're willing to ask Cooper if you can date his Brynncess."

"You're worth the risk."

With that one simple sentence, I was done. Crush on Chase Reilly, reactivated. With a vengeance.

He tucked my hair behind my ear again—*oh my god, please do that forever and ever, Chase*—and just about knocked me over with his smile. "So, what do you think? Can I ask you out? Maybe get another shot at that kiss?"

I was trying so hard to play it cool—and failing miserably. *Don't giggle, Brynn. Don't giggle.* "Yeah, that sounds great."

"Awesome." He stared at me for a moment and licked his lips. "I should get going before..."

Before you kiss me and I drag you inside and rip your clothes off? "Yeah."

For a second, I thought about kissing him anyway, Cooper be damned. He was so close, I could pop up on my tiptoes and reach. He'd kissed me without warning yesterday, so why not return the favor?

But he slipped a hand around my waist, gently drawing me closer, and pressed his lips to my forehead. He lingered there, his hand lightly caressing my lower back, his mouth touching my skin. I closed my eyes and took a deep breath. His scent was an intoxicating combination of fresh, clean soap mixed with engine oil and grease. I wanted to bury my face in his neck.

Slowly, as if he was reluctant to do so, he pulled away. "I'll call you, okay?"

"Okay."

He reached out and caressed my cheek with his thumb, then walked out to his truck.

It probably made me look like a smitten little girl, but I stood there watching him until his truck disappeared down the gravel drive.

Of course, *smitten* didn't even cover it.

I was falling for him, and we hadn't even had a real date yet. It wasn't just that I'd crushed on him for years. That was little girl stuff, based on his adorable smile and gorgeous body. What I was feeling now was different. I wasn't crushing on Chase just because he was cute.

That guy who'd just spent the last few hours with me? I liked him. A lot.

It was exhilarating, but also scary. I wasn't dumb, I knew about his track record with girls. I knew he didn't date very often—mostly just picked up random girls or had short-term flings.

But he wasn't asking me for that. If all he wanted was to get in my pants—if I was some sort of forbidden conquest—why would he wait to talk to Cooper? And why would he come over just to hang out and talk?

I was positive he'd never shared things with any of those other girls. He hadn't told them about his parents, or his childhood, or how it all made him feel. If he had, they'd never have let him go. They'd have poked holes in every condom so they could get knocked up with his babies just to keep him.

But he had opened up to me, and I knew that meant something.

I still didn't know where this was going. But I was pretty excited to find out.

TEN

CHASE

I DIDN'T REALLY HAVE a reason to be at Salishan. Cooper was out of town, so it wasn't like I was meeting him. And their machinery was all functioning properly, so I didn't need to stop there for a repair. Or even scheduled maintenance. But I still pulled into the grounds after work on Monday and parked near the Big House.

Brynn was like a freaking magnet. Her pull was irresistible. I'd thought about her all day. I'd almost texted her at least ten times, but I didn't want to be that guy. Things were fine between us. I'd laid my cards on the table, let her know I was into her. Thankfully, she hadn't shot me down. I had a chance with her, which was all I wanted at this point.

Actually, I wanted a lot more than a *chance*, but I had to take things one day at a time.

Still, I could come see what she was up to. That wasn't a big deal. I'd keep my hands—and other things—to myself. I was a horny bastard most of the time, but I wasn't an animal.

Besides, Brynn was going to be worth the wait.

My phone buzzed in my pocket, so I pulled it out to

check. When I saw the text, I almost dropped it, like it was suddenly on fire. Before I could even open the first one, there were three in rapid succession.

Shelly: *thinking about u*
Shelly: *are you busy?*
Shelly: *wanna hang out?*

I scowled down at my phone. No, I did not want to *hang out*. What was wrong with her? I'd broken up with her— twice. It wasn't like I'd been stringing her along. I'd told her we were over. She'd done this last time, too. She'd been angry as fuck at me, then a little time had gone by, and she'd started this *let's hang out* crap.

I wasn't getting sucked in again. I didn't bother to reply —just stuck my phone back in my pocket and went in search of Brynn.

She was over near the guest cottages, struggling beneath the weight of a big box. I jogged over and grabbed it at the base.

"Here, let me get that for you."

"It's okay," she said, her voice strained. "I've got it."

"Yeah, but if you give it to me, you'll make me feel needed and important, so really you're doing me a favor."

"Okay, tough guy." She laughed and let me take the weight of the box.

I shifted it, so it leaned against my chest and peeked at her around the outside edge. "Where am I taking it?"

She pointed away from the cottages. "Storage shed. We're actually moving a bunch of stuff around."

"I guess I came at a good time, then."

"Yeah, you did. I'll go grab something else—a lighter something else, I guess—and follow you over."

She caught up with me near the storage sheds; there

were two on this end of the property. Ben came out of one, carrying another box.

"Chase." Ben nodded to me. "That can go in the newer shed. This one's letting in a lot of moisture, so we're clearing it out."

Mrs. Miles came out of the second shed and brushed her hands together. "How are we looking?"

"Do you want to go through these?" Ben asked.

"Nope," Mrs. Miles said, her voice decisive. "Dump it all."

Ben grinned at her. "As you wish."

Brynn leaned closer and lowered her voice. "That stuff was my dad's."

"Gotcha."

"All right, Chase, I hope you came to work," Ben said. "We need to clear everything out of this one and rearrange things in the second shed so there's room for the stuff Brynn needs to store."

"I'll feed you dinner for helping, how about that?" Mrs. Miles asked.

"I won't say no to that, Mrs. Miles. But I'll help either way."

She smiled at me. "Honey, you know you can call me Shannon."

"Yeah, I know." I winked at her. She'd been telling me I could call her *Shannon* since I was in high school, but I never did. It didn't seem right to use her first name.

I got to work, moving boxes out of the old shed. A lot of the stuff had belonged to Brynn's dad, so Ben and I hauled it over to Ben's pickup and tossed it in the back. I had a feeling Ben had no problem helping with this particular task. Kind of wondered if he'd take Mr. Miles' shit to the dump, or light it all on fire somewhere. Hell, I wanted to light it on fire. I fucking hated that guy for what he'd done to his family.

Brynn still had some things to move out of her cottage, so Ben and I helped her take them to the shed. Mrs. Miles poked through a few more boxes before declaring them trash, so we took those out to Ben's truck.

As Ben and I walked back toward the girls, Mrs. Miles came out of the old shed. She stumbled and sank onto the ground, clutching her ankle. Before I could blink, Ben was already sprinting toward her.

Brynn was closer. She crouched down, and I heard her asking if she was okay. Ben got to her while I jogged the rest of the way to catch up.

"I'm fine. Really." She winced as she rubbed her ankle and lower leg. "I think I just twisted it."

Ben carefully stretched her leg out and removed her shoe and sock. With gentle fingers, he prodded her ankle and turned her foot. "Let me just check. Does this hurt?"

She winced again. "A little."

"I'll go get an ice pack," Brynn said and started off toward her mom's house.

"Just help me up," Mrs. Miles said. "I'm sure it's fine."

Ben raised an eyebrow. "You stay put until we're sure."

"Benjamin," she said, although the hint of scolding in her tone wasn't sharp.

"I'll get you a chair so you can rest it a bit before you try walking," Ben said. "But that's my final offer."

Before he had to ask, I grabbed a folding chair I'd seen in the shed. I got it set up for her, and after Ben shook it a little to make sure it was steady, he helped her into it.

"You don't need to make a fuss," she said.

Ben obviously had things well in hand. He knelt in front of Mrs. Miles and started checking her ankle again. I suppressed a smile and wondered how big of a party Ben was going to throw when Mrs. Miles' divorce was final.

There were a few boxes left in the old shed, so I went in to get them. One was up on a shelf, the contents sticking out of the top. *Brynn's Room* was scrawled in bold letters across one side.

I took it down, eying what was inside. This stuff had definitely been Brynn's. There were some yearbooks, and picture frames that looked like she'd hand-painted them. The pink sign that had once hung on the outside of her bedroom door, with *Brynn* in fancy letters. There were also some books and what might have been a makeup bag or maybe a case for pens and pencils.

I brought the box outside, but the bottom was loose, like the tape wasn't sticky enough to hold the weight of its contents. Before I could adjust my grip and support the middle, the bottom ripped open and Brynn's stuff started spilling out onto the ground.

"Shit."

I crouched and set the box down. Luckily the ground was dry. Brynn was still off getting ice for her mom's ankle, so I started putting things back in the box. I'd have to get some tape to reinforce it, but if I was careful picking it up, it should be fine.

Among some dog-eared paperbacks, I picked up a pink and gold journal. On the outside, she'd written *Brynn's Diary*.

Well, shit, this was tempting. But I wasn't going to look inside. Even if it was old, that was a dick move. But then I turned it over and glanced at the back. There was a heart drawn in black sharpie, and inside were the initials B.M. with a plus sign, followed by C.R.

Wait, C.R.? Those were my initials. That was funny.

I didn't remember Brynn having a boyfriend before college, but maybe she'd had a crush on some kid at school. It was weird to feel a brush of jealousy. This journal was probably from when she was in high school. It wasn't like it made a difference now if she'd been into some other guy.

But I kind of wanted to know who he was. I glanced up, but there was no sign of Brynn. Ben was still trying to coax Shannon into staying seated. They weren't paying attention to me. I left a few of the books on the ground—giving myself cover in case Brynn came back—and flipped through the pages of her old diary.

Her handwriting was smooth and even, with little curls and flourishes. There were some journal entries, complete with dates and beginning with *Dear Diary*. I didn't read them, just skimmed for names. I thumbed through some more pages and stopped, staring.

She'd written my name surrounded by little doodled hearts and flowers. On the facing page, she'd written *Brynn Reilly*, over and over, like she'd been practicing a signature.

Her signature with my last name.

I shut the journal and put it back in the box, but I was reeling. Had Brynn had a thing for me? I guess there was no other reason she'd have written my name surrounded by hearts. Or practiced writing her name with mine.

God, she was adorable.

Had she really had a crush on me back then? I'd never known. But of course, I hadn't paid attention to her. And it wasn't like I would have been able to act on it at the time, even if I'd realized.

But the fact that she'd thought about me that way hit me hard. She'd once dreamed about taking my name? About being Brynn Reilly? How often had I wished I was part of *her* family? The idea that Brynn had indulged in this little fantasy tugged on something in my chest. Made it a little hard to breathe.

And fuck, the weirdest part was how much I liked seeing her name with mine. Even though it was from years ago—just the doodles of a teenage girl—the sight of it stirred up a primal urge I'd never known I had. The desire for someone to belong to me. For me to belong to her.

I gathered up the rest of her stuff and carefully brought it to the other shed, making sure to support the bottom. There was some packing tape sitting out, so I repaired the box and found a place for it among Brynn's other things.

If you'd asked me about marriage a few weeks ago, I'd have waved it off as unimportant. It was fine for other people, but I wasn't interested in getting married. Being with the same woman for the rest of my life? It sounded complicated. Like a lot of work.

But maybe I'd just never met anyone who was worth it.

Brynn was turning me upside down and inside out. I was feeling things I'd never felt before. Thinking about things so differently. I had no business thinking about marriage when I wasn't even officially dating her. That was legit crazy. But the thought of her becoming Brynn Reilly felt kind of awesome.

"This is the last of it."

I jumped at Brynn's voice behind me. "Shit."

"Sorry," she said with a laugh. She put her box down and scooted it to the side. "Didn't mean to scare you."

The light was fading as the sun went down, and the last rays illuminated her from behind through the shed's open doors. Her face was framed with a soft glow, her hair shining.

"That's okay, I just didn't hear you. Is your mom's ankle okay?"

"Yeah, I think so. Ben convinced her to go home, but she was insisting she'd still cook everyone dinner."

I shook my head. "She doesn't have to do that."

"I know, and that's what Ben told her, too. He's going to grab some takeout instead. Want to join us?"

"Yeah, I'd love to."

She smiled again and I shit you not, it was like those little doodled hearts popped up in the air around her face. "Good."

Yep, I was a goner.

ELEVEN

BRYNN

THIS WAS NOT HAPPENING. I turned the key again. Nothing. No hum of the engine. No lights. Was my battery dead? I turned the key a few more times, as if somehow my car would magically start when it hadn't the first ten times I'd tried it.

I banged my fist against the steering wheel. I'd driven it yesterday, and it had seemed fine. Why wasn't it working now? I didn't have time for this. I had a test to get to.

Cooper was gone, so I couldn't call him. I tried Roland, but he didn't answer. Zoe was busy. There was an event at the Big House later today—a corporate lunch or something —so I couldn't bug her. Mom's ankle was still hurt. I knew she'd come if I asked her to, but I didn't want to make her drive. And Leo... well, Leo hadn't left the winery grounds in years, so he wasn't going to help.

Maybe Chase...

He was probably at work, but it wouldn't hurt to ask. If he was busy, he could just say no. I wouldn't put any pressure on him.

I swallowed hard, forcing down the prickles of nervousness as I brought up his number.

"Hey, you," he said. "Everything okay?"

"Yeah, except my car won't start."

"Uh oh. Do you want me to come look at it? I can swing by tonight."

"Um, yes... but... I'm sorry, I know you're working. But I have a test in less than an hour and I'm starting to freak out a little. I can't miss it."

"I'll be right there."

"Are you—"

He'd already hung up.

I smiled down at my phone. God, that guy.

Chase had been clear that he wasn't going to ask me out, officially, until he'd had a chance to talk to Cooper. And my brother was still out of town. But he seemed to find excuses for us to hang out almost every day.

Nothing had happened. He hadn't so much as hugged me. Sometimes he just hung out while I did homework. I'd sit at the little table with my books spread out, laptop open, while he lounged on the couch. He'd even helped me study for my test, quizzing me on the facts I needed to remember.

The rest of the time, we talked. Endless conversations about everything. I knew more about Chase after a week than I'd known in the entire twenty-one years before. He'd been pouring his heart out to me. Talking about his parents. His job. Things he loved, and things he hated. I knew he had a soft spot for sappy movies. That he loved old-school country music. That he secretly followed an Instagram poet, and he didn't want Cooper, or his other friends, to find out.

He'd told me about starting his business when he was twenty-two. How scary it had been to sign the lease on his shop, and how he'd taken extra business classes to make sure he knew what he was doing. What it had felt like the first time he'd billed a client.

I knew he loved brownie edges and hated carrot cake. That he and Cooper grilled ninety percent of their food, regardless of whether it was meant to be grilled. That about half of the things Cooper got in trouble for when they were kids had actually been Chase's ideas.

And I'd found myself telling him all about me. I left out the part about having a crush on him for most of my life. But I talked about my parents. About growing up with my dad, and how I felt about my mom. I talked about my brothers. About my hero-worship of Zoe and how hard it had been when she and Roland got divorced. We even talked about Leo, which I hadn't done before, with anyone.

I talked about going to business school. About my classes—the ones I liked, and the ones I didn't. About my worries for the future—what would come after I finished school. I told him about Grace, and what meeting her had been like.

I'd never bonded with another person so quickly, and so thoroughly, as I had with Chase. And every moment I spent with him made me fall for him a little bit more.

Which was dangerous, and I knew it. But my heart was not listening to that little voice in my head, warning me to be careful. Reminding me that we'd shared one stolen kiss, and since then, nothing more. We weren't really dating. We were just hanging out.

Except we'd shared so much more than just that kiss.

Chase pulled up in his black Toyota pickup and leaned out the window with a grin. "Hey, you're kinda cute. Need a ride?"

Yeah, I was screwed.

I got in the truck. "Thank you so much."

"It's no problem."

I fastened my seatbelt and arranged my backpack on my lap. "I'm so sorry to pull you away from work. I don't know what's up with my car, but I can't miss this test."

"Don't worry about it. I'm glad you called me."

Giddiness bubbled up through my tummy and my cheeks felt warm and flushed. Chase drove out of the winery grounds and through town toward the highway.

"Are you ready for your test?

"I think so." I shifted my backpack. It was heavy with all my books.

"Would it help if I quiz you again?" he asked. "Or are you past the point where last-second cramming is going to help?"

"It couldn't hurt."

He started asking questions about the material. It was hard to concentrate on answering. Not because I didn't know the answers; I did. He'd quizzed me on this stuff several times over the last week. It was hard to focus because I couldn't believe *he* remembered. He stumbled over a few things and didn't remember all the right things to ask. But even that helped, because it gave me a chance to explain what I knew.

It was hitting me hard that Chase *cared*.

By the time we got to campus, I was pretty sure I'd rock this test. And also sure if I didn't get the chance to kiss Chase very soon, I was going to go out of my mind.

"What time do you think you'll be done?" he asked.

"I have another class at two. And I can hang out at the student lounge until you're done with work. It's fine."

"Just text me when you're done."

"Okay, but don't rush out here or anything. I know you have stuff to do."

The corner of his mouth hooked in a grin. "Don't worry about it. I've got you."

I had to bite my lip to keep from giggling. He kept making me feel so giddy. "Thanks."

After I got out of the truck and headed toward the building, I glanced back. He was still there, parked in a loading zone, watching me. I wiggled my fingers in a little wave, then kept walking. Just before I went into the building, I glanced again. He smiled and gave me a chin tip. I had a feeling he wasn't going to leave until I went inside.

This. Guy.

AFTER MY TEST—WHICH I was pretty sure I'd rocked —I went to my two o'clock class. It felt like time slowed to half speed. I was fidgety, constantly checking the time. Wishing it would be over. Thinking about Chase.

Class finally ended, and I went over to the student lounge. It was part cafeteria—and the food wasn't bad—part study area. There were tons of tables where students spread out their books, sipped coffee, ate pre-packaged sandwiches and baked goods, and studied for tests.

It was usually busy in the afternoon, and today was no different. I found a table toward the back and set my stuff down, then pulled out my phone to text Chase.

Me: Finished, but no rush.

Chase: Be there in a few

Me: I'm in the student lounge. Text when u get here.

Chase: Np

I got out my statistics book and lay it flat on the table.

That class was going to be the death of me. I went over the last few chapters, taking notes as I went. Some of the material was finally starting to click. I wrote down a few more notes to help solidify everything in my mind. Maybe stats wasn't going to kill me after all.

"Hey, Brynn."

The voice sent a tremor through my stomach. Images of walking into my apartment to find my roommate fucking my boyfriend ran through my mind.

I glanced up. "Austin."

"Hey." He smiled, but it faded quickly, and he adjusted his backpack. "How have you been?"

"Fine."

"Good. That's good. How are your classes this semester?"

Why the hell was he talking to me? This guy had broken my heart. I'd thought we were getting serious. Turned out, he'd been banging my roommate behind my back.

"Do you need something?"

"No." He adjusted his backpack again. "I was just wondering how you are."

I shrugged. "Like I said, I'm fine."

"Do you want to go get some food or something?"

"What? Why?"

"I thought we could talk," he said. "It's been a while, you know?"

Was he serious? I tilted my head. There had to be a reason this asshole was talking to me. "Let me guess: Carrie dumped your cheating ass and now you don't have anyone to suck your dick. Sorry, not interested."

"Come on, Brynn, don't be like that."

I don't know how I knew. I wasn't sitting near the front

doors, and a steady stream of people walked in and out. But somehow, the second Chase walked in, I felt his presence.

He paused just inside and looked around, finding me quickly. Our eyes met, and a slow smile spread across his face. He was wearing his old baseball cap and a black jacket over his faded blue t-shirt and jeans. He walked straight for me, his eyes not leaving mine, and I realized I was smiling as big as he was.

"How did your test go?" he asked as soon as he got to my table.

"I think I nailed it."

"Of course you did." He seemed to notice Austin and his smile faded. "What's up with herpes guy?"

The color drained from Austin's face. "What?"

Chase leaned closer to me and lowered his voice, as if trying to keep Austin from hearing. "You should be careful. I think I saw this guy on a herpes poster."

I knew it. Cooper and Chase *were* behind all those posters. They'd denied it for weeks after it had happened, but I'd known it had to have been them.

Although right now, I couldn't even be mad.

"Really? Gross." I gathered up my things and put my bag over my shoulder. "Ready?"

Austin stared at Chase, open-mouthed. Chase didn't even have to be a dick to him. He just brushed my hair back off my shoulder and smiled at me. His eyes flicked to Austin once, then back to me—a clear dismissal. Everything about Chase's casual and confident demeanor sent a message to Austin: *I'm not worried about you, because you don't matter.*

I'd never been so turned on in my entire life.

My brothers? They ran guys off with glares and threats. Cooper had even dragged Kieran out of a restaurant by his shirt. Chase? He didn't need to threaten or bluster. He just put his hand gently on the small of my back and led me through the student lounge. No jealous glares. No pissing testosterone all over the room. Just a calm assurance that he was in another league, and Austin had no hope of reaching him.

He was right.

"Thanks again for the ride," I said as he opened his truck door for me.

He met my eyes and smiled—that slightly crooked, confident smile that made me a little melty every time he did it. "Of course. I told you, I've got you."

Yeah, you do, Chase. You really do.

TWELVE
CHASE

I'D BEEN FINE, until today. Fine with waiting. Tempted by the sweet girl sitting in my truck, certainly. But I had shit under control. Today? Something about Brynn was driving me out of my mind.

I went around to the driver's side and got in. Maybe it was the way she smelled. Was she wearing some new perfume? It didn't smell artificial, or even that strong. It just smelled like her. But she was putting off some goddamn powerful pheromones. It was taking a lot of self-control not to grab her and kiss the hell out of her.

As I drove away from campus, heading toward the highway, I glanced at her a few times. She was so fucking beautiful. Ever since I'd started seeing her with clear eyes, I'd been struck by how gorgeous she was. But now? Now that I knew her better? Jesus, this woman was everything.

Over the past week, I'd spent almost every spare minute with her. Props to her for not getting sick of me. That was a good sign. I'd tried really hard to let her study and do homework when she needed to. Even helped her, which had done weird things to my insides. Given me a mix of pride—

because I knew she was going to kill it on her test—and satisfaction that I could actually help her.

But mostly, she'd listened.

She'd listened to me talk about everything. Some of it had been casual stuff, things I could discuss with anyone. Work, and what it was like running my own business. Random stories about shit Cooper and I used to pull.

But I'd also told her things I'd never uttered aloud before. Things I'd never felt comfortable talking about with anyone—even Cooper. I'd talked more about my parents, and what my childhood had been like. How ignored I'd felt, and the lengths I'd gone to get them to notice me. It was as if once I'd started, I hadn't been able to stop. It had all poured out.

I'd glossed over all the partying and girls. I figured she knew enough; I didn't need to make a thing out of it. I already felt like that was in the past, anyway. It was so weird how quickly my outlook had changed.

There was life before Brynn, and life now. They were largely separate things. Old me never would have spent so many hours with a girl knowing it wasn't going to end with me getting in her pants. I loved women, and I loved sex, and it had seemed like there wasn't much more to it. Why make it complicated?

But spending time with Brynn was doing something to me. She was tugging on something in my chest I hadn't known was there. Opening places inside me I hadn't realized were closed. And it felt good. It felt so fucking good, I couldn't get enough—made me crave her in a way I'd never experienced before.

I peeked at her again, from the corner of my eye. Her tongue slid out to wet her lower lip and she crossed her legs.

She shifted a little more, a subtle movement of her hips, drawing my eyes to the apex of her thighs.

With a deep breath, I tore my gaze away and focused on the road. What was she doing to me? I'd never been so attracted to a girl. Never wanted someone like this. Like my whole body needed her. Every nerve ending flared to life, desperate to feel her.

And don't even get me started on my dick. Just thinking about her got me hard, no matter what I was doing. It had made for some awkward moments at work. But now? Being alone in an enclosed space? It was killing me.

"Music?" My voice sounded strained and I swallowed hard. I needed something to distract me from this voodoo sex magic Brynn was giving off.

Her lips lifted in a subtle smile, and her voice was soft. "Sure."

Nothing about that helped.

I turned on the radio and tried to focus on the road. Conversation might have been a good way to calm the insistent pressure of my erection—give my brain something else to focus on—but I couldn't think of anything to say. I was afraid if I opened my mouth, it would either come out as gibberish, or some version of I want to fuck you senseless right now.

And of course, every song on this station was about sex. Literally.

Sparks flared between us as I drove down the highway. I could feel them, pinging back and forth, bursting against me. She shifted in her seat again, hips moving, her hands on her thighs. God, was she feeling this too? The music hummed, the lyrics promising a night to remember, the bass reverberating through us both.

The arousal didn't end in my groin. It thrummed

through my body, teasing through my chest, down to my fingertips. I was on fire for her. By the time I pulled off the highway into Echo Creek, I was wondering if I'd survive the blaze.

"So... I don't have any studying to do tonight," she said. "Do you want to go hang out at your place?"

Say no, Chase. Tell her you can't. Anything but yes. You're not equipped for this today. "Sounds good."

There I went doing the idiot thing again. Damn it. But it was like I physically couldn't say no. And the truth was, I wanted her around. I didn't want to drop her off at the winery and say goodbye. I wanted her with me. The fact that she wanted to be with me, too? Completely irresistible.

I drove us over to my place, telling myself I could handle it. Yes, I wanted her so badly it made me ache. And yes, she was giving off a fuck-me vibe that was short-circuiting my brain. But we'd been hanging out for more than a week without any issues. I'd loved the time we'd spent together.

Cooper would be home in a few days, and then I'd talk to him. And once that happened, it was game on. Tonight? I'd enjoy the fact that she wanted to spend more time with me. No problem.

IT WAS ACTUALLY A BIG PROBLEM.

Ten minutes after getting to my place, we were sitting on the couch with the TV on. I pretended to pay attention, but I couldn't have told you what we were watching. All my senses were attuned to Brynn. My fingers twitched with the desire to touch her. My heart thumped hard in my chest. Every time she moved, I caught a whiff of her.

This girl was killing me.

"How was work?" she asked.

"Not bad..." *That's awesome, Chase. Way to keep the conversation alive.*

She adjusted, turning her body toward me. Her legs were crossed, and she'd taken off her shoes, leaving her feet bare. Her toes brushed against my leg and I almost groaned.

"Thanks again for giving me a ride."

"Of course."

I couldn't take my eyes off her. Her skin looked soft, flawless. Her lips wet and shiny. She blinked those big eyes at me and her mouth turned up in a slow, sexy smile.

My heart beat faster as a litany of dirty thoughts poured through my mind. What I'd do to that mouth. How I'd suck on her skin. I wanted to slip my fingers into her pants and play with her pussy. Explore her beautiful body until I knew every inch. Until I knew how it worked.

She shifted closer. I didn't move away.

"Is it just me?" she asked, her voice quiet.

"Is what just you?"

A glimmer of uncertainty passed across her expression. She looked so vulnerable. It made me want to pull her into my arms and hold her.

She moved even closer, so her thigh leaned against mine. When she spoke again, her voice was a whisper. "Do you feel it, too?"

Not daring to move an inch—almost afraid to breathe—I nodded.

I saw the second she made the decision. Resolve shone in her eyes and she dragged her teeth across her lower lip. "Good."

She leaned in, tilting her chin up. I stared at her,

watching her close the distance between us, unable to move. And then her mouth was on mine and I was fucking done.

I pushed her back onto the couch and spread her legs with my knee. Kissing her deeply, I settled on top of her. My tongue slid into her mouth, tangling with hers. They were desperate, messy kisses, filled with a heady mix of relief and mounting tension. I'd been holding back, keeping myself in check, and I was ready to unleash.

Dry humping wasn't sex, but it was fucking awesome foreplay. I ground my erection against her, rubbing her pussy through our clothes. She slid her hands up my back, beneath my shirt, and rolled her hips. Our bodies moved together in a slow rhythm, the heat and pressure building so fast I wondered if she was going to make me come in my fucking pants.

Her fingers dug into my back and I groaned into her mouth. Just kissing her felt so good, I never wanted to stop. Our first kiss had blown me away, but this? Every press of our lips and caress of our tongues was a blissful explosion of sensation and desire. I couldn't get enough.

"Jesus, Chase, this is why we made a room rule."

I froze. That was Cooper's voice. I hadn't heard the door open, but I'd been a little lost. Why was he home?

"Seriously, I don't want to see your balls again." The clink of keys hit the table. Shoes dropped to the floor. "Come on, man, we have these rules for a reason. And check your fucking phone. I texted you saying I was on my way."

Brynn's eyes were wide and she wasn't moving either. God, we were so fucked.

Cooper's footsteps moved around the apartment and I heard the refrigerator open. "Sweetheart, are you staying?

I'm going to grill some chicken. Should I make extra? I don't know about you guys, but I'm starving."

She winced and mouthed, *What do I say?*

I don't know, I mouthed back. Fuck. This was bad. I wished he'd go into his room so we could at least get up. I glanced over, and he was behind the open refrigerator door.

Brynn nudged my chest, so I shot another look into the kitchen and got off her. She stood and quickly smoothed down her hair and clothes.

"I'll sneak out," she whispered. "I can call Zoe for a ride. She'll be cool about it."

Fuck, I hated this. I didn't want to hide her. It felt so wrong. The whole thing felt wrong, and I knew there had to be a reasonable way to handle it. But if she didn't want Cooper to see her here, I wasn't going to make her stay.

"Are you sure?"

"Yeah, it's better this way." Her eyes flicked toward the kitchen, and I caught the unspoken message: *Talk to him.* She picked up her backpack and smoothed her hair down again. "Text me later?"

"Definitely."

She made it all the way to the door before Cooper popped out of the kitchen.

"Shit, I'm sorry. Sweetheart, you don't have to go. Is it the chicken? If you don't like chicken, we can just order pizza. Or you guys do your thing, it's cool. We have good insulation in this place. You won't even know I'm—" He stopped, his last word snapping off like a breaking twig. "Brynn?"

She slowly turned toward him, her hand still on the doorknob. "Hey, Cooper."

He stared at her, unmoving except for a few twitches of his fingers. "What are you..."

"Cooper, it's fine," she said, reaching out toward him. "Please don't."

His face swung toward me, his eyes blazing. I stood my ground, keeping my back straight, but didn't say anything.

"What the fuck?" he asked.

"Cooper—"

"Don't even fucking start." His voice was low, missing his usual stream-of-consciousness quality. That was not a good sign. "You had my sister on our fucking couch? My *sister*?"

"Cooper, stop," Brynn said.

I held up a hand. "It's not what you think."

"Oh really? That's a fucking relief. Because I think I just caught you dry humping my sister on our couch. Am I mistaken? Is the other girl in the bathroom and Brynn just got here?"

"No, but—"

"What the fuck, Chase?" Cooper looked between me and Brynn.

Brynn stepped toward him. "This isn't his fault."

"What the fuck were you thinking?" Cooper asked, ignoring her. "This is fucked up, dude. I never thought I'd have to worry about you pulling something like this."

"I'm not pulling anything," I said.

"She's not on the fucking menu," Cooper said, his voice rising. "What kind of asshole do you have to be not to know that?"

"On the menu?" I asked. "That's not what this is, Coop."

"Don't fucking call me that."

"Cooper, listen to me," Brynn said. "*I* kissed *him*, okay? He was going to talk to you, but—"

"Talk to me about what?"

"About us. About me and Chase."

"There's an *us*? You mean you've been hiding this from me? Are you fucking kidding me right now? How long have you been hooking up with my sister behind my back?"

"Will you just listen? I'm not hooking up with her."

"No shit you're not." Cooper swiped his keys off the table and grabbed Brynn's arm. "Let's go."

She wrestled her arm away. "Stop it. You're not listening."

"I'm taking you home."

"No, you're not."

He grabbed for her again and I almost launched across the room to stop him.

She sidestepped out of his grasp. "Damn it, Cooper, I knew you'd overreact."

"I'm not overreacting," he said. "You should know better."

"Know better?" she asked. "What does that even mean? It's Chase."

"Yeah, it's Chase, which is such a goddamn mind fuck I don't even know what to do right now. What the fuck am I supposed to say when I come home and find you on that couch with him? You know how many girls he's had on that thing?"

"Hey," I said. "Wait a fucking second."

"What if I don't care?" Brynn asked. "It's none of your business anyway. If I want to make out with Chase on your stupid gross couch, I can."

"No, you can't," Cooper said. "Let's go."

I tried to interject. "I'll take her—"

"Shut the fuck up right now," he said, pointing at me. "I need to take my sister home. We'll finish this later."

"No," Brynn snapped, and her eyes brimmed with tears.

"You shouldn't talk to him like that, and you're not taking me home."

"Brynncess—"

"Do *not* follow me," she said as she whipped the door open and stormed out.

Cooper twitched, like he was struggling to decide if he would follow her outside or not. He seemed to decide to let her go, moving with unnatural slowness as he closed the front door. He didn't look at me—kept his eyes on the floor, his teeth grinding and fists clenched. I'd never seen him so angry.

I gestured toward the door. "What the hell was that?"

His gaze swung to me, his eyes narrowed. "You're not asking the questions right now, asshole. Why the fuck did you have my sister on that couch?"

"I was going to talk to you first."

"What the fuck does that have to do with it? I didn't think I needed to say anything about Brynn. I thought you understood. How the fuck could you do that to her?"

"Do what? I'm sorry you found out like this, but I didn't do anything to her."

"You were making out with her on the couch," he said, gesturing wildly.

"You say that like I did something horrible to her."

"You *did* do something horrible to her."

That hit me like a blow to the chest. "What? Why is it horrible?"

"Because you can't make out with your best friend's sister, you dick. Did you sleep with her? If you slept with her, I swear to god..."

"You swear to god what? You'll kick my ass to protect her virtue? Why is that your job? Why do you think you get to decide who she's with?"

"She's my—"

"Yeah, she's your fucking sister, we've established that. And apparently the thought of me being with her is enough to make you lose your mind. Is that what you think of me? Am I that big of a piece of shit?"

"Don't turn this around on me," he said, pointing at me again. "That's not what this is about. You don't pull this shit, Chase. You don't mess with a guy's baby sister."

"She's not a baby, Coop."

"I thought you were better than this." He threw open the door and walked out, slamming it shut behind him.

THIRTEEN
BRYNN

I'D COMPLETELY FORGOTTEN about my car problems until I went to leave for class in the morning. But when I turned the key, the engine hummed to life, as if nothing had been wrong yesterday. That was weird.

It was cold outside, so I turned up the heat and waited a minute to let the car warm up. I wondered if I should bother going to class today. I wasn't in any frame of mind to concentrate on accounting and statistics. Not after the nightmare that was yesterday. But my statistics professor was known for pop quizzes. Besides, if I was at the winery all day, I'd probably run into Cooper. And if I did, I was liable to murder his face.

I'd never been so angry at my brother. He'd pulled some ridiculous overprotective crap before, but this was so much worse. Obviously I hadn't wanted Cooper to walk in on me and Chase making out. That was awkward. But did he have to lose his freaking mind? It's not like I was a child and Chase was a predator. Chase was a good guy, and Cooper shouldn't have treated him like that.

I felt bad for leaving the way I had. Maybe I should

have stayed to help Chase explain. But I'd been too angry to think straight. And rational-Cooper hadn't been home, so it probably wouldn't have done much good anyway.

The strange thing was, Cooper hadn't texted me since. Usually when I got mad at him, he'd blow up my phone, trying to make me laugh. But there was no string of texts with ridiculous gifs and reminders as to why he was the best brother in the world. He'd gone silent. It wasn't like him.

Chase had texted last night to ask if I was okay. I'd replied that I was and wanted to know if *he* was okay. I knew his *yeah* was a lie. I just didn't know how *not okay* he was. Had he and Cooper worked things out? And where did that leave me?

I'd foolishly thought Cooper would understand—maybe even be happy. After all, he loved Chase like a brother, didn't he? Why was it so awful for his best friend to be with his sister? It wasn't like we were getting married. We were just... dating. Or almost dating. We hadn't even gotten that far.

One thing I knew for sure. I couldn't ask Chase to choose between me and Cooper. Even if that meant whatever was happening between us never had the chance to get off the ground.

The thought of losing Chase before I'd really had him made my heart ache. Why did Cooper have to be so insane? Why couldn't he be a normal brother?

I drove out to campus and my classes went by in a blur. My stats professor did surprise us with a quiz, which I probably bombed, but that was better than missing it and getting a zero.

After my last class I headed home. I still hadn't heard from Chase again. Or Cooper, for that matter. Their radio silence was disconcerting—seemed like a bad sign. I wondered if I should try to talk to Chase—text him or stop by. I had no desire to talk to Cooper. I was still too angry. Until he decided to apologize, I didn't want to deal with him.

When I got back to Salishan, I walked over to the Big House. It was open, but there weren't many guests. Just one group in the tasting room. I went upstairs to Zoe's office, hoping she was still here. I really needed to talk to someone, and I didn't think my mom would understand.

I knocked on her half-open door. "Hey Zoe. Are you busy?"

"Hey." She looked up from her messy desk. "No, I'm just finishing up a few things. Come on in."

My hero worship of Zoe had never quite gone away. She was beautiful, with long dark hair and blue eyes. She had a tiny stud in her nose and little tattoos on her wrists that were so *her*. Even dressed in a very businesslike blouse, she still looked like Zoe—had a little edge.

"Thanks." I sank down into the chair on the other side of her desk.

She took a small notebook and waved it in front of her face. "Is it hot in here?"

"Not to me, but I just walked over and it's cold outside. How are you feeling?"

"Terrible with a side of always hot," she said. "So far being pregnant sucks. But I'll survive. What's up?"

I took a deep breath. Where did I even begin? I might as well just say it. "Um, so... Chase kissed me the other day."

She stopped fanning herself and her eyes widened. "You mean, my goofball Chase? Chase Reilly?"

"Yes."

"Whoa," she said and resumed fanning.

"I don't know how it happened the first time. I—"

"The first time?"

"Well, yeah."

"I'm sorry. Keep going."

"I was yelling at him for... well, he helped me with my car, but that's not the point. I was frustrated, and he was kind of in the wrong place at the wrong time. He kissed me, and it was really surprising. But then Roland came over, so he left really fast."

"Well at least he was smart enough to do that."

"Yeah, what is going on with my brothers lately? Wait, don't answer that, I'll come back to it in a second. So the next day, Chase came over. He brought a movie—"

"Please tell me it wasn't a Disney movie."

I laughed a little. "No, but he did make me promise not to tell what it was."

"God, I love him," she said. "Sorry, go on."

"We didn't just watch the movie. We talked. A lot. And before he left, he said he really liked me and he wanted to know if he could ask me out. But he needed to talk to Cooper about it first, and Cooper was out of town."

Zoe's eyebrows drew in. "Huh. Okay."

"We saw each other every day after that. He helped move my stuff into storage and helped me study for a test. And I hung out with him at his place a few times. Nothing happened. We just talked. Like, about everything. There was so much about him I didn't know."

Her expression grew more bewildered by the second.

"So yesterday, my car wouldn't start. He gave me a ride to campus, which was so nice of him, because I'm sure he was supposed to be working. And then he picked me up and... god, Zoe, I don't know. There was so much tension. It was driving me nuts. I asked if he wanted to hang out again, so we went to his place. And that feeling—all that tension between us—it didn't go away. So I asked if he felt it too, and he said yes, so I said fuck it and kissed him."

Zoe nodded slowly.

"And then... Cooper wasn't supposed to be home until tomorrow."

"Oh Jesus," Zoe said, leaning back in her chair. "No wonder you called me for a ride home last night. How bad was it?"

"It was so bad." A lump started forming in my throat, and I tried to swallow it down. "He caught us making out on their couch."

"Okay, that couch is kind of gross, so maybe next time just go straight for the bedroom," Zoe said. "Or stick to your place."

I rolled my eyes. "Thanks for the tip, but that's not really the point. And I don't know if there will be a next time. Cooper was so angry. He went off on Chase about how he should have known better and I'm off limits. Then he tried to drag me out of there and take me home."

"Which is why you called me."

"Yeah, exactly," I said. "I stormed out and now I feel awful for leaving. Maybe I should have stayed to help Chase get through to Cooper."

Zoe started fanning herself again. Her cheeks were a little flushed. "Don't beat yourself up about that. When Cooper decides to be unreasonable about something, it's pretty hard to get through to him. And lately, anything to do with you makes him unreasonable."

"I know. What's up with that? Yeah, our dad sucks, but why does Cooper think that means I suddenly need a body-guard and a chastity belt?"

"It's not just you," she said. "He's doing it to your mom, too."

"Oh god, my poor mom."

"Your mom is an expert Cooper-handler. I need to process this for a second, because I think you're telling me that Chase was getting ready to tell Cooper he wants to date you, and that's just... I'm having a hard time internalizing that information."

"Why?"

Zoe put the notebook down and gathered her hair up off her neck. "Because Chase doesn't date. Well, that's not entirely true. Once in a while he sees the same girl for a few months or something, but that barely counts. I don't think the guy's ever had a long-term relationship. Except for Cooper. But not with anyone he's sleeping with."

I shifted in the chair. I knew that, but I didn't really like hearing it. "Yeah, I know."

"You guys go to pound-town yet?" she asked.

My cheeks warmed. "God, Zoe. No."

"Sorry, I don't know what's wrong with me lately," she said. "It's like my filter is completely broken. Yesterday I told one of my brides her centerpieces were ugly."

"What?"

She waved it off, like it was no big deal. "It sounds worse than it was. She agreed with me. Anyway, where are things now?"

I shrugged. "I'm not sure. Cooper doesn't seem to be speaking to me. Or he's taking his time getting to the part where he sends me five hundred funny texts in a row. Chase texted me once last night to ask if I was okay, but I haven't heard from him since."

Zoe paused, letting her hair fall back around her shoulders. "This is tough, Brynn, I'm not gonna lie. Making out with your brother's best friend... that's touchy. And when the brother is Cooper, it's downright dangerous."

"I know. I didn't mean for him to find out like that. And Chase didn't do anything wrong. I'm the one who messed it up by giving in to my stupid hormones."

"I guess the question is, what do you want now? Were you just fooling around with Chase? Because, honestly, if that's all it was, I think you should walk away."

"Why should I let Cooper's temper dictate who I date?"

"You shouldn't," she said. "That's not what I mean. All that stuff Chase did? It's not very Chase-like. I've known him for years, and I've never seen him put that much effort into a girl. He's usually all about having fun, and if there's even a hint of it getting complicated, he's out. This was going to be complicated from the start—and he knew it— and he was still willing to take a chance on you. So what I'm saying is that if you're just having a little fun, maybe it's fine to let it go. Unless..."

"Unless, what?"

"Unless that look on your face means you're not just indulging in a *brother's best friend* fantasy, and you really like him."

I blinked away the sting of tears. "It's the second one."

"I kind of thought so," she said, her voice soft.

"But how can I get between him and Cooper? I can't ask him to choose between us. Plus, I haven't heard from him since last night. I think you're right about him bowing out as soon as things get complicated. And this is beyond complicated."

"You think Chase is going to bail?"

"Don't you?" I asked. "We weren't even really dating yet. And it's not like he has any problems meeting girls."

"Well, maybe you weren't technically dating, but spending all that time together counts for something." She paused for a second. "Do you want my advice?"

"Yes."

She picked up the notebook and fanned herself again. "Give Chase a little time. He needs to make this decision for himself. This is probably putting a level of strain on their friendship that they've never dealt with before. Let's be honest, those two have been sailing through life like it's an endless party. It seems to me that Chase just found a pretty compelling reason to grow up, and Cooper's going to struggle with that."

"Yeah. Plus he doesn't want me to date anyone. Ever."

"I know, he's taking his overprotective thing to new heights right now," she said. "It's how he's coping with your dad."

I took a deep breath. "Yeah, but it still sucks. I know it hasn't been very long, but... Chase and I were... I don't know. Is it weird to say we were good together?"

"It's not weird. It's actually pretty awesome. I've been waiting for the day when a girl would bring Chase to his knees." She gave me a reassuring smile. "I know it's hard. He could still decide he's better off walking away. But I don't think he will."

"What do I do about Cooper?"

"Give him time too," she said. "If Chase backs off, I'm sure Cooper will be falling all over himself to convince you not to be mad at him. And if Chase doesn't..."

I raised my eyebrows, hoping she'd tell me she knew Cooper, and she was sure he'd accept that Chase and I wanted to be together.

"If Chase decides that what he feels for you is too big to let Cooper get in the way, you have a decision to make, too. You have to decide if what you feel for Chase is worth pursuing, even if Cooper isn't okay with it. And then accept the fallout until he gets his head out of his ass."

"What if he never does? What if Chase and I date and Cooper's never okay with it?"

I got the feeling Zoe didn't want to answer that question —or didn't know what to say. She stared at her desk for a long moment. "I don't know, Brynn. Cooper has a huge heart. He doesn't know how to do anything small, you know? When he cares, he cares with everything he has. You're his baby; it's not like he's going to disown you. He'll have to figure it out."

"Yeah, I guess so. Thanks."

She smiled. "Anytime. I'd offer to take you out for a few drinks, but I'm exhausted. I'd probably fall asleep on the bar. Plus, you know, pregnant."

"That's okay. I'm exhausted, too." It was barely dinner-time, and I was already thinking about bed. "I think I'm going to go change into pajamas and eat ice cream for dinner."

"Good plan."

I got up and hugged Zoe before going back to the cottage. She was probably right about giving Chase time. Whatever was going on between him and Cooper, I needed to let him decide what he was going to do about it.

The problem was, I had a feeling he was going to decide I wasn't worth it.

How could a week make that much of a difference? Maybe Chase liked me, but that wasn't enough. And despite the fact that I knew we had potential—I felt it deep in my soul—we probably weren't going to get the chance to find out what this could have been.

And that hurt more than I would have imagined.

It hurt more than when my ex had cheated on me. When I'd caught them, I'd been so furious, I almost couldn't remember it happening. But this wasn't the hot flare of rage that would die down to a simmer and quickly fade. I'd gotten over Austin pretty fast because I hadn't been in love with him.

Was I in love with Chase? It seemed stupid to even consider it. Sure, I'd known him forever, but the sparks between us were so recent. Still, I *had* known him forever. And getting to know him in a new way this last week... it had changed everything.

I checked my phone for what felt like the millionth time, wishing Chase would text. Or call. Or... anything. The longer the silence stretched out between us, the more convinced I became that he wasn't going to. That I wouldn't hear anything, and the next time I ran into him, he'd give me a half-hearted apology. Shrug and say sorry, but it was too complicated.

Rain pattered against the cottage roof and ran in rivulets down the windows. I was about to go run a bath—the best part of these guest cottages were the big jetted tubs —when someone knocked on the door.

I opened it to find Chase, standing in the pouring rain. He looked miserable, with water streaming down his face, soaking his clothes.

"I'm sorry, Brynn, but I just can't."

My chest clenched with anguish. I knew this would happen. *Damn it, Cooper.* Why did he have to ruin this for me? "It's okay. I understand."

He stepped closer. "No, I don't think you do. I'm falling in love with you, and I can't let you go."

FOURTEEN
CHASE

THERE, I said it. I'd never told someone I was falling in love with them before. But I'd never been in this position before. I'd never been in love before.

"I know it's crazy." I was soaking wet, but the cold barely registered. "I'm sorry if this is too soon. But it's the truth. I can't walk away from this, Brynn. No matter what else happens, I can't let you go."

She stared at me, her lips parted. My chest tightened and for a second, I thought I'd made a horrible mistake.

"Oh my god, Chase, I'm falling in love with you too."

Those were the sweetest words I'd ever heard. I stepped in and pulled her close. I needed to kiss her like I needed to breathe. Our lips met, and I practically shuddered with relief. The cold and rain were nothing compared to the fear I'd felt on the way over here. I'd known I was going to say it—put my heart out there. I hadn't known if she'd crush it or take it gently in the palm of her hand.

"Oh my god, come in, you're getting soaked." She led me inside and shut the door behind me.

Water dripped down my clothes onto the floor. "Sorry."

"It's okay. Let me get you a towel."

She disappeared into the bathroom. I stood next to the front door, dripping wet, equal parts miserable and elated. Miserable because the last twenty-four hours had been the worst of my entire life. Elated because Brynn had just told me she loved me. And that made everything worth it.

"Come here." Wrapping a towel around my shoulders, she led me to the couch.

I sank down onto the edge and held her hips while she gently toweled off my hair. The cold was finally starting to seep into me and I shivered. It was pouring out there.

"Let me put this in the dryer."

She lifted my shirt over my head, but I didn't want her to leave. I pulled her down into my lap and she let the shirt drop to the floor.

"You're so cold," she said, wrapping her arms around me.

I buried my face in her neck and nodded. Her body was warm and soft. I took a deep breath, taking in her scent, and wrapped my arms around her. She caressed my back with slow strokes, her hands trailing gently across my skin.

She pulled a blanket from the back of the couch and wrapped it around us both. I settled into the cushions with her still in my arms.

"I'm sorry I didn't come over sooner. I was hoping I could work this out with Cooper first."

"What happened?"

I took a deep breath. "He left last night not long after you did. I waited up for him, but he came home drunk, so I just made sure he got to bed okay. Then I came over here to fix your car."

"Wait, you fixed my car in the middle of the night last night?"

"Yeah, of course. I knew you had to get to school today."

She blinked at me a few times, her lips parted. "Chase, that's... thank you."

"It was just your battery. No big deal. Anyway, Cooper left again early this morning, but he was there when I got home from work."

"Why do I have a feeling it didn't go well?"

"It didn't." I paused, the sick feeling in the pit of my stomach flaring again. "If anything, he was more pissed off. I tried, but..."

"But he wouldn't listen."

"Nope. Then I got mad and left. I drove around for a while because I needed to think. And then I came here."

She tilted her chin so she could look up at me. "Chase, I can't ask you to choose between me and your best friend."

"I know." I shifted her so I could look her in the eyes. This was important. "I don't want to lose Cooper. But Brynn, I *can't* lose you. If I walked away now, I'd never forgive myself. Not when I had a chance with you. This isn't just because you're beautiful—which you are—or because I want you more than I've ever wanted anything in my entire life—which I do. This is too big. It's too real. I've never felt anything like this before. I'm an idiot a lot of the time, but I'm not stupid enough to let you go. No matter what it costs me."

She touched my face and leaned in to softly kiss my lips. "I'm so sorry."

"It's not your fault."

Her nose brushed against mine and her voice was a whisper. "Did you really say you love me?"

"Yes. And I meant it. Did you really say it back?"

"Yes. Are we crazy?"

I slid my hand to the back of her head. "Maybe. But I don't care."

Leaning in, I drew her mouth to mine. The softness of her lips felt so good, like she could heal all the broken places inside me. I kissed her slowly. Gently. Tasted her lips with my tongue.

This was why I was here. Why I couldn't let her go. I kissed her deeply, feeling the empty space inside me fill with her. With beautiful, sweet Brynn Miles who'd once dreamed of being mine.

Now, she would be. I was already hers. I'd do anything for her. Give up anything. That realization would have terrified the old me. I'd never thought another person was worth this kind of risk. But love was a powerful force. It had knocked me on my ass. As I kissed her, I knew I'd made the right call. Letting her go would have been a fucking tragedy.

She shifted, her legs straddling my lap. I ran my hands up her thighs and grabbed her ass, still kissing her. I was done holding back. Tonight I was going to love every inch of her.

I grabbed her and stood, picking her up, and easily carried her into the bedroom. I laid her down on the bed and climbed on top of her, kissing her neck and running my fingers through her silky hair.

The heat between her legs beckoned me, even through our clothes. My dick was achingly hard, desperate to be inside her. I growled into her neck as I rubbed my erection against her.

"Chase, wait."

I stopped. It didn't matter how much I wanted her. She needed to be ready. "I'm sorry, I didn't mean to push."

"No, that's not it. I want this. I just feel like everything is about to change."

Touching her face, I looked deep into her eyes. "It already has, Brynn. Everything is different, and I don't ever want to go back."

She wrapped her hand around the back of my head and pulled my mouth to hers. There was no hesitance in her kiss. She was giving herself to me. Giving me permission to touch her, kiss her, love her. It was unbelievable.

I slipped her shirt off, leaving her in a pink bra. Taking my time, I kissed down her neck, past her collar bone. I tucked my finger beneath the fabric of her bra and drew it down over her nipple. Holy shit. It was hard and dark pink. So fucking lickable. Flashing her a grin, I traced the outline with my tongue.

"Baby, you're going to have to show me what you like."

"So far, I like everything you do."

I took her nipple in my mouth and sucked it gently. Then harder. She gasped, arching her back, and a shudder ran through her body. I unfastened the clasp in the center, revealing her full round tits. Palming one, I sucked on the other while she trembled beneath me.

Working my way down her body, I lavished kisses across her ribs, over her stomach. She lifted her hips so I could take off her pants. The fact that I was getting her naked almost short-circuited my brain. She was petite, but those fucking curves. Her narrow waist flared out to her hips, and she had enough meat on her to give me plenty to grab onto.

"Holy fuck, Brynn, look at you."

Her cheeks flushed, and she nibbled her bottom lip.

I quickly kicked off my shoes and took off my pants and underwear. My dick stood at attention, hard as steel for her. She looked me up and down, taking me in, licking her lips. I loved seeing the desire in her eyes. The flush of her cheeks.

"Baby, you are sexy as fuck. I can't wait to be inside you."

She tilted her knees apart and her full lips curled in a seductive smile. "Come here, then."

I got a condom out of my wallet, tore open the package, and rolled it on. With deliberate slowness, I crawled on top of her and settled between her legs.

Touching her face, I looked into her eyes while I slid inside her. I took my time, pushing into her inch by inch. As our bodies joined, I was overcome with a rush of emotion. It hit me in the chest and spread through my body—a warmth I'd never felt before.

Her eyes fluttered closed and she sighed my name. I buried myself deep inside her and held there, letting the sensations wash over me. The feel of her pussy. Her skin against mine. Her scent enveloping me. The way her chest moved with each breath. I felt connected to her. Open and vulnerable, but the intensity was addictive. I wanted more. I wanted to devour her. Claim her. Own her and let her own me.

I plunged in and out, starting slow. Her body moved with mine, her hips lifting to meet my thrusts. Our mouths crashed together, tongues dancing.

Oh my god, I was fucking Brynn Miles. And it was better than I could have imagined.

She moaned beneath me as I drove into her harder. Long, powerful thrusts of my cock that sent shockwaves of sensation through my body. Scorching heat radiated through me, the feel of her consuming me.

Her delicate curves melded with my hard edges, her skin silk under my rough palms. I kissed her, licked her, sucked on her skin. Felt the warmth of every inch of her body that touched mine.

Her hands traced along my back and arms, making my skin tingle. I was so aware of her. Not just of her pussy—although that was fucking spectacular—but her entire body. She held me, kissing me, touching me. She was making me *feel* and I couldn't get enough.

Sex had never been like this before. I'd had no clue what I'd been missing.

"You feel so good," I whispered in her ear, then kissed down the side of her neck. "Tell me what you want."

"Harder," she said.

She didn't have to tell me twice. I drove into her, feeling the satisfaction of her fingers digging into my back, her soft moan in my ear. Moving faster, I plunged in and out, sinking my cock in deep.

The pressure building in my groin was going to make me lose my mind. I kept thrusting, letting the heat grow. Feeling the steady escalation of pleasure, my cock hardening, pulsing, ready to unleash inside her. The walls of her pussy clenched harder with each thrust. She was close.

She lifted her arms over her head and her tits moved as I fucked her. Holy shit, she was beautiful. A blush crept across her skin and she closed her eyes. The sound of my name on her lips and the way she looked beneath me was almost too much.

I shifted down to my forearms so more of our skin would touch and buried my face in her neck. Thrusting hard, I kept a steady rhythm. She whimpered into my ear and her pussy tightened around me. Oh god, I was going to come so fucking hard.

Growling into her neck, I drove harder. Faster.

"Chase... yes... don't stop."

There was no chance of that. We were coming and we were doing it together. Almost there...

Her pussy clenched hard and I came undone.

She bucked her hips against me and called my name as she came. The feel of her orgasm sent me over the brink. Hot pulses swept through me, my muscles tightening. The pressure unleashed in a rush so intense, I couldn't think. My cock throbbed, over and over, until there was nothing left.

I held myself on top of her, breathing hard. She wrapped her arms around my neck and held me tight.

"Chase, that was amazing."

It was. It was more than amazing. It was better than any sex I'd ever had in my entire life. It was fucking mind-blowing.

"Yeah." It was completely inadequate for what I was feeling, but it was all I could get out. My brain wasn't quite working yet.

I kissed her softly, then got up to deal with the condom. When I got back in bed, I gathered her in my arms and kissed her again. I had no words. I was too overcome.

"Will you stay?" she whispered.

I rarely stayed. I was always itching to go—to get away. Not now. Not with Brynn. I wasn't going anywhere—not until she kicked me out.

"I'll stay as long as you want me, baby."

She traced her fingers across my chest. "What if I want to keep you forever?"

For the second time today, I was hearing the sweetest words I could possibly imagine. *Forever*. I already knew I'd be hers forever. I didn't care that this was new. That didn't matter to me. I *knew*, deep in my soul, that Brynn was it for me.

"Then I'll stay forever."

FIFTEEN
CHASE

IT HADN'T BEEN *FOREVER,* but three months later, Brynn hadn't kicked me out.

She lay with her head on my bare chest, her body tucked against mine. It was a Sunday, but we'd woken up early and enjoyed some delicious, sleepy morning sex. Now I held her close, drifting in a post-orgasm glow.

"I should probably go home today," I said.

She lifted her head and stuck out her lower lip. "No, you should stay."

I traced her lip with the tip of my finger. "You've said that every day this week. I'm out of clean clothes."

"Just do laundry here. I don't care if you're naked."

I laughed. "You aren't sick of me hanging around?"

"No, of course not." She laid her head back down, as if the matter was settled.

I did go home occasionally, mostly to get clean clothes and take care of my share of the bills. Cooper still wasn't speaking me, so being at my place was miserable. It wasn't so bad if he was gone, but when he was home, I had to live with the constant reminder of his silence.

I'd tried. I really had. I'd texted and offered to meet so we could talk. Tried to tell him I was serious about Brynn. He didn't want to hear it.

At this point, I was as angry as I was hurt by the whole thing. He was being a childish dick. It pissed me off that he'd let this go on so long.

Was my dating Brynn really so bad? The rest of her family was fine with it. Mostly, at least. Her mom and Zoe were cool about it. Granted, I was pretty sure Roland and Leo had plans in place to make me mysteriously disappear if I ever hurt her. But as intimidating as that could have been, I wasn't worried. Because I wasn't going anywhere.

I hated that Cooper and I were still fighting, but despite that, the last three months had been the best of my entire life. Brynn was everything. I loved her so fucking much, and the fact that she loved me back still blew me away. Every day I looked at her and wondered what the hell I'd done to deserve her.

Tracing my fingers across her back, I kissed her head.

She looked up at me again, resting her chin on her hand. "I need you to stay and help me study for my test, anyway."

"I thought you had study group today."

"I already told them I wouldn't be there. I like studying with you better."

I squeezed her gently. I loved that she'd rather be with me. Maybe it was selfish, but I wanted her all the time. We were both busy, so I lived for the time in the evenings and on weekends when we could be together. I took her out on dates pretty often, or sometimes we just hung out together at her place. And I spent the night here more often than not.

"Your test is way more important than clean clothes."

"Exactly," she said.

"How about I drive you to class tomorrow? I can pick you up after your test and take you out."

"Ooh, date night? I like it."

I kissed her forehead again. "Where do you want to go?"

"We can just go out for pizza or something. There are some good places near campus."

"Pizza?" I raised an eyebrow. "Baby, you've been working your ass off for this class. You deserve better."

She kissed my chest. "You're so sweet. But you don't have to keep spoiling me all the time."

"Of course I do. You're my girl. Plus, I like showing you off. Let's be honest, you make me look awesome. I like the attention I get for being seen with a beautiful woman all the time."

She shook her head, laughing.

Looking back, it was hard to imagine why I'd been so anti-relationship before Brynn. Having a girlfriend was the fucking best. Although, to be fair, the right girl made all the difference. My forays into dating had always been short-term, but I'd never *wanted* more. I'd never been with anyone who made me feel like Brynn did.

She sat up, holding the sheet to her chest. "I could stay in bed with you all day, but I really do need to study."

"Tell you what. I'll make breakfast and then we'll get to work."

"Why are you so amazing?" She leaned in and kissed me, her lips soft against mine.

"Because I love you."

"I love you too."

I DROPPED Brynn off at campus early Monday morning so I could get to work. I was a little behind lately. Nothing I couldn't handle, but jobs were piling up. I usually worked weekends when things got busy like this, but I'd been spending most of my free time with Brynn.

After getting caught up on a few things at my shop, I had to make a trip out to Salishan. Ben had called to ask if I could come take a look at their bottling machine. It was acting up again, and it was always easier to fix things before they stopped working entirely.

Ben and I found the issue. Luckily it was an easy repair. I still had half an hour before I needed to head to Tilikum to pick up Brynn, so I went over to the Big House to see how Zoe was doing.

I found her in her office with her head down on her desk. "Hey, Zoe. You okay?"

She lifted her head and blinked sleepy eyes at me. Her skin was pale and some of her hair stuck to her cheek. "This baby is trying to kill me."

"Still feeling sick?"

"Don't worry, they said. You'll feel better after the first trimester, they said. Newsflash. I don't fucking feel better."

Zoe had been sick off and on since she found out she was pregnant a few months ago. At first, having a baby coming seemed to cheer up Brynn's family, especially her mom. But the pregnancy being so hard on Zoe was tough for everyone. Roland was always on high-alert, ready to rush her to the doctor. Mrs. Miles was worried, and everyone insisted Zoe was working too much. Brynn and her brothers had been helping with events as much as they could, and the rest of the Salishan staff were pitching in as well. Still, Zoe kept insisting she'd rather go to work than lie around at home.

"You look like shit." I pulled a package of M&Ms out of my pocket. "Chocolate?"

Her eyes brightened a little. "It's the weirdest thing, but these are one of the only things I can eat without puking them up."

I knew that already. After I'd eaten the M&Ms in her break-up box and forgotten to replace them, I'd started bringing her M&Ms whenever I saw her. It had become kind of a joke. After she got pregnant, I'd noticed her actually eating them, even when she was sick and couldn't seem to eat anything. So I made sure to bring her more when I stopped by.

"What else can you eat?" I got the five other bags of M&Ms out of my coat pocket and stacked them on her desk.

"Nothing that makes sense. Grapefruit. Some days eggs, but only if they're scrambled. Oh, and those sea salt crackers we have down in the tasting room. I've been eating those by the box."

"Brutal. Well, I've got your back with the chocolate."

She cracked a small smile. "Thanks, Chase. How are you doing?"

I knew by the way she said it, with that glimmer of sympathy in her eyes, that she was thinking about Cooper. Everyone knew he wasn't speaking to me.

"I'm good. Brynn has a test today. I'm picking her up in a little bit so I can take her out afterward."

"Look at you, being such a good boyfriend. I'm proud of you, goofball."

I grinned. I couldn't help it. Thinking about Brynn always made me smile. "I'm probably messing up somewhere, but I'm crazy about her."

"I can tell. I've never seen you like this." Her eyes filled with tears. "Sorry, it's just so great to see you happy."

"Jesus, Zoe, don't cry."

"I know, I know." She wiped her eyes. "Everything makes me fucking cry lately. This is definitely Roland's baby. They both make me insane. What about... you know. He still won't talk to you, will he?"

It wasn't something I wanted to talk about, even with Zoe. Luckily, Roland came in behind me, saving me the need to reply.

"Zo, what are you still doing here? I thought you were going home."

"I just have a few more things to do," she said.

He went around the other side of her desk and took her hands, like she needed help to stand. "Come on, honey. You're doing way too much. You need to lie down. I went to the store earlier, so we have a fridge full of eggs and grapefruit."

Her lip quivered, and her eyes filled with tears as she stood. Her belly was just starting to show. "I'm sorry. I'm fine. You're just being so sweet."

Roland gave me a mystified look, as if to say *I have no idea*. "Okay, baby. Let's go."

"Sure," she said, the tears coming harder. "I really love our house. Have I mentioned that lately?"

He put his arms around her and rubbed her back while she cried into his shirt. I gave him a *good luck with that* look and backed out of her office—slowly, so I didn't do something to make her cry more.

Downstairs, Mrs. Miles was in the lobby, talking to Leo. She looked over at me and smiled. Leo did not. But he didn't smile at anyone very often.

"Hi, Chase," Mrs. Miles said. "Were you upstairs with Zoe? How is she?"

"About the same. Roland's up there."

She sighed, and I could see the concern in her eyes. "Poor thing. I was sickest with Brynn, but it was never this bad. Is Brynn around?"

"No, I'm heading out to pick her up. Then I'm taking her to dinner."

"That sounds nice," Mrs. Miles said.

Leo nodded to his mom, then narrowed his eyes at me before he left. He might as well have mouthed *I'm watching you, punk*. I'd have bet a million dollars he was thinking it.

Roland was bringing Zoe down, so I said goodbye to Mrs. Miles and ducked outside. I didn't know what to do with this weepy Zoe. I figured I'd just keep throwing M&Ms in her direction and hope she started feeling better soon.

Snow blanketed the ground, although we hadn't had any new snowfall for about a week. Salishan was beautiful in the snow. It sparkled in the daylight, coating everything in white. I paused outside the doors to get my keys out of my coat pocket. When I looked up, Cooper was standing a few feet in front of me.

It wasn't the first time I'd seen him. We'd been home at the same time, and I'd run into him here. We'd had to suffer through the holiday dinners at his mom's house, both staying as far away from each other as possible when we had to be in the same room.

Anger flared in my gut. I wouldn't have blamed him for being so mad if I was screwing over his sister. But I wasn't, and I wasn't fucking going to. It hurt that he thought so little of me, after knowing me for so long.

His jaw clenched tight and his nostrils flared. Without a word, he walked past me and opened the door to the Big House.

"Really?" I asked as he passed. "This is still what we're doing?"

He went inside without answering.

"Fuck," I muttered under my breath.

I went out to my truck. Brynn would be finished with her test soon, so I needed to get out there to pick her up. I hadn't let Cooper's assholery keep me from Brynn so far, and I certainly wasn't going to start now.

Half an hour later, when I pulled up to the curb near the student lounge and saw my girl, Cooper was the last thing on my mind. She was all bundled up and adorable in a knit hat, scarf, and a thick jacket. She hurried over to the truck and got in.

"Oh my god, it's cold out there."

"I'm sorry. You weren't waiting long, were you?"

"No, not at all." She rubbed her hands together and I turned up the heat. "But I think they had the heat way up in the classrooms today, so it feels extra cold outside."

"Don't worry, baby, I'll warm you up." I winked at her.

She took off her hat and ran her fingers through her hair. "You bet you will. Hopefully more than once."

God, I loved her. "Date first, though. I'll buy you dinner before I destroy your pussy. Because I'm a gentleman."

"You keep talking like that and we won't make it to dinner."

I grabbed her hand, twining our fingers together, and brought them to my lips for a kiss. "How'd your test go?"

She smiled. "I won't know for sure until I get it back, but honestly? I nailed it. I'm looking at a four point oh this semester."

"Baby, I'm so proud of you."

"Thanks."

I leaned over and kissed her. "Time to take my girl out. You ready?"

"Definitely ready."

She smiled and my heart melted a little. I didn't think I'd ever get over the way it felt when she smiled at me like that. Because she was smiling at *me*. And it was nothing short of amazing.

SIXTEEN

BRYNN

CHASE WAS LITERALLY the best boyfriend in the world.

The guys I'd dated at school had thought *dating* meant going out for pizza and banging afterward, usually with roommates on the other side of the wall. If Chase took me out for pizza, it was because we were both in the mood for it. Other nights, he took me to nice dinners, always insisting he liked showing me off.

He'd taken me skiing at Stevens, and night-sledding in this little out-of-the-way spot up the highway. We'd gone to movies, and even to a local community theater production of *A Christmas Carol* back in December. Other nights, we stayed in—snuggled up on the couch together to watch a movie with wine and popcorn.

For New Year's, he'd splurged on two nights in the cutest little cabin about an hour from home. It was secluded with a big bed and a hot tub. We'd sat in the warm water, watching the snow fall, while the clock struck midnight on New Year's Eve.

I loved it. I loved being with him, no matter what we

were doing. Even when he was just sprawled out on the couch while I did homework, I loved having him there. I never wanted him to leave. Technically, he still lived with my brother, but he spent more nights at my place than he did at home. I was pretty good at convincing him to stay.

He held my hand as we walked out to his truck after dinner. I'd kicked ass on my test earlier, and our dinner date had been fantastic. It was a restaurant we'd been to before, and both loved. I was full from the meal and relaxed from my glass of wine.

My brother was still being a total pain in the ass. He wasn't speaking to Chase at all, which was such bullshit. He was distant with me, although lately it seemed like he was trying. He was prone to drive-by hugs while I was working in the tasting room—popping in and grabbing me in a bear hug, then leaving without saying a word.

I knew he was hurting too, but trying to talk to him about Chase hadn't helped. I kept waiting for him to get over it—or remove his head from his ass—but so far, he was being as stubborn as I'd ever seen him.

The winery grounds were quiet, the snow dampening any sound. I loved winters here. Everything was sparkling white, and my cottage was cozy. It was especially cozy with Chase to keep me warm.

He parked next to my car and turned his sweet, sexy grin on me.

"Are you coming in?" I asked.

"I am if you're inviting me."

I leaned over and brushed my lips against his. "Yes, please."

He cupped my cheek and ran his thumb along my bottom lip. "Good."

We went inside and took off all our cold-weather gear—hats, boots, gloves, coats. He seemed to know exactly what he wanted. As soon as my coat was off, he cupped my face and backed me into the bedroom, kissing me while we walked.

His lips played with mine and his tongue slid out with quick, teasing strokes. I could feel him smiling against my mouth as he kissed me.

"Get these fucking clothes off," he growled into my ear. "I'll get a condom."

"You know, I'm on the pill. What do you think about not using those?"

He looked at me for a long moment, then brushed my hair back from my face. "I trust you. But I'm not risking your future. We'll use them at least until you're done with school. Then... we'll see."

"Are you sure?"

"Yeah. I don't mind them. Honestly, I've never *not* used one, so it's fine."

It felt good to hear him say that. He kissed me again, then went for the box of condoms in the drawer while I started unfastening my pants.

He paused next to the nightstand and watched while I hooked my thumbs in the waistband of my jeans and slid them down. I took my time, turning slightly so he could watch my backside while I bent over. Arching my back, I glanced at him through my hair. His eyes were glued to me. I took my time straightening to a standing position, then turned to face him.

"This is fun," he said, the corner of his mouth hooking in a grin. The condom packet dangled from his fingers. "Now the shirt."

I giggled and pulled at the hem of my shirt a little before

bringing it up over my head. I slid my arms out and dropped it to the floor.

"We need music for this." He took his phone out and turned on a song.

The idea of stripping for him made me giggle again. I laughed while I slid one bra strap down my arm.

"That's it, baby." He looked me up and down. "Keep going."

I rolled my eyes, feeling a little silly, and moved the other bra strap down. The music hummed a slow rhythm, but I couldn't seem to move my hips and unfasten my bra clasp at the same time. I finally got it off and tossed it aside.

"Fuck, you're sexy. Touch yourself a little."

The fun was melting out of this. I felt more goofy than sexy. "Chase, I'm not sure what you want me to do."

"Just move to the music."

I let out a breath and tucked my hair behind my ear.

"Here, I'll go first and show you, how about that?"

Now that sounded fun. I plopped on the bed and waited while he found a song on his phone and set it on the nightstand.

He backed up toward the door and took off his shirt. He started with slow body rolls, his abs flexing as he moved his hips. His hands slid over his chest and across his abs, then he pounded his fists against his hips while he thrust hard.

Sliding his thumb over his lower lip, he sauntered closer to the bed. I loved the way he moved. He knew how to use every inch of that muscular body. With a flick of his hand, he unfastened his jeans, then slowly lowered the zipper.

A real stripper would probably have pants that ripped off, but the way Chase pulled them down was sexy as hell. His erection was thick beneath his underwear, the tip peeking out the top. He did another body roll, then grabbed his dick, and I was surprised my panties didn't evaporate into thin air.

I saved him the trouble and slipped them off while he moved his hips, those delicious abs flexing. He got close to the bed and took off his underwear, using them to tease little glimpses of his cock. Then he put both hands on the bed, one on either side of me, and rolled his hips, his body moving in slow waves.

Heat pooled between my legs as I watched him dance. I grabbed the condom he'd dropped on the bed and unwrapped it. He paused long enough for me to roll it down over his hard length, grinning while he watched me do it.

I backed up onto the bed, but he wasn't finished. He knelt in front of me and put my legs up on his shoulders. Holding my ankles, he gyrated a few times, his hips hitting the backs of my thighs.

He let my legs fall to either side of him and braced himself with his arms. With long, slow thrusts, he mimicked grinding into me, then pushed himself up again. His chest dragged across my skin, making my nipples harden, and his cock brushed against my opening. This mock fucking thing he was doing was driving me crazy.

I grabbed his ass, trying to guide his cock into me, but he just smiled. His hips pressed into mine, but he rolled his body again.

"What do you want, baby?"

I giggled, moving my hips so his cock slid against me.

"Tell me," he said.

"I want you to fuck me, Chase."

Groaning deep in his throat, he plunged into my wet pussy. The sudden pressure of his cock filling me made me cry out. It was sweet relief and desperate need all at once.

He fucked me hard, his thrusts relentless, like he

needed this as much as I did. I lifted my legs to take him in deeper, and held onto his muscular back.

His perfect rhythm pushed me to the brink so fast, I could barely breathe. My muscles clenched and tightened around him, pulsing with tension. Heat bloomed from my core, spreading across my belly to my hips and between my legs. Pressure built until I was ready to burst.

Reaching back, he grabbed my leg to pull it higher. A few more hard thrusts and I was done for. The tension exploded, sending sparks racing through my veins. I closed my eyes, gasping with the intensity as the orgasm overtook me. He didn't stop, his cock stretching out the pleasure as he drove it in and out of me.

My orgasm faded, leaving me breathless. Chase paused his movements and kissed down my neck, giving me a second to recover.

"God, I love feeling you come," he said.

Without warning, he pulled out and flipped me over, his hands rough and aggressive. He grabbed my ass, lifting it into the air, and plunged into my pussy. With gentle pressure, he pushed my head down to the bed and draped his body over mine.

His mouth was next to my ear and he nibbled and licked at my earlobe and neck while he fucked me from behind. His breath was warm on my neck and he grunted and growled with every thrust.

"Fuck, baby, I love you so much."

"I love you, too."

The thickness of his erection stretching me open still felt so good, even after an orgasm. I loved when he took what he needed. He always made sure I came first—every single time—and I loved it when he'd unleash on me afterward.

His rhythm was heating me up again, making my pussy throb. I loved the feeling of being at his mercy—trusting him with my body like this. He pinned me down, fucking me hard from behind, growling in my ear. His need drove me crazy, making my core muscles clench around his cock.

"I need you to come again," he murmured in my ear. He nibbled on my earlobe and thrust a few more times. "Does my baby want to come?"

"Yes."

He drove his cock in, grunting. "I want to feel you come again, baby. I love it when you come all over me."

I was about to tell him I didn't think it was going to happen unless we moved, but then he slid his hand down my body and reached between my legs. His fingers found my clit and involuntarily, my body jerked backward into his. He stroked my clit with his fingers while his cock drove in and out.

He kept going, breathing hard, groaning into my ear while his fingers made magic happen. The sound of his low murmurs and growls, the feel of his cock filling me, and the rhythm of his fingers sent me spiraling out of control. I cried out, rocking my hips back, as the world came apart.

His grip on me tightened and his cock thickened and pulsed. He thrust into me hard as he came, grunting as he drove his cock in deep.

"Fuck, I love you." Thrust. "I want to marry you."

I was so far gone in the throes of my own orgasm, his words almost didn't register. I murmured an *I love you* in answer as the pulses surged through me.

Chase pulled out and collapsed next to me. He was quick to take his condom off; he was always so good about cleaning up after himself. Before I had a chance to catch my breath, he'd gathered me in his arms and held me close.

With my body curled up against him, his fingers tracing gentle circles over my skin, I wondered if I'd imagined him saying the words *marry you*. Was he going to mention it? Did he even realize he'd said it?

"Um, Chase?"

"Yeah, baby?" His voice was sleepy and sex-drunk.

"Did you say that on purpose?"

"Yeah."

Wait, was he serious? "I'm not sure if we're talking about the same thing. I don't mean the *I love you* part. I mean what you said after that."

"What?" He lifted his head to look at me. "That I want to marry you?"

"Yes, that part."

His mouth hooked in that mischievous smile I loved so much. "Yeah."

I sat up, covering myself with the sheet. "Okay, but... why did you say it? You didn't just propose while you were coming in me, did you?"

He cleared his throat. "No, I guess... of course not. That was just... I don't know."

"Just heat of the moment?"

"Yeah. Exactly."

There was a glimmer of something in his eyes I couldn't quite place, but just as quickly as it had come, it was gone. He pulled me down and wrapped his arms around me. We lay together in silence for a few minutes.

"So how long have you been moonlighting as a male stripper?"

He laughed. "That was my first time. But maybe I should consider it. I bet it would be a good way to make some extra cash."

"That was *not* the first time you've ever done that. You

were amazing. How is that possible?"

"I don't even want to tell you why I know how to do that. This story does not make me look awesome."

"Okay, now you *have* to tell me."

He groaned. "Fine. It's mostly Zoe's fault. She brought over *Magic Mike* for movie night at least ten times in a row. I don't know if she actually liked the movie, or if she just liked torturing us. We let her get away with it for a while, but then we took away her movie picking privileges."

"So you watched the movie and figured out the moves?"

"No, that's just what started it. One night Cooper and I were kinda drunk and we got into an argument about who would make a better stripper. We ended up trying to prove it by showing each other our moves, except we realized neither of us had any moves. Not stripper moves, at least. So we stayed up all night using YouTube tutorials to learn how to do it. I don't really want to get into more detail. It involves a chair and each of us standing in for the girl while we figured out how to do the lap dance stuff on each other. It wasn't pretty."

I started laughing so hard I curled up, clutching my stomach. "Oh my god, you gave my brother a lap dance."

"Shut up. I was pretty drunk. And you can't ever tell anyone."

"Who was better? Come on, be honest. Who gave a better lap dance?"

"Me, obviously."

"After that performance, I believe it."

He laughed again and kissed my forehead. I relaxed against him, enjoying the warmth of his body next to mine. I was so in love with him, and as I lay there, I realized something. I wished he had been serious when he said he wanted to marry me. Because if he had been, I would have said yes.

SEVENTEEN
CHASE

I HADN'T EXACTLY MEANT to propose to Brynn, so the way it had gone down shouldn't have bothered me. I'd blurted it out without thinking. But I hadn't expected her to basically shoot me down. And I wasn't sure what it meant that she had.

Mulling it over while I worked was driving me crazy. I kept going around in circles. I'd told her I said it on purpose. And then she'd tossed the ball back, with *you didn't just propose while you were coming in me, did you?*

Sure, it wasn't a candlelight dinner with a big ring and classical music playing in the background. But she hadn't said, "Hey, dork, maybe you should do it right, but shit yeah, I want to marry you." She hadn't said that at all. In fact, she'd changed the subject pretty fast.

I didn't know what it all meant, and I was making myself nuts worrying about it.

About a week later, I cut out of work early and went over to Zoe's house. I'd texted her to see if she was at Salishan, but apparently Roland had forced her—her word, not mine—to go home and lie down.

She and Roland lived close to the winery, in a house they'd bought last fall. It was a nice two-story with a big wrap-around porch. It looked like it would be a great place for a kid to grow up. I paused outside, looking at the snow-covered yard, the path cleared to the porch stairs, and it hit me how lucky their baby was. The little thing wasn't even born yet, but he or she was coming into a family that was going to love it to pieces.

I knocked and heard Zoe's *come in*, so I went inside and took off my coat. She was lying on the couch, half-covered with a blanket, a large empty bowl on the floor next to her.

"Puke bowl?" I asked.

"Just in case. I haven't needed it this afternoon, but you never know."

"Shit, Zoe, I'm sorry." I pulled a few packages of M&Ms out of my pocket. "Want these?"

She winced. "You're the sweetest thing ever, but not today. I did eat some toast earlier, so I have that going for me."

"If you're feeling like crap, I don't want to bug you." I jerked my thumb toward the door. "I can go."

"No, you're fine. Actually, I'm bored as fuck, but I'm too exhausted to do anything, and Roland won't be home for at least another hour. I'm glad you came over. We hardly ever hang out anymore."

I sat down in an armchair next to the couch. "Yeah, I guess it's kind of hard with, you know... everything."

"Yep. This." She held up her hand to show her wedding ring. "And this." Pointed to her belly.

"And the fact that Cooper won't speak to me because I'm dating his sister."

"That too."

I ran my hand through my hair. "She's actually why I need to talk to you."

"Uh-oh."

"What?"

"Please tell me you're not about to ask me how to break up with her. I can't go there, Chase."

I leaned back and looked up at the ceiling, taking a deep breath. "I'm not the fuck-up everyone seems to think I am, Zoe."

"What? I never said that."

"I know, but the first thing everyone assumes is that I'm going to screw her over. That's why Cooper's so pissed. If he knew..." I trailed off, shaking my head. "I know I wasn't much of a relationship guy before. But I never wanted one before Brynn. And now that I have her, I don't ever want to break up with her."

"Wait, Chase, what are you saying?"

"I'm saying I'm going to marry that girl."

Zoe stared at me. "Is the baby giving me hallucinations now, or did you just use the words *marry that girl* in a sentence referring to Brynn Miles?"

"Yes, I did."

"Wait, wait, wait." Her eyes were wide. "Are you engaged? Did you ask her already?"

"Not exactly. I kind of did, but I didn't get the reaction I was hoping for."

"Oh god, did she turn you down? There's no way Brynn said no to you. You must have screwed it up somehow because that's not possible."

I scowled at her. "Great, I'm glad you have so much confidence in me."

"I'm just saying, Brynn is insanely in love with you. If it wasn't obvious that you're insanely in love with her too, I'd be worried about her. But you have it just as bad as she does."

Leaning forward, I put my elbows on my knees. "I don't know. I said I wanted to marry her, and she acted... confused."

"How did you say it?"

"Just... pretty much like that. That I want to marry her."

"Where were you? I'm guessing it wasn't planned, but was it a good moment?"

"Um, we were kind of in the middle of having sex."

"Okay... when you say in the middle, what exactly does that mean?"

"Jesus, Zoe, you want a play-by-play?"

"Do you want my help or not? Come on, it's me."

I got up and started pacing around the living room. "I guess... I was coming when I said it. I said I love you, and then I said I want to marry you. It just kind of came out, you know? It felt right to tell her."

"And then what happened?"

"We finished—it was her second orgasm, by the way— and then... well, I needed a minute. You know guys can't think right after we come. There's no blood in our brain. So she started asking me questions, and I told her yeah, I said it on purpose. And then she said, *you didn't just propose while you were coming in me, did you?* And I got a little flustered, because I actually had, but it seemed like she didn't want me to. I wasn't sure what to say to that."

"And have you talked to her about it since?"

"No."

She rolled her eyes. "What is it with men and not talking?"

"Are we going to male-bash, or can you help me?"

"Help you what, exactly?" she asked. "If you want to propose to Brynn, propose. Just do it right."

"But I did, and—"

"No, you didn't. You were in the middle of blowing your load. Do you think any girl trusts a thing a man says while he's coming in her?"

I sank back down into the armchair. "Okay, that's a good point. I hadn't thought about it like that. So... you mean I could still ask her and she'd say yes?"

"Yeah, I do, but can we back up for a second? You're sure about this? I mean, this is marriage, buddy. That's some deep stuff."

"I know. I'm serious as fuck, Zoe. I love her. I blurted it out, but that's because I keep thinking about it. I keep thinking how stupid I'd be to screw this up. How I can't ever let her go. I keep thinking about forever, and what that means. She's it for me. I'm done. I get it, marriage is huge. But anything less would be a mistake I'd never get over. I'm telling you, I want it all with her. A house and a dog and a bunch of kids. I can't imagine anything better than getting to spend the rest of my life with her."

"Holy shit," Zoe said. "Yeah, you definitely need to marry her."

"See?"

She laughed. "Okay, so now you need a ring. And a plan."

EIGHTEEN
BRYNN

I GOT HOME from class around four and dropped my backpack by the door. This semester was kicking my ass. Usually I had one class that was easier than the others, giving me a bit of a break. Not so much this semester. I was stuck with heavy workloads and more tests than I wanted to think about.

However, it was Friday, and I'd already decided to give myself the night off. I had to work in the tasting room tomorrow, but I'd have time to study afterward.

Hopefully Chase would be around this weekend. I hadn't seen him in a couple of days. He had a big job with a client a few towns over, so he'd been leaving early and getting home late. I missed him like crazy. I'd made him promise he'd text me when he got back into town tonight, no matter what time it was. I wanted him to come over, even if it was just to sleep. Being away from him this long felt like going through withdrawal.

I hung up my coat, but something caught my eye on the couch. There was a small white envelope with my name on the back sitting in the center of the cushion. It gave me a momentary chill, a little coil of fear making my heart beat faster. I made a quick check of the bedroom and bathroom, but no one was here—not even Chase behind a door, ready to jump out and scare me.

The envelope beckoned, with its crisp white paper and my name in blue ink. Inside, I found a folded half-sheet of paper with a typed message. No name or any indication who had left it for me.

JUST A TASTE *of you was all it took.*
A taste will help you find the next clue.

THIS HAD to be from Chase. What was he up to? I glanced around again, still half-wondering if he was going to pop out at me. What did he mean by *a taste will help you find the next clue?* Was this a scavenger hunt?

A taste. He'd had a taste of me when he'd kissed me the first time, but that had been right here. But a taste could mean something else. Maybe the tasting room?

Intrigued, I put my coat back on and walked over to the Big House. It was quiet this time of year, even on a Friday. There was a couple at a table, but no one sitting at the bar. I said hi to Lindsey, who was working tonight, and went behind the bar to look around. I found another white envelope tucked beneath a bottle of chardonnay.

A MESSAGE *in a bottle might not reach you.*
But a bottle will lead you to the next clue.

. . .

A BOTTLE. We had bottles of wine everywhere. Here, in the kitchen, in the cellars. My mom had her own private wine cellar. But that didn't seem right.

But what about the bottling room? Chase often worked on the machinery in there. I glanced around, wondering if I was being secretly filmed. Or followed. But I didn't see anyone. If Chase was watching, he was doing a good job of staying hidden.

I walked out to the bottling facility. The machinery wasn't running today, leaving the cavernous room oddly quiet. Ben was on the far side, working on a piece of equipment.

"Hey Ben. Have you seen an envelope in here anywhere?"

He put his tool down and wiped his hands on a rag. "An envelope? Did you lose something?"

There was a hint of amusement in his voice, making me wonder if he was in on this.

"Not exactly. But I think it might be in here."

"Hmm. I don't know, Sprout. I haven't seen anything."

Ben was literally the only person in the world who didn't make me feel like a child when he used one of my old nicknames. He'd been calling me *Sprout* since I was a baby. I actually liked it, coming from him. It was sweet.

I also didn't believe him. He knew exactly where it was. "Fine, don't help. I'll find it myself. But am I in the right place?"

"You might be." He winked.

He definitely knew where it was. I wandered around, checking in and around the bottling machine. As I moved farther toward one side of the room, Ben cleared his throat. I glanced at him and changed direction, and he gave me a subtle nod.

I finally found it on the conveyor belt, half-hidden by a cardboard box. It looked just like the others—plain white with my name on the outside. I slipped out the paper and read the note.

IT TAKES *you where you need to go.*
The next clue can be found with the turn of a key.

WHERE YOU NEED to go and turn of a key. I wondered if that meant my car.

Ben came up next to me, a soft smile on his face. He put an arm around my shoulders and gave me a quick squeeze. "Find what you were looking for?"

"Yep. But I'm not sure what's going on."

"Hmm."

"You're not going to give anything up, are you?"

"Not likely," he said. "But you have a nice time tonight."

"Thanks. What about you? Have a hot date?"

He shook his head. "None of that for me these days."

"Why not?" I was pretty sure Ben had a bit of a crush on my mom. I saw the way he looked at her. And now that she was getting divorced... "A woman would be lucky to have you in her life."

He started wiping his hands on the towel again, looking at them as if it was critical he get them clean. "Thanks, Sprout. That's nice of you to say."

It hit me, in that moment, how much I wished Ben and my mom would get together. Some kids dream about their parents reconciling after they split. I wanted my mom to get divorced already so she could be free—maybe even free to find love again. And if she found it with Ben... that would be pretty amazing. But it wasn't my business, and I didn't want to put him on the spot.

"I guess I should see if I can find the next clue. Have a good weekend."

"You too," he said.

I walked back to the cottage and looked in and around my car, but I couldn't find an envelope. Maybe I'd misunderstood the clue. I thought back to that day Chase had kissed me. He'd been out here, working on my car. I'd found him underneath it.

Crouching down, I looked under the car. Still no envelope. I was about to get the last note out to check it again when I got an idea. I popped the hood and lifted it.

Sure enough, there was the envelope. Wasting no time, I opened it to read the next clue.

GRAPEVINES IN LONG ROWS.

Into the clearing you go.

I KNEW EXACTLY what that meant. The south vineyard.

The sun was going down and with it, the temperature. I ran inside to get my keys, then drove out to the vineyard. My car bumped along the dirt road and butterflies fluttered their way around my tummy. I had a feeling I knew what this was about, and I couldn't quite believe it was happening. Why else would he plan something so elaborate?

I drove up the hill and Chase's truck came into view. Forget butterflies. My tummy was full of bursting fireworks. I parked behind him and got out. He wasn't here, but there was a note taped to his truck with an arrow pointing the way.

It was a short walk to the clearing. My brothers used to build fires here when they wanted to hang out with their friends—or girlfriends—away from the house. Chase not only had a fire going, but two big propane heaters stood on either side. He'd set up a little table, complete with a tablecloth and candles.

He stood next to the fire, looking adorable in his black coat and knit hat. He looked me up and down as I walked toward him, a sweet grin on his face. "Hey."

"Hi." I stuffed my hands in my pockets to keep them from shaking. Oh my god, this was really happening. "I hope I didn't keep you waiting too long."

"You got here faster than I thought you would, actually," he said. "I almost didn't have time to finish getting ready."

I stepped closer to the fire and the warmth of the propane heaters seeped into me. It was almost warm enough to take off my coat. "Getting ready for what?"

"Our date," he said, gesturing to the table and chairs.

He said it with such nonchalance, I thought I might have misread the situation. Maybe this was just a date. Maybe he wasn't going to—

"And I got you a little something."

As he reached into his inside pocket, my heart hammered in my chest. I bit my lip to keep the tears at bay. But the box that he pulled out wasn't small or square. It was long and rectangular. Maybe jewelry, but certainly not a ring.

The last thing I wanted was to seem disappointed or ungrateful. He'd blurted out something about wanting to marry me in the middle of sex. I couldn't expect to hold him to that, no matter what he'd said afterward. He hadn't been serious. And now he'd brought me a present, which was so sweet.

With a slow breath to calm my frayed nerves, I took the box. "What's this?"

"Open it."

He looked so excited—like an eager little boy. I slowly opened it. Sure enough, it was a necklace. A gold chain with my initials. Except my initials were BM, and this said BR.

I stared at the letters on the necklace, as if I'd been frozen by a spell. I couldn't move. I could barely breathe. BR? R was Chase's initial. Chase Reilly. Did this mean...

I tore my eyes away in time to see Chase lowering himself to one knee.

"Oh my god."

It was the smile on his face that did it. He beamed at me like he'd never been happier in his entire life. Like no Christmas morning, no birthday party, no crazy stunt with my brother could ever compare with this moment. And he was giving that smile to *me*. I started sobbing before he could get a word out.

Gently, he set aside the box with the necklace and took my hands in his. "I have a confession."

"What?"

"Do you remember that day I helped you move some of your stuff into storage?"

"Um..." I didn't understand why he was bringing this up while he was down on one knee in front of me. "I guess so, yeah."

"Your old diary was in a box. It fell out and I peeked inside. Don't be mad, I didn't read the entries. But I did see something you wrote that I'll never forget."

"What's that?"

"Brynn Reilly."

I bit my lip and sniffed. "That's... kind of embarrassing."

"No," he said with a smile. "It was amazing. I think that was the moment I knew I loved you. It hit me like a ton of bricks that you were always meant to be mine. I know we haven't been together for a long time. But I don't need more time. You're all I want, and I've known it almost from the start. I love you. I want to build a life with you, have a family, *be* a family for each other."

"Oh, Chase."

He squeezed my hands, then let go to reach into his pocket again. This time he pulled out a box that was small and square. He opened it and took out the ring. My eyes were almost too cloudy with tears to see straight.

Taking my hand again, he held the ring just in front of my finger. "Brynn Miles, will you marry me?"

"Yes," I said, barely managing to get the word out through my tears. I was sobbing again, but I didn't care. This was the single most incredible moment of my entire life. "Yes, oh my god, yes."

He slid the ring on my finger and before he could even stand, I threw my arms around his neck. He held me tight while I cried happy tears into his shoulder.

"Holy shit, I love you so much," he said.

"I love you, too," I sobbed.

He laughed a little as he stood and brushed the hair back from my face. "Did you just say you'll marry me?"

I nodded.

Cupping my cheeks, he kissed me. Or tried to. He couldn't seem to stop smiling. Although, neither could I. I was going to marry Chase Reilly.

NINETEEN

BRYNN

I'D NEVER BEEN SO nervous. Not for my SATs, or my first day of college. Not for my first date, or the first time I had sex. I couldn't think of anything that had left me as riddled with anxiety as the prospect of telling my family I was engaged.

Last night I'd been tempted to text everyone to give them the news. Once I'd stopped crying, and Chase had stopped kissing me, we'd calmed down enough to enjoy the dinner he'd brought. Between the fire and the heaters, we'd been cozy and warm, and the food had been delicious. I was excited to tell my family, but I'd decided to wait until I could see them in person.

But it wasn't supposed to be now.

Chase and I had come up with a plan. Zoe already knew—she'd helped Chase with the scavenger hunt—so we'd tell my mom first. I didn't anticipate my mom having a problem with it. She'd be surprised, but I was confident she wouldn't be against our engagement. Roland and Leo would probably do the big brother thing and be too practical for their own good. That was fine. I'd assure them we'd thought this through and that I knew exactly what I was doing.

Cooper? I wasn't sure what he would say. The only dark spot on our engagement night had been the unspoken knowledge that Cooper hadn't been in on it. He hadn't been the one to help Chase plan for one of the most important moments of his life.

I was desperately hoping this ring would show Cooper what Chase and I meant to each other. Why we were willing to be together despite his months-long temper tantrum. This wasn't a fling, an experiment, or some kind of fantasy fulfillment. This was real. Chase and I were getting *married*. Cooper had to get on board now.

I stood in the doorway of the tasting room, our plan falling to pieces before my eyes. Because my family—every last one of them—were here. I was coming in to work, although we obviously didn't have any customers. I'd had no idea they'd all be here. And unless I was going to slip the ring off my finger and hide it, chances were one of them was going to notice.

For a second, I thought about ducking outside to text Chase. He was at his shop, getting caught up on work. I knew he'd come over here if I asked. But my mom caught sight of me.

"Hi, sweetie," she said. "Impromptu Miles tasting. Want to help?"

"Um, sure."

I went behind the bar and helped her get glasses for everyone. Someone had already put out snacks—a few plates of crackers and cheeses.

Leo sat on the end, looking like he wanted to be here about as much as I did. His hair obscured his face and he was thumbing through something on his phone. He barely looked up when I set a glass in front of him.

Zoe had more color in her cheeks than I'd seen in a while, and she smiled at Roland. Instead of work clothes, he was actually wearing a t-shirt and jeans. That seemed like progress for Roland. Zoe was loosening him up again. He kissed her forehead and I noticed his hand straying to her belly. She wasn't big yet, but you could tell she had a baby in there. And the way Roland looked at her was awfully cute.

I set a glass down for Zoe—she might have a sip, although I wasn't sure—and Cooper grabbed me from behind. I held still for his bear hug, but before I could say anything, he let go and wandered around to the other side of the bar.

Mom opened a bottle of white and poured. "This is one of our spring releases. I've really been looking forward to adding this to our offering. It's so light and refreshing."

I took my glass and went through the motions, not really looking at the wine. Swirled it. Brought it to my nose. But I wasn't thinking about the intricacies of flavor as I sipped. I was thinking about Cooper. And Chase. And the ring on my finger that so far, no one had noticed.

Then I met Leo's eyes. He was staring at me, his glass untouched. He knew. He'd seen it. He raised his eyebrows and opened his mouth, like he was going to say something.

I blurted it out. "I'm going to marry Chase."

Everyone went silent, the sound of their voices disappearing in an instant. For what felt like an eternity, my family all stared at me.

Mom was the first to break the shocked silence. "Honey, what did you just say?"

"Chase asked me to marry him." I held up my hand, showing my ring. "I said yes."

Zoe's face broke into a wide smile and tears shone in her eyes. For a second, I thought all my fears about telling them were unfounded. They were going to be happy for me. And maybe Cooper would finally stop being an idiot.

I was wrong.

"You're kidding, right?" Roland asked, setting his wine glass down. Zoe smacked his arm. "Ow, what was that for?"

"Brynn, you're not even finished with school," Leo said.

Mom put a hand to her chest. "Oh honey, this is unexpected."

"Did he get you pregnant?" Cooper asked, his voice sharp.

My mouth dropped open. He had to be kidding me. "What? No, I'm not pregnant. God, Cooper, really? That's the first thing you have to say?"

"Why else would you be getting married this fast?" he asked.

"Because we love each other. Is that so hard to believe?"

"Brynncess, you can't do this. You're way too young to get married. You need to finish school and grow up before you even think about tying yourself to some guy for the rest of your life."

"Some guy? We're talking about Chase, not *some guy*."

"I swear to god, I'm going to fucking kill him."

"Cooper," Mom said.

"No, this has gone too far." Cooper started pacing around the room, his wine still in his hand. "He can't marry her. Jesus. She's twenty years old. What the hell is he thinking?"

"I'm twenty-one, genius. And Roland and Zoe got married at nineteen."

Cooper gestured wildly at them, sloshing wine onto the floor. "And got divorced."

"And now they're married and having a baby," I said. "What did their age when they got married the first time have to do with anything?"

"She was too young, just like you. Do you think they're normal? Most people fuck it up forever and don't recover."

"At least I'm willing to take a chance," I said. "Do you think I haven't thought this through? I'm not stupid, Cooper. I grew up in the same house with the same parents as you. I know what can go wrong."

"Hey," Roland barked at me, and Mom crossed her arms. "Watch it."

"I'm sorry, Mom. I know it wasn't your fault."

"You should know better," Cooper said.

"Chase isn't Dad." I was yelling now, but I didn't care. "He's a good guy, and you know it. You *know* him. And me being young doesn't change anything. I know what I want for my future, and Chase is part of that. He's not going to screw me over and he's not going to hold me back. He loves me and supports me. We're really great together. But you wouldn't know anything about that because you've been acting like a child."

"I'm acting like a child?" Cooper asked, still walking and flailing his arms. "You're rushing into marriage, and we're supposed to applaud you for your maturity?"

"Are they really rushing, though?" Zoe asked. "It's not like they started out as strangers. She's known Chase literally her entire life."

"But why make what could be a permanent mistake?" Cooper asked. "She already said she isn't pregnant. Why get married?"

"Would it be better if he'd knocked her up?" Zoe asked.

"Isn't being in love and committed to each other a good enough reason to get married? Quite honestly, I can't think of a better one."

Cooper pointed at her. "You're not helping. That ba—"

"You better shut your mouth, Coop, because if you even imply that the only reason I'm on her side is because pregnancy is making me irrational, I'm going to punch you in the balls."

He closed his mouth, scrunching his face like that was exactly what he was about to say. "Still not helping."

Leo spoke without looking up. "Brynn, is this because of Dad?"

I sighed and put my glass down. "You think I want to marry Chase because I have daddy issues?"

"I'm not trying to be an asshole here," Leo said. "But I think it's a fair question."

I glanced at my mom. I'd kept most of my feelings about Dad to myself. I didn't want to make this harder on her than it already was. She met my eyes, her expression full of concern. She was thinking the same thing as Leo. I'd lost my dad, so I was trying to replace him with another man.

Squaring my shoulders, I took a deep breath. "It's not like I had a good relationship with Dad. He was hardly ever around. He was barely a dad to me at all."

Mom's eyes were clouded with guilt. "Oh, honey."

"No, you don't understand. I didn't lack anything. I've always had so many good men in my life, it never bothered me that Dad wasn't the greatest. I had my brothers, and Ben. We all did. I'm not getting married because Dad left. I want to marry Chase because I love him. I've loved him for most of my life. And he loves me just as much, and do you know what that is? It's magic. It's what so many people long for, and some never find. Maybe I found it young, but that doesn't make it wrong."

"Brynncess—"

"Stop, Cooper. Just stop. What gives any of you the right to think you know what's best for me? I'm more than ready to commit my life to him. I'd do it tomorrow if I could. I'm going to marry him, and you can all either accept it or stay out of our way."

I walked out, ignoring the voices calling my name. Maybe it was childish to pout, but I was sick of taking the high road—of constantly trying to prove I was mature. Right now, I wanted to have a good old-fashioned tantrum.

I understood them being concerned that this was fast. But did they have to gang up on me like that? Did they have to assume we were too young and stupid to realize what we were doing?

When I got back to the cottage, I sprawled out on the couch and buried my face in a pillow. This sucked. I'd dealt with Cooper's stubbornness for months and I'd put so much hope into the idea that this would fix things. This would make them understand.

Clearly I'd been wrong. And right now, I just wanted this day to be over.

TWENTY

CHASE

BRYNN ANSWERED SO FAST when I knocked, I wondered if she'd been waiting at the door for me. She grabbed my shirt and pulled me inside, shutting it behind me.

She barely let me take my coat off before she was twining her arms around my waist and burying her face in my chest.

I gently wrapped my arms around her, hoping I didn't smell too terrible. I was dirty from working all day. "Hi, baby."

She said something, but it was muffled by my shirt.

"You okay?"

"Mm-hmm." She nuzzled her face against my chest, so I held her tighter. I wasn't sure what she was up to, but I wasn't complaining.

I ran my hands down her hair and eased her over to the couch. She didn't let go, just melted into my lap as I sat. I scooted back so she could tuck herself around me and just held her for a moment, enjoying the feel of her. She was warm, and she smelled so good. I took a deep breath, my brain lighting up at the hit of her scent. She was the most potent drug I'd ever taken, and I had no intention of giving her up.

She nestled tighter against me and I couldn't help but laugh. She was so fucking adorable. Was this some kind of post-engagement clingy phase? If it was, I hoped she never got over it.

I'd stopped being surprised by my reactions to Brynn months ago. Everything was different with her, and that was a good thing. But *wanting* a girl to be clingy? That struck a chord. *Don't date a clinger* was rule number four. Clingy girls meant trouble. That's what we'd told ourselves, at least.

But if Brynn wanted to cling to me like this for the rest of my life... sign me up. I fucking loved it.

Running my fingers through her silky hair, I kissed her head. "What's going on?"

She took a deep breath, sliding her cheek along the side of my neck, but didn't answer. Her hands slipped beneath my shirt and she pressed herself against me, like she was trying to get closer.

Something was wrong. I didn't know what it was, and I wasn't sure if I was supposed to ask or wait for her to tell me. I was still figuring out all this boyfriend—now fiancé—stuff. But I could sense that something was bothering her.

However, the way she was moving in my lap was making it hard to concentrate on anything else. She shifted so she was straddling me, and I instinctively moved my hands to cup her round ass-cheeks. I breathed her in again while she nuzzled against me, her face in my neck. Fuck, she felt good.

She rubbed against my erection, and I groaned, deep in my throat. I held her tighter as she peppered kisses up the side of my throat.

"Baby, I should get cleaned up. I'm all dirty."

"I like you dirty." She pulled my shirt up over my head and tossed it to the side.

Her touch spoke of desperation. Of need. She didn't just want sex. She needed me right now. I could feel it. I didn't know why, but I'd give her everything.

I held the back of her neck and went in for a kiss. My tongue lapped against her lower lip and slid into her mouth. She clung to me like she couldn't get enough. Like she needed to be closer. I pulled off her shirt to feel more of her soft skin. Ran my hands over her beautiful body while I kissed her.

She reached between us to unfasten my pants. This was moving fast; she obviously didn't need me to give her a warm-up. I shifted my hips so I could take them off.

"I need you to fuck me," she breathed in my ear.

I groaned, my dick achingly hard. "Then take your fucking panties off."

The couch was too limiting for what I wanted to do to her. Those primal instincts she'd awakened were kicking into high gear. I needed to possess her. Consume her. Own her and give her everything in return.

She took off her bra and panties, letting them drop to the floor. I grabbed her, hoisting her over my shoulder like a goddamn cave man, and took her to the bedroom.

I tossed her onto the bed and took a second to look at her. The soft line of her neck. Her tits with those sweet pink nipples. The slope of her stomach to her hips. Those legs that wrapped around me perfectly. God, she was gorgeous.

She lay on her back, biting her lower lip, and tipped her legs open. I got out a condom and quickly slipped it on. I needed to be inside her, and I needed it now.

I climbed on top of her and thrust inside. She was

already so wet, I slid in easily. She clung to me, holding me tight, shifting her hips to draw me in deeper. I growled into her neck, reveling in the sweetness of being inside her.

"Fuck me, Chase. Please. Fuck me hard."

What my baby wanted, my baby got. I plunged in and out, increasing my pace. Thrusting deeper. Harder. She moaned, digging her fingers into my back. The sharp pinch of her fingernails sent a rush of heat straight to my groin.

I could have come in her right then. The tension built so fast, my balls tightening, it would have taken almost nothing to pull my trigger and unleash inside her.

But that wasn't what she needed. And I never came first.

Slowing down, I kissed along her neck. Her skin tasted so good. I lapped my tongue against the soft spot behind her ear. Sucked on her neck while she moaned beneath me. I wanted to devour her. I bit her shoulder lightly, nibbling my way to her neck, and she gasped, tilting her head to bare more of her delicate skin to me.

Her nipples against my chest felt good, but I wanted to taste them. Grasping her tit in my hand, I licked her hard peak. She moaned again, sighing my name. I sucked on her nipple then gently pinched it between my teeth. Her back arched and she cried out, sending a shock wave of heat through my veins.

Conscious thought fled, replaced by pure carnal instinct. I pulled out and flipped her over, pushing her down flat on the bed. Sinking my hips over her ass, I drove into her from behind.

"Oh god, yes," she whimpered.

Fisting my hand through her hair, I tilted her head back to expose her neck. I sucked on her skin, grazing her with my teeth, while I plowed into her. Hard, swift thrusts, pushing my cock deep inside her hot pussy.

She was totally in my control. A heady sense of euphoria swept through me. Brynn was mine. She trusted me with her body, and her heart. She was going to fucking marry me—be mine forever.

I drove into her harder. Pulled back on her hair. She whimpered *yes* over and over while her pussy clenched around my cock. I was fucking her hard, pinning her down, biting her neck, pulling her hair. She arched her back and every gasp and moan spurred me on.

"What do you need, baby?"

"I need to come," she said, her voice soft and desperate. "And I need you to come inside me."

A few more hard thrusts and I pulled out so I could flip her to her back. Staying on my knees, I put her legs over my shoulders and sank my cock in deep.

Her tits were flushed pink, bouncing as I drove in and out. She was so fucking sexy. I leaned down, squeezing my glutes to drive into her harder. Our mouths crashed together, tongues licking out, messy and wet. The heat in her pussy built. She was close. I could feel it.

I could feel *her*. I'd never felt so close to anyone. Never realized how amazing this could be. Sex with Brynn wasn't just fun—a way to feel good and get off. It was deep and intense, connecting me to her. Not just to her body. Our spirits mingled as we fucked, like we were two parts of a whole. For this brief, blissful moment, everything was as it should be.

"I love you so much."

She kissed me again, moaning into my mouth. "I love you too."

I couldn't hold back much longer. The pressure in my

groin was ready to explode. I moved back, and she took her legs off my shoulders to wrap them around my waist.

I was deep inside her, but it wasn't enough. I needed to be closer. She held onto me while I draped myself on top of her, feeling every inch of skin. I buried my face in her neck, growling with every thrust. Her pussy was so hot I could barely stand it.

Her muscles clenched around my cock and she moaned loudly as she started to come. It was enough to make me lose my fucking mind. I plunged into her hard, feeling the tension hit the breaking point. My balls drew up tight, my back stiffened, and for one heartbeat, my body teetered on the brink.

Until I came undone.

White hot waves of pleasure crashed over me as I started to come. My cock pulsed, over and over. I drove into her, releasing all the tension and pressure. All the heat and passion. I gave it all to her.

When my climax subsided, I stayed inside her, holding her tight. I didn't want to let go—didn't want to disconnect. She wrapped her arms around me, her breath warm on my neck. I held her close, my chest filled with so much emotion, I didn't know what to do with it all.

I lifted to kiss her softly. Her lips, her cheeks. The soft skin of her throat. I pressed my lips to her, covering her with kisses. I needed her to know how much this meant to me. How much I appreciated her sharing her body with me. How much I fucking loved her.

Our mouths came together again in a slow, deep kiss. When I pulled away, she touched my face, laying her palm against my hand.

"How did you know?"

I kissed her lips again. "How did I know what?"

"How did you know what I needed?" she asked. "Everything you just did was... perfect. It was like you could read my mind. I didn't ask for anything, but I needed it all."

"I don't know." I brushed my nose against hers. "I just did what felt right."

Her eyes glistened with tears. "Thank you. I needed that so badly."

"Baby, what's wrong? Did something happen?"

She nodded, and my chest tightened with concern. I pulled out of her and quickly dealt with the condom, then gathered her in my arms.

"Tell me."

"I saw my family today," she said, her voice almost breaking. "I didn't know they'd all be there, but it was quiet at the Big House, so I guess my mom called everyone down to sample one of the new spring wines."

I was afraid I knew where this was going. Damn it, we were supposed to tell them together.

"I didn't want to talk to them without you, but they were there, and Leo saw my ring, so I sort of blurted it out. And then everyone jumped all over me about it."

"What did they say?"

"Cooper asked if I was pregnant."

Anger coursed through me and I fought to keep it out of my voice. "Are you kidding me?"

"No, it was the first thing he said. And that I'm too young and rushing into this. Zoe stuck up for me, but that's basically what they all said. Leo even asked if this was because of my dad."

I squeezed her and kissed her head. We'd both known her family would be surprised. But what the fuck was Cooper's problem? Apparently it was stupid to have hoped this would change his mind. That he'd see I wasn't fucking around. It wasn't why I'd proposed to her—that had nothing to do with anyone else—but I'd thought it might make Cooper realize how wrong he was about me.

"They weren't happy for you at all?"

"Zoe was. But the rest of them just ganged up on me."

I stared at the ceiling, trying to keep my breathing even. But this fucking hurt. I'd grown up with this family. I'd thought they knew me. Had they let me hang around all those years out of pity? Was I just a stray they'd let in? Good enough to feed once in a while, but not good enough to let into the family? Certainly not good enough to be with one of their own.

Yeah, Brynn was young. But she wasn't a child; she was mature and put-together. She'd always known what she wanted out of life and had never been afraid to go for it.

What was so wrong with finding love young, anyway? Did they want her to go through a string of losers who would break her heart before she settled down? How much baggage did a person need before they were ready?

Looking back, I wished I could tell my old self to calm the hell down and stop all the meaningless flings. What had that done for me? It had been fun in the moment, and to be fair, I hadn't really known better. I'd had no idea what loving someone felt like—the sheer power of it. What I had with Brynn was so much more than great sex. And the sex was fucking insane, so that was really saying something. But I didn't look back on my past and feel like it had been necessary. She wasn't missing out on anything by finding love now.

"You know what?" I rolled to my side and propped myself over her. "They'll come around. I don't know what it will take, but we'll prove them wrong. Someday they're going to look back on how they reacted and wonder what they were so worried about. We're in this together, baby."

She brushed her fingers across my jaw. "I love you so much."

"I love you too. Don't worry. I've got you."

Wrapping her arms around my neck, she pulled me close. I didn't want her to be upset, but I felt like I might burst. Brynn needed me. No one had ever needed me like this before and it was so overwhelming—so incredible—it almost brought tears to my eyes. This was what I'd always been missing. This was why I knew we were meant for each other.

This was why I'd never let her go.

BRYNN'S PHONE kept buzzing with texts until late that night. She didn't tell me what they said, but she didn't have to. As much as I wanted to march over to her mom's house and set everyone straight, I didn't. Brynn needed time to calm down, so we turned off her phone, put on a sappy movie, then went to bed early.

The next day, I knew exactly what we needed to do. I wasn't going to let this stretch out, or make Brynn face it on her own. Like I'd told her, we were in this together.

Of course, I wasn't ruling out just flying to Vegas to elope. If Brynn said the word, I'd book the tickets. But I was pretty sure she wanted a real wedding, and I was going to make sure she got everything she wanted.

After breakfast, we went over to her mom's house. I could tell Brynn was dreading it, and in a way, I was too. I wasn't sure how this was going to go down. Was I about to hear they didn't want me to marry Brynn? I didn't know how I'd handle it if that was what they said.

I took Brynn's hand as we walked inside. We found her mom sitting with Zoe in the living room. Zoe looked pale again. She had a thick blanket wrapped around her shoulders and a big bottle of water in her lap.

Mrs. Miles stood when she saw us. The tension in the room heightened and I fought down a flare of anger. Mrs. Miles had been good to me—not just good, she'd been great. She'd been more of a mother to me than my own in a lot of ways. I needed to keep my anger in check until we'd both said what we needed to say.

"I'm glad you're here," she said. "Do you want coffee? Tea? Breakfast?"

"No, Mom, it's okay. You don't have to play hostess," Brynn said.

"I feed people," Mrs. Miles said with a shrug. "It's what I do. Especially when I'm worried."

Her gentle smile put me more at ease. Maybe we weren't in for a lecture about why we shouldn't get married.

"She's been trying to get me to eat something all morning," Zoe said.

Mrs. Miles glanced at her. "I'm just trying to find something that won't upset your stomach. Roland said you haven't been eating enough."

"My doctor says I'm fine, all things considered," Zoe said. "The baby is growing. I just puke a lot. The cure is giving birth, but unfortunately I have to wait until July for that."

"Where's Roland?" Brynn asked.

"He had to go out of town for two days, and god forbid I be unsupervised," Zoe said with a roll of her eyes.

"He's just making sure you're taken care of," Mrs. Miles said. "Which is exactly what he should be doing."

I didn't think any of us missed her meaning. There was a certain satisfaction in her tone. She was proud of Roland for his concern—for making sure his wife was cared for. Something she'd probably lacked in her own marriage.

"Well, come in, you two," Mrs. Miles said, beckoning for us to sit.

Brynn took a deep breath. I squeezed her hand and kept her close as we sat on the couch across from Zoe.

I'd already decided I needed to take the lead on this. It was Brynn's family, but it felt like my place to explain. "I'm just going to come out and say what I need to say. I love your daughter. I love her more than anything. I know our engagement came as a surprise to everyone. But I want to assure you that I plan to take good care of her and do everything in my power to make her happy."

"I'm sorry for reacting badly," Mrs. Miles said. "You're right, it was a surprise. It's not because there's anything wrong with you, Chase. I didn't expect Brynn to want to get married so soon."

"I don't know how to say this without sounding like I'm being a brat," Brynn said. "But I'm not a little girl. I'm not playing house or getting into something I don't understand. I love Chase. He's good for me, Mom. This won't change anything about school or what I do afterward. So you don't need to worry about that."

"That's good to hear," Mrs. Miles said.

"I don't think he'd let me marry him if I said I wasn't going to finish school," Brynn said, nudging me with her elbow.

"That's actually true," I said. "I don't know how else to reassure you that we've thought about this and we know what we're doing. Except to say that I love her. She makes me want to be a better man and when you find someone like that, I think you have to hold onto them. Brynn is amazing. I swear to you, I'm going to love her for the rest of my life."

Zoe had the blanket up over her mouth and nose, but I could see that she was crying again. Damn it, she kept freaking me out when she did that.

"We would have said all this when we told you," Brynn said. "I didn't know you were all going to be there yesterday. I don't think me blurting it out like I did helped the situation, but Leo saw my ring and I panicked."

"Of course he noticed," Mrs. Miles said with a slight shake of her head. "I've said this before, and I have a feeling I'm going to keep saying it. Having adult children is hard. It's so difficult not to project your own mistakes onto your kids. But Brynn, what you said yesterday was right. Chase isn't your dad. I have to go on record saying I'm nervous that you're moving too fast, but if you're sure about this, I'll support you."

Brynn and her mom stood, her mom wrapping her in a hug.

"Thank you, Mom."

Mrs. Miles let go and gestured for me to get up. I stood, and she hugged me. "You've always been like a son to me, Chase. I want you to know that." She pulled away and put her hands on my arms. "And now we get to make it official."

Well, shit. Now my eyes were misting a little bit. I cleared my throat, hoping to god I didn't actually shed a tear in front of the three most important women in my life. "Thanks, Mrs. Miles."

"Oh, honey, now you really have to start calling me Shannon."

I let out a long breath. I didn't know why, exactly, but this felt like a big deal. "Okay... Shannon."

Brynn was sniffling hard, Zoe was full-on crying, and Mrs. Miles—Shannon—swiped the corners of her eyes.

"We need to celebrate." Shannon disappeared into the

kitchen and when she came back, she had a bottle of wine and three glasses. She poured and handed us each a glass of sparkling white. "To Brynn and Chase."

We held up our glasses—and Zoe held up her bottle of water—to toast.

Shannon sat back down on the couch next to Zoe, her wine glass in her hand. "Have you thought about the details at all, or are you going to wait?"

Brynn glanced at me. "Well, it has to be here."

She was so right. There was no better place for us to get married than her family's winery. "I agree."

"It's such a relief to hear you say that," Shannon said. "I was a little bit afraid the next thing you were going to say was that you were eloping in Vegas so you didn't have to deal with your obnoxious family."

I didn't mention I'd been thinking about that very thing earlier.

"No, I've always wanted to get married here," Brynn said. "It doesn't need to be a huge wedding. Just family, really."

"And I don't have a big family, so that won't add a lot of people," I said. In fact, I hadn't even bothered to call my parents to tell them I was getting married yet. I'd have to do that soon.

"So I guess the first thing to do is set a date," Shannon said.

"I don't mean to add fuel to the fire," Zoe said. "And if you're thinking long engagement, I'm not trying to pressure you to get married sooner. But I did have a cancellation for early June. Otherwise, we're all booked up on weekends for most of the year."

"June?" I asked. "I guess if we have to wait until June, that's okay."

"If we have to wait?" Brynn asked. "When did you think we'd get married? Next weekend?"

I shrugged. "I don't know. Sooner is better, but I can live with June if you can."

Zoe laughed. "Goofball, you're such a guy."

"What?"

"June is close to when the baby's due, though," Brynn said.

"If you take the June date, I'll have a month until the baby is due," Zoe said. "Between me and Jamie, and you and Shannon, I don't think it'll be a problem."

June seemed like a long time to wait, but I didn't know anything about planning a wedding. Four months? That had to be enough time. I certainly didn't want to wait until next year. Now that I'd decided, I was all in. I wanted to make Brynn my wife.

"I think we should do it," I said.

Brynn's eyes were bright, her smile lighting up her face. "Really?"

"Yes, really. I didn't propose because I want to be engaged forever. I want to get married. Let's do this."

Shannon looked between Brynn and Zoe. "I guess we have another wedding to plan."

TWENTY-TWO

BRYNN

ADDING *plan a wedding* to my to-do list felt a little bit insane. I was already busy with school and working weekends at the winery. Chase was busy too, with more jobs than he could handle most weeks. Zoe's knowledge, and connections, did help, and things were coming together. But the last couple of months had been crazy.

I'd also started helping Chase at his shop a few afternoons a week. Accounting was his least favorite part of business ownership. He'd been doing all right, but he wasn't as organized as he could be. And he had to force himself to get through things like invoicing.

I loved that stuff. Numbers and spreadsheets and reports. I'd started by helping him get caught up on some paperwork, then reorganized his filing system. Pretty soon, I was handling most of his accounting.

It gave me so much satisfaction that I could work with him like this. He told me constantly how much he appreciated my help. But I loved doing it. Crunching numbers and organizing things gave me a little buzz.

I glanced at the ring on my finger as I drove out to the

shop. I did that at least a thousand times a day. It was so pretty, and just looking at it gave me all kinds of warm fuzzies.

With my mom and Zoe on Team Wedding, Roland and Leo had quieted down with their protests. They'd still both felt the need to point out that we could opt for a long engagement, rather than getting married in June. Chase had shut them both up by saying if a guy wasn't sure he wanted to marry a girl, he shouldn't give her a ring in the first place. They didn't have anything to counter that.

Chase wasn't the least bit interested in a long engagement. He'd said more than once that he didn't ask me to marry him to *get engaged*. He asked me to marry him to *get married*. I was pretty sure he'd been serious when he'd said June was a long time to wait. He didn't give two shits that most people took a year or more to plan their weddings. To him, that was a silly waste of time.

Cooper remained on my shit list. Fortunately for him, I hadn't been there when Zoe told him Chase and I set the date for June. He'd apparently gone on a tirade about all the reasons we shouldn't get married. If he'd have subjected me to that nonsense, I probably would have punched him in the nuts. My desire to maintain my maturity only went so far.

I got to the shop and went inside. Chase was beneath a large tractor, his booted feet sticking out.

"Hey," I said, tilting so I could look under the huge engine. "How's it looking under there?"

"Dirty." He rolled out and grinned at me. "And not the sexy kind."

"Bummer."

"I'm glad you're here." He stood and gave me a quick kiss. "I have something to show you."

I followed him back to the office. Stopping in the doorway, I looked around. He'd rearranged the furniture and added a second desk. Now one faced each wall, with two chairs sitting back to back.

"What's all this?" I asked.

"I got you a desk."

I walked over to the new desk and traced my finger along the wood. He'd bought matching desk organizers, all in a pretty shade of blue.

"This is so sweet."

"I figured you should have your own space," he said. "This place is yours as much as it is mine."

This meant so much to me, I didn't know what to say. "Thank you. I love it."

"Yeah? You sure? I know you like blue, but if you want another color, we can order anything."

"It's perfect."

He smiled and pulled me close. "I'm glad you like it. School is still the priority, obviously. But I love having you here, so this is pretty great."

"It's so great."

"I even left you a spot to put a wedding picture on your desk. Not that you can't just swivel your chair around and look at me. But that's a thing, right? Putting pictures on your desk?"

I laughed. "Yes, that's a thing."

"Awesome. I have room on my desk for pictures, too."

God, he was so cute. "Speaking of wedding, can you make it to cake tasting this afternoon?"

He pulled away. "Shit, baby, I can't. I have to get this thing running before I can leave. It's being a bastard. I'm sorry."

"That's okay. As long as you don't mind me choosing without you."

"Yeah, whatever you want is fine," he said. "But it's kind of killing me that I have to miss cake."

"I'll bring some home, how about that?"

He hugged me again and kissed my forehead. "Thanks, baby. You're the best."

———————

BEFORE I WENT to the bakery, I stopped by the winery. Since Chase couldn't make it to the cake tasting, I figured I'd see if my mom was around. She might like to go.

I found her in the Big House, back in the kitchen. "Hey, Mom. I'm about to go sample cakes. Want to join me?"

"Oh sweetie, I'm sorry. I can't get away. Zoe had to go home, and we have a big group coming in less than five minutes. Jamie needs my help."

Cooper's voice carried from the hallway and Mom raised her eyebrows.

I knew exactly what she was about to suggest. "Mom, no."

"Just ask him," she said.

"He won't come."

"It's *cake*."

I knew what she was doing. She wanted me to try to make nice with my brother. Admittedly, cake was probably a good way to do it.

"Fine, I'll try."

I caught up with Cooper just as he was heading out the doors. "Cooper, wait."

"Hey, Brynncess." He shoved his hands in his coat pockets.

"I'm going to the bakery for cake tasting." I paused,

noting how his eyes lit up a little at the mention of cake. "Do you want to come?"

He narrowed his eyes and pressed his lips together, like this was an extraordinarily difficult decision. "Cake?"

Damn it, why did he make it so hard to stay mad at him? He wasn't even trying to make me laugh, but I couldn't help it. "Yes, cake. Lots of it. Samples of all different kinds."

"Yeah, well, it's probably better if I go. If someone else picked, you'd end up with shitty cake."

I rolled my eyes but decided to take this as a small win. At least he wasn't ranting about the fact that I was getting married. Maybe this was progress.

The bakery was just down the road, so we walked. Cooper started talking about grilling meats and I let him talk. Sometimes I got tired of his endless rambling. But things had been so strained between us, this moment of normalcy was nice. Even if I did hear more than I ever wanted to know about the relative merits of marinating versus his homemade steak rub.

When we got to the bakery, Cooper held the door open for me and the little bell jingled.

"Oh my god, it smells good in here." He walked in and started eying cupcakes and cookies in a glass case. "Can I get one of everything?"

"You're ridiculous."

A woman in a crisp white apron came out from the back. She looked young, maybe mid-twenties, and had blond hair pulled up in a bun. "Hi, can I help you?"

"I'm Brynn Miles. I'm here for a wedding cake tasting."

Cooper sighed heavily, but I ignored him.

"Great," she said. "You two have a seat and I'll bring out the samples."

I sat at a little round table, but Cooper paced along the

glass case, then over to the window. He glanced outside, then went back to the case.

"You can sit," I said.

He scowled but took the seat across from me. His leg bounced, and he bobbed his head slightly, almost like he could hear music.

The baker came back and set a tray filled with small cake samples on the table in front of us. "I have them labeled, but if you have any questions, just let me know. I find it's better to leave couples to it, rather than hover."

Cooper swiveled toward her, his mouth turning up in a crooked grin as he looked her up and down. "I'm not part of the couple. She's my sister. I'm just here for the cake."

"Oh, I'm sorry," she said. "Well, it's nice of you to help her choose. Let me know if I can get you anything else."

"We will absolutely do that," he said, still grinning at her.

Her cheeks flushed, and she bit her lip. I swear, the woman almost giggled. Cooper didn't take his eyes off her until she disappeared into the back again.

"Seriously?" I asked. "Do you have to flirt with every woman in existence?"

"What?"

"Don't pretend like you're not aware of what you're doing."

"Relax, I'm just playing," he said. "She's married anyway. Has a ring."

"She's married and you still eye-fucked her like that?"

Cooper lowered his voice. "I did not eye-fuck her. What do you know about eye-fucking, anyway?"

"I'm a woman. I know plenty about being eye-fucked."

He groaned. "No one should be eye-fucking you."

"My fiancé can eye-fuck me all day long," I said, crossing my arms. "In fact, he can—"

"Stop." Cooper put a hand up, palm out. "Don't say it. I swear to god, Brynncess, I am not equipped to deal with this, so you need to shut up right now."

"Why are you being such a pain in the ass?"

"I'm not," he said, and the poutiness in his tone made me want to strangle him. "I'm here, aren't I? I'm helping you pick a... cake."

"A wedding cake."

"Whatever."

I shook my head and laughed. "Can we just taste these, please? I need to choose one before we leave."

With a deep breath, he picked up his fork. "Fine."

I took a bite of white cake with buttercream and strawberry filling. Basic, but it was good.

Cooper put a bite in his mouth. "Hmm. This one tastes like bitter lies."

"That's carrot cake."

"Interesting." He took a bite of the next one. "This one's not bad. Unrealistic expectations."

"Cooper."

But he was on a roll. He sampled the next piece. "This might be the one, Brynncess. Life-altering-mistakes with you're-too-fucking-young frosting."

"Wow, I'm so glad I brought you," I said, my voice flat.

He took his time finishing his bite, then went on to the next one. His fork slid through the spongey cake and he made a show of taking a dramatic bite.

"Oh, yeah, this one. This is good. Same you're-too-fucking-young frosting, but this betrayal cake is fantastic."

"I hate you right now."

He licked the frosting off his fork. "No you don't."

"Yes, I really do. I want to smack that smug grin off your face."

"So violent," he said. "You don't need to resort to threats to get your point across. I thought I taught you better than that."

"You taught me to stand up for myself."

"Good, I'm glad to know you were listening. Why am I here, anyway? Shouldn't *he* be here picking cake with you?"

"He had to work late."

He took another bite of chocolate with whipped mousse filling. "Kind of a shitty excuse, don't you think? Shouldn't he be making this a priority?" He pointed to another cake sample with his fork. "You should pick the carrot cake."

"Chase doesn't like carrot cake."

"I know."

I barely resisted the urge to smack my head against the table.

The baker came out again and smiled at Cooper. "How are we doing?"

"We're doing excellent, sugar." He wiped his hands on a napkin and stood. "You have an amazing talent and quite frankly, we're lucky you share it with the world."

She blushed a deep scarlet. "Thank you."

"I have to get going, but I think my sister knows what she wants."

"Oh, okay." She twisted her hands together. "Would you like a complimentary cookie before you go?"

Cooper turned up the heat on his grin. "I would love one. Can I pick anything I want?"

"Of course."

I rolled my eyes. Naturally he'd get a free cookie. The guy played women like a piano prodigy.

He picked a cookie—chocolate chip with walnuts—and

she got it out of the case. She handed it to him in a little white bag.

"Thank you, sugar. This is the best thing that's happened to me all day," he said to her with a wink. "Although if you didn't have that ring on your finger, I'd be sampling your cookie tonight."

"Cooper!" I had no idea how he got away with that stuff.

She giggled behind her hand, seeming to have forgotten my existence. At least she wasn't offended by Cooper's ridiculousness.

He took his cookie and paused next to my table on his way out. "Choose wisely. If you have shitty cake, I'm not coming."

"Maybe we won't invite you."

"Then it'll be the worst wedding ever."

"Ha." I pointed at him. "You said wedding."

"Fuck." He glanced back at the baker. "Whatever, she gave me a cookie."

The bell jingled again as Cooper left. I tasted the other cake samples while I waited for the baker to come back to reality after being Cooper-ified. She'd taken the full force of his charm. I was impressed she was still standing.

I ate the last bite of chocolate cake with whipped mousse frosting. This was definitely the one. It was delicious, and Chase would love it.

I put in the order, confirming the date with the baker. My phone buzzed with a text from Cooper, so I checked it on my way back to the winery.

Cooper: It's not too late to back out. We can eat the cake anyway.

Me: Stop being ridiculous

Cooper: Just saying. We don't need excuses to eat cake.

Me: How's your cookie?

Cooper: Amazing. Did she give you a cookie?

Me: No

Cooper: See?

Me: See what? What's your point?

Cooper: That I'm awesome.

I shook my head and put my phone away. I didn't know if I'd ever understand my brother.

I TOOK my coat off as I walked. It was warm for the beginning of spring. Living in the mountains, the spring weather could be anything from freezing cold with a late-season snow to hot enough for shorts and flip-flops. Today was somewhere in between, but I didn't need the coat I'd worn to campus.

I'd been to class, and now I was meeting Grace for coffee. The café we usually went to was a short walk from campus. Grace and I had been getting together at least once every few weeks since last fall.

I don't think either of us had quite known what to do with each other at first. She'd been an only child until she was in high school. I'd grown up with three brothers. Neither of us knew much about having a sister.

But early on, we'd seemed to both come to the same conclusion. It didn't matter what having a sister was *supposed* to look like. We'd form our own relationship and figure it out as we went.

So we met for coffee or lunch sometimes. Grace lived in

Tilikum, not too far from campus, so it was easy to get together on days I had class.

She was already at a table when I got to the restaurant. I got my coffee, then went to her table and hung my coat on the back of the chair.

"Hey," she said. "Isn't it gorgeous out there?"

I sat. "Yeah, it's so nice."

"How have you been? How are the wedding plans coming?"

"Good so far," I said. "There's a lot to do, but I think we'll manage."

"I'm excited for you," she said with a smile.

"Thanks. I wish everyone was."

"Is Cooper still mad?"

I sighed. "He's being such a pain in the ass. He's still not speaking to Chase. I brought him with me to the bakery for cake tasting yesterday and he kept referring to the cake flavors as things like *bitter lies* and *you're too fucking young frosting.*"

She laughed. "I'm sorry, I shouldn't laugh. But I grew up next door to a family with five boys. I'm well acquainted with the mantrum."

"Mantrum?"

"Man-tantrum," she said.

"That's my new favorite word. He's throwing the biggest mantrum ever." I took a sip of my coffee. "I don't even know why he's mad anymore."

"I'm sorry," she said. "I know how hard that is."

I thought about the ring on Grace's finger. She didn't talk about her fiancé very much, except to say that he was away and they couldn't get married until he came back. I wondered if he was in the military—maybe involved in something top-secret and she couldn't talk about it. Leo's military service had been a bit like that. There was a lot he couldn't talk about. Whatever her reasons, I always felt like I shouldn't ask too many questions. But it seemed like maybe she'd given me an opening.

"Does your family like your fiancé?" I asked.

"Yeah, our families have known each other forever," she said. "But there are people in my life who think I'm stupid to wait for him."

"Really?"

She nodded. "I'm used to it, though. And honestly, it's none of their business. They don't need to understand."

"I admire your attitude," I said. "And your self-assurance."

"Thanks. I'm not always so confident about it. But honestly, the people who are judging me don't know the truth because they only see what they want to see. And it's not up to me to change their minds. Although I'm not dealing with a brother who's being a pain about my wedding, so your situation is a little different. What about the rest of the family? Are they on board?"

"My mom is, for the most part. So is Zoe. Roland and Leo are... reluctantly supportive."

She smiled. "Your brothers—I'm sorry, I should say *our* brothers, but I'm not used to it yet—they're good guys."

"They are. Even when they're being ridiculous and driving me crazy. Which is often." I took another sip of coffee. "So, there's actually another reason I wanted to see you today. I was wondering if you'd be a bridesmaid."

"Oh my god, Brynn." She touched her mouth and took a deep breath. "I'm so honored. I would love to."

"Yeah? I'm so glad. I really want you to be a part of it."

We both stood and hugged. Tears stung my eyes and I sniffed a little.

"This is so exciting," she said. "I've never been a brides-maid before."

"Really?"

"Nope. I don't have any other sisters, and I'll be shocked if my best friend gets married before she's fifty."

"Oh, so she's the female equivalent of Cooper?"

Grace tilted her head. "Actually, a little bit. Cara's a fire-ball. It's going to take one hell of a guy to handle her."

"She sounds pretty cool."

"Yeah, she's great. I'll invite her along for coffee one of these times." Her phone rang, and she peeked at the screen. "Sorry, it's my mom. I'll just see what's up, if you don't mind."

"No problem."

"Hi, Mom. I'm having coffee with Brynn." Her face fell as she listened. "Oh my god, don't even open the door. Did you talk to him? What did he want?"

I waited, feeling bad for listening in. But I had a feeling I knew who she was talking about.

"You're sure he's gone?" She shook her head, rolling her eyes. "I swear. I know I shouldn't but god, Mom, he's such an ass. I can't believe he did that. No, I'm coming over. Yes, now. It's fine, I'm positive she'll understand. Okay. See you in a few."

Grace hung up and put her phone away.

"Why do I have a feeling that was—"

"Dear old Dad? Yeah. He showed up out of nowhere a little while ago. I don't remember the last time he tried to contact my mom. Do you know what he's been up to? Why he might be trying to weasel in on my mom again?"

"I have no idea. We haven't heard from him in months. My mom might have, through her lawyer, but everyone assumes I'm too young and fragile to participate in grown-up discussions so they don't tell me things."

"That's annoying. I'm sorry to bail on you, but I can tell when my mom's upset, even when she's trying to hide it. And Dad showing up always upsets her. Plus I need to find out if Elijah saw him."

"Speaking of Elijah... I don't want to push if your mom isn't comfortable with it, but we'd love to meet him."

She smiled. "Yeah, we'll have to do that soon. The whole thing has been a little overwhelming for my mom. She doesn't want to keep him away from any of you, but she's struggling a bit with how to handle it. He's very... literal. And inquisitive. He's going to have so many questions."

"That's understandable. None of us want to step on your mom's toes."

"Thanks. I'll talk to her about it again and see what she thinks." She stood, so I followed and hugged her again. "Thank you so much for asking me to be in your wedding. I can't wait."

"I'll let you know when we go dress shopping."

"Perfect. And if there's anything I can do to help, just text me."

We said our goodbyes and Grace left. I sat back down and stared at what was left of my coffee. Why had Dad come here? Was he trying to see Grace's mom? Or did he want to see his kids?

He hadn't once tried to come see me. He hadn't called, or texted. Not a single attempt at contact.

I felt such a confusing mix of emotions. I didn't want him bothering my mom. It would have made me angry to hear he'd come to Salishan. So why did this hurt? Why did knowing he'd tried to visit his other family make me feel so awful inside?

Whatever his reasons, I needed to let someone know he'd been here. I texted Leo.

Me: I was just with Grace. Dad showed up at her mom's house.

Leo: When?

Me: A little bit ago.

Leo: Where are you?

Me: Coffee shop near campus.

Leo: Come home.

Me: Why?

Leo: Just to be safe. I don't trust Dad.

Me: He's our dad. He's not going to hurt me.

Leo: Don't care. No chances.

Me: I'm fine.

Leo: Did you tell Chase yet?

Me: No, I texted you first.

Leo: Call him now. I want him to know.

Me: You're weird, but OK.

Leo: That's how this works now. Chase takes point.

Chase takes point. That seemed like a big concession, coming from Leo. Oddly, it took the sting out of my dad's general shittiness. And I did want Chase to know. In fact, what I needed right now was to sink into Chase's arms.

I left my coffee and walked back to my car, texting Chase as I went. As soon as I got his reply, I felt better. Chase always made me feel better. He'd meet me at my place, and I knew as soon as I was with him, he'd give me everything I needed.

CHASE WASN'T there when I got to the florist. He was supposed to meet me, but his truck wasn't in the parking lot, and no other customers were inside. I checked my phone again, but he hadn't texted. Hopefully he was on his way.

The florist was down a side street, not far from Chase and Cooper's apartment. It was a cute little shop with flowers and greenery spilling from potted plants and hanging baskets. The sweet scent of flowers wafted on the light spring breeze, intensifying when I opened the door.

"I'll be right with you," came a voice from the back. It sounded like Mona, the head florist. I'd spoken to her on the phone already. Zoe and Jamie both said she was the best. I had some ideas for bouquets, but I was excited to see what she had in mind.

The bell above the door jingled, but when I turned, it wasn't Chase. It was Cooper.

"What are you doing here?"

"Nice to see you too, Brynncess." He nudged my arm. "Aren't you happy to see me? I even showered first."

I waved my hand in front of my nose. "You sure about that?"

He lifted his arm and sniffed his armpit, then tried to shove it in my face. "Yeah, I smell great."

"Oh my god, get off me," I said, pushing him away.

He snickered but backed off. "So what are we doing?"

"We? I know what I'm doing, but I'm not sure about you."

"Mom said you were down here."

Lovely. My mom was trying to orchestrate a truce between us again. "I don't really need you to give me sarcastic commentary about all my flower choices."

He gasped, his eyes widening as if he were shocked. "What? I would do no such thing. I'm never sarcastic."

"Cake that tastes like bitter lies? Yeah, you were enormously helpful in choosing my wedding cake."

He laughed and pretended to wipe his eyes. "God, I'm fucking hilarious."

I crossed my arms, determined not to laugh at him. I wasn't even going to give him the satisfaction of a smile.

Mona came out with a stack of large binders in her arms. "Sorry about that. Let's go to the table in the back and we can take a look. If you have ideas already, that's wonderful. But I have plenty of options if you're not sure where to start."

Cooper put his hands in his pockets and followed me back. Apparently he'd decided he was helping me choose flowers. Truthfully, I was glad to have someone else here to weigh in. I wasn't sure what I wanted, and it would be nice to get a second opinion. If Cooper decided to behave, that is, which was doubtful.

I took a quick peek at my phone again, just to see if Chase had texted. No messages.

"Are you sure she has time to get her order in?" Cooper asked. "There's no need to be impatient, right? It would probably be better if she waited another year. Or five."

"Cooper."

Mona smiled. "No, as long as we finalize the order in the next few days, it's fine."

Scowling, he crossed his arms.

"Don't mind him, he's just being an obnoxious older brother," I said.

"Obnoxious? I'm offended, Brynncess. I haven't even started to be obnoxious."

Mona just chuckled as she opened the first binder. "Now, June is a traditional month for weddings, so if you want, we can stick with classic white roses. Maybe something like this."

She showed me a picture of a bouquet of white rose buds together in a tight bundle.

"That's really pretty, but I think it's more formal than I want."

"No problem," Mona said, turning the pages. "Maybe something along these lines?"

Cooper stepped closer. "Oh my god, I love calla lilies. They hold their shape so well."

Mona nodded. "They really do. They're great to work with and they make gorgeous bridal bouquets."

He started flipping through the pages, pointing out different flowers. The next thing I knew, he and Mona were deep in a discussion about the properties of certain plants and flowers.

The bell above the door jingled again.

"Sorry I'm late." Chase stopped just inside the shop, his eyes sliding from me to Cooper.

Cooper stiffened, and my heart skipped a few beats.

Great, were these two going to throw down in the middle of the flower shop?

"As you were saying, Mona?" Cooper said, dramatically turning his back on Chase.

Chase rolled his eyes and walked to the back of the shop. He was dressed in a battered t-shirt, stained jeans, and his work boots. His rough hands looked dirty, but I could tell he'd washed them. They often looked like that after he'd been working all day.

I stepped close and slipped my hands around his waist. He was a little grimy, but god it was sexy. I leaned in to smell his neck, trailing my nose across his stubbly skin, feeling his Adam's apple bob in his throat.

"Careful," he said quietly. "I probably don't smell very good."

"Mm," I hummed into his neck. He smelled amazing. The hint of perspiration on his skin was intoxicating. "You smell good."

He held me tighter and I felt the hardness of his erection pressing against me. I loved that he responded to me like this. Inappropriate to make him hard in the middle of a florist appointment? Probably. A turn-on? Definitely.

Cooper cleared his throat behind me.

"Cockblocker," Chase murmured.

I giggled and stepped back.

"Sorry I'm late," he said. "I meant to leave work early enough to go home and shower, but I didn't have time. I came straight here."

"That's okay. I'm glad you made it." I trailed my fingers down his chest. "I know it's just flowers and you probably don't care that much. But I wanted you to at least see the options."

He touched my face, his hand rough against my cheek. "Of course I care. This is important to you, so it's important to me."

Cooper cleared his throat again.

I looked over my shoulder. "No one invited you."

"Mom did."

"Are we ten?"

"No, last I checked, you're twenty-one and only on the brink of adulthood."

I clapped a hand to my forehead and ground my teeth together. God, he was driving me crazy. But getting in digs about my age was better than hostile glares at Chase, so maybe this was good. It was hard to tell with Cooper.

Chase glanced at him, and I could see the uncertainty in his eyes. It was more than uncertainty. It was pain. He was hurting over the rift with Cooper. I was hit with potent mix of guilt, sadness, and frustration. I'd never meant to cause this between them. I hated that I was the problem. If Chase hadn't wanted to be with me, he and Cooper would still be off doing... whatever it was they did. They'd both be happy again.

I took a deep breath and clasped Chase's hand. He squeezed mine back and we went to the table to look at flowers with Mona. And Cooper, apparently.

"Brynn, will you remind Chase that he left pizza in the fridge at home and it's going to go bad?"

"Um, he's right here. He can hear you."

"Hmm," Cooper said, flipping idly through the binder pages. "Just tell him he needs to clean up his shit."

Mona stifled a laugh.

Chase just shook his head. "So, what are you thinking for the flowers? These look nice."

"Tell Chase those aren't in season in June. They're better for fall."

"Cooper, stop."

"That's okay, you can tell Cooper his knowledge of flowers is impressive. As is the depth of his assholery."

"Brynn, please tell Chase there's only one asshole in this room, and it isn't me."

I stifled the urge to shout at both of them. "I'm not playing this stupid game."

Cooper cast a glare at Chase, then flipped the pages of the binder backward. When he spoke, his voice was softer, no longer laced with sarcasm. "These are a good choice for June, Brynncess. They'll be in season, so they'll cost less. It might be more color than you were looking for, but I think they'd look really nice."

I looked at the arrangements he was pointing to. They had a mix of roses with purple hydrangea and white calla lilies. "They're beautiful."

"He's right," Mona said. "These are lovely and very easy to get this time of year."

"My work here is done," Cooper said. He yanked on my ponytail as he walked past me, heading for the door. "Coopster is out."

"If you want to go with this, I can show you what the rest of the flowers will look like," Mona said. "We can make the bridesmaid bouquets and everything else match."

I glanced up at Chase. "What do you think?"

"They look great to me. If you're happy, I'm happy."

Mona took us through the rest of the flower choices. She really did know her stuff, and she was conscious of our budget, which I appreciated. I made a mental note to thank Zoe—for the hundredth time—for pointing me in the right direction.

After we finished, Chase led me outside with his hand on the small of my back. His phone dinged and he pulled it out. Looking at the screen, he groaned.

"Is something wrong?"

He rolled his eyes. "Honestly? This girl I was dating last year keeps texting me."

That raised my hackles. I didn't want to be jealous of some past girlfriend. It was easier to not think about the girls Chase had been with before me. And I didn't worry that he would ever be unfaithful. I trusted him. But hearing that a girl was texting him did not sit well with me.

"That's not cool."

"No, it's not," he said. "I don't know why she's doing it. I haven't seen her in months. Not since... well, not since before you. And I quit replying to her texts before that, but she keeps coming up with crazy bullshit to suck me back in."

"Maybe you should block her number?" *And delete her contact information. And block her on every social media channel you use. And maybe see if we can get her to move out of state or something.*

"I think you're right," he said. "This shit she's trying to pull? Just, no. It's time."

He tapped a few things on his screen, then pocketed his phone. "There. That's finished. I feel better already." He wrapped his arm around my shoulders and kissed my head. "Hungry?"

"Yeah, I am."

"Cool. Let me buy you dinner. I suggest Ray's because I think they're the only place in town that will let me in like this. If you want something nicer, I need a shower and clean clothes first."

I popped up on my tiptoes to kiss his mouth. "I love Ray's. Maybe we should ask for the back booth."

He nibbled on my bottom lip. "I like the way you think."

TWENTY-FIVE
CHASE

IT WAS weird having Brynn in my apartment—reminded me of the day Cooper had caught us on the couch. Plus, we never hung out here. If we weren't going out, we always spent time at Brynn's place. I slept there more often than not. But I was home doing laundry and taking care of a few things. She'd been in class all day and was helping with an event over at the winery tonight, so she'd stopped by in between.

"I'm so ready for this semester to be over," she said, putting her backpack down. She looked tired.

"You sure you're doing okay?"

"Yeah. There's just so much going on."

I pulled her close and kissed her. We were both feeling the pressure of everything. Work. Her classes. The wedding. "I know, it's a lot. Are you sure you have to work tonight?"

She took a deep breath. "Yes. They really need me."

I touched her face and kissed her forehead. "Fair enough. Are you hungry?"

"A little."

"I'll see if we have anything."

I went into the kitchen and poked around, but there wasn't much food. Cooper had some leftovers in the fridge, but I wasn't about to offer her his half-eaten dinner. I found a bag of chips in the cupboard and grabbed them. Better than nothing.

When I came out of the kitchen, I didn't see Brynn. "Hey, where'd you go?"

Her voice came from my bedroom. "In here."

She was standing in my room, looking around. "Sorry. I just realized I've never really been in here."

"Yeah, it's... a bedroom, I guess."

It was pretty fucking empty, actually. I hadn't changed anything. There had never been a lot of stuff in here to begin with. It looked like a single guy's room. My bed was just a mattress on the floor. I had a dresser, and a shelf with a few things sitting out. Clothes in the closet. Cheap blinds on the window, nothing on the walls. It was kind of sad, when I thought about it.

Brynn sat on the edge of the bed. "I always wondered what it would be like to crawl into your bed."

"You've been in bed with me lots of times."

She plucked at the sheets. "We've been in my bed. Yours seems different."

"Yeah, I guess it does."

"Can I tell you a secret?"

I grinned. "Only if it's dirty."

"Stop," she said with a laugh. "Once when we were younger, I overheard you talking to Cooper about sneaking a girl into your room, and I got so jealous. I took it out on Cooper. I was mean to him for like a week and he had no idea why. I still feel a little bad about that."

The last thing I wanted to talk about with Brynn was

me sneaking other girls into my room. Or other girls in general. And there was something about Brynn being in this room that felt off. It wasn't about Cooper. I had no idea when he was coming home today, but I was past caring if he saw us together. Part of me wanted to drag her into his bedroom, fuck her on his bed, and leave him a note saying I'd done it.

But this room was the past—a relic of the old me. That guy had brought a lot of random girls here. Brynn was not some random girl. She was the love of my life. So even though she was nibbling her bottom lip and had a *let's be naughty* look in her eyes, I knew I wasn't fucking her on this bed. Ever.

"I shouldn't mess with you," she said. "I have to go to work, so I don't have time to play."

"That's okay."

She stood and ran her hands up my chest. "Do you want to come over tonight? I have to work late, but I like it better when you're there. Even if we're just sleeping."

I kissed the tip of her nose. "Yeah, I'd love to come over. But we won't just be sleeping."

"Good." She lifted up on her toes for another kiss. "I have to go. I'll see you after work."

"Do you want these?" I lifted the bag of chips.

"That's okay. I can eat over there. Thanks, though."

"Love you."

"Love you, too."

I walked her out and after she left, I went back to my bedroom. I stood in the doorway for a few minutes, staring at my bed.

Cooper and I had made a bonfire out of his mom's mattress after she'd kicked her husband out. We'd done it as a joke at first. But it had turned out to be a cathartic experience for the Miles family. Even I had felt good about watching that mattress go up in flames.

Then we'd done it to Zoe's bed. That had been Roland's idea, although Cooper and I had egged him on about it. It had been symbolic. A sign that Roland and Zoe's lives apart —and the potential for sleeping with other people—were in the past.

I was at a similar crossroads. I'd left my past behind without any doubts. Brynn was my future. I'd proposed, given her a ring, and in a month, I'd marry her. But I felt like my transformation wouldn't be complete until the mattress burned.

Pulling the comforter and sheets off, I left them in a heap on the floor. The mattress was more awkward than heavy. I tipped it up and slid it over to the door. I could drag it downstairs myself and hoist it into the back of my truck. Then take it out to one of the unused fields on Salishan land to burn it. A lot of their property was used as vineyards, and they had a big pear orchard that they leased out to another farm. But there were acres and acres of empty land—forest, mountainside, even open fields. Cooper and I had spent most of our childhoods out there, so I knew it well.

I got the mattress halfway out of my bedroom and had to make a tight turn into the living room.

"What the fuck?"

I hadn't heard Cooper come in. I looked around the edge of the mattress to find him standing just inside the door, his hands on his hips.

"Are you fucking moving out?" he asked.

"No, but I don't know why you care."

"Because you live here, or you used to. I'd like to know what the hell is going on. Jesus, Chase, keep a guy in the loop."

I leaned the mattress against the wall so I could let go. "Are you fucking kidding me? This is the most you've spoken to me in months. I sleep here once every week or so. You're telling me you'd be surprised if I packed my shit and left?"

"If you're not moving out, what the fuck are you doing with your bed?"

"Burning it."

He stared at me for a second, mouth half-open, eyes intense. "What?"

"I'm burning my mattress."

"Why?"

"Is that a serious question?"

Cooper just kept staring at me. I had no idea what he was thinking. Which was weird, because normally the time between Cooper having a thought and saying the thought was too small to be measurable.

I was so sick of this shit. "You know what? At this point, you can go fuck yourself. I'm sorry it was her. I'm sorry your sister and I fell in love, but we did."

He still didn't say anything.

I didn't really intend to keep talking, but once I started, I couldn't seem to stop. "I don't think you understand what that means to a guy like me. Everybody fucking loves you. Have you ever felt alone, even once in your life? I know your dad is an asshole, but the rest of your family is great. And they love the shit out of you, even when you're being a fucking nutjob. You know that as long as they're around, you'll never really be alone.

"I never had that, Coop. I spent my whole life knowing my parents didn't really want me. Do you know what that does to a guy? That fucked me up. But now I have someone who wants me—who chose me. I'd do anything for her. And the craziest part? She'd do anything for me. Jesus, Cooper, that's fucking insane. When you find that, you can't let it go."

He crossed his arms and widened his stance but kept silent.

"I know you and I had a good thing going and it was really fucking fun. Work hard, play hard, right? But is that really how we were going to live the rest of our lives? Are we really those guys? Because I know where those guys end up. They either make a huge mistake and get tied to some crazy girl for the rest of their lives, or they die alone and miserable."

"That's really fucking bleak, dude."

"I know, and I'm not making that mistake. Look, I didn't mean for you to find out the way you did. I swear to you, I was trying to do the right thing. And I wouldn't have done this for any girl. You have to know that. I never gave a shit before because there was always someone else—always more women. But Brynn isn't just some girl to me. I love her, Cooper. I fucking love her. And I'm not going to do the idiot thing this time. I know a good thing when I have it and I'm not going to let her go. Ever. She's my life, dude. She's the most important thing in the world to me and I'm going to spend the rest of my life trying to make her happy."

"Holy shit," he said. "You're going to burn your mattress."

"Are we still on the fucking mattress? Were you even listening to me?"

"You're going to burn your mattress because you love my sister," he said. I wasn't sure if he was talking to himself, or to me. "Oh my god. What the fuck have I done?"

His eyes were wild, and he ran his hands through his

hair, messing it up as he started pacing around the living room.

"What the shit? You were... and I thought... so I figured you just... and what the fuck? How did I even think that? Cooper, what the fuck is wrong with you?"

I waited for his brain to calm down. It wouldn't do me any good to interject while he was on a rant like this. He needed to get it out so he could think clearly again.

"Because that meant you... and she was... God, how did I not get that? How did I get this so fucking wrong? This is a goddamn disaster." He stopped dead in his tracks in the middle of the living room and stared at me. "Jesus, Chase. I fucked this up."

I hadn't expected that, so I didn't know what to say.

"You're really going to marry my sister."

It wasn't a question—thank god, because if he threw that at me like an insult, I'd probably punch him in the face. "Yeah, asshole. I'm going to marry your sister."

Then Cooper did something I'd never seen, not even once in the entire time I'd known him. He got tears in his eyes.

We stared at each other for a long moment. Between any other two guys, it would have been enormously awkward. But between us, it wasn't. It was necessary.

When he finally spoke, his voice was unnaturally subdued. "Chase, I'm sorry."

He barreled into me before I had a chance to reply, wrapping me in a tight hug. Now my eyes were stinging with tears. I hugged him back. This was prime gay-joke fodder, but we'd get to that later. For now, I just bear-hugged my best friend.

When he finally let go, he stepped back and wiped his

eyes. "You piece of shit, you made me fucking cry. You owe me a cookie."

"I didn't make you cry, dumbass. And if anyone owes cookies, it's you."

He cleared his throat. "Let's get this mattress out. Fucker needs to burn."

WE TOOK the mattress and box spring out near the south vineyard, not far from where I'd proposed to Brynn a few months ago. A healthy dose of gasoline and it lit up the night sky.

Cooper and I sat in camping chairs watching the fire. Neither of us had said much since leaving home. We'd been busy with the mattress and getting the fire started. Now we sat with beers in hand while the flames licked at the edges.

"Is there any way we can be cool?" he asked, finally breaking the long silence. "Or did I fuck this up forever?"

I thought for a minute before I replied. "I don't know, man. I get that she's your sister, and she's really important to you. But I thought you'd get over it sooner, you know? I thought if you understood that I was serious about her, you'd get on board."

"That isn't why you proposed so fast, is it? To prove it to me?"

"No. Believe it or not, it wasn't about you."

He took a drink of his beer. "Okay, buddy, real talk. You might think I overreacted when I saw you guys on the couch, but I stand by that. It was a shitty thing to come home to."

"Yeah, but—"

"Hold on, I'm not finished. I fucked it up after that, and

I'll own it. I didn't give you a chance to explain—just stayed pissed off. But dude, it was hard. I was so fucking mad. Yeah, I was an asshole for thinking you'd hurt Brynn. But you have to admit, it's not like you have a track record of being the perfect boyfriend. Not that I do, either. But come on, if you had a sister, would you let her anywhere near me?"

"Fuck no."

"See? Neither would I. Although if I *wanted* to be a good boyfriend, I'd be the best fucking boyfriend on the planet."

I tipped my beer bottle to him. "That's true, bro. You would be."

"I just want Brynn to be happy," he said. "Actually, that's not true. I want more than that for her. Happy is awesome, but it's just a feeling, you know? I want her to be safe, and secure, and living a good life."

"I'm going to give that to her. I promise."

He glanced at me, the firelight dancing in his eyes. "You really are, aren't you?"

"Yeah, I really am."

"I am sorry," he said. "I mean that. I should have trusted you. I've been a shitty friend. But the good news is, I guess that means I can tell Leo and Roland to call off the plan."

"What plan?"

He grinned. "Now you'll never have to know. Although if you fuck things up with my sister, we'll kill you. You know that, right?"

"Oh yeah, I know."

"Just so we're clear."

I shook my head and finished my beer. He'd been a dick for longer than he should have, but forgiving Cooper was a foregone conclusion. We had a history that went too far back for this to break us. I loved that motherfucker too much. He was the only person besides Brynn I'd ever really loved who had loved me back just as hard.

"There's just one more thing we need to talk about before this is finished," I said.

"What's that?"

"I need a best man. I don't know if you know a guy who might be free that weekend, but I could really use someone to stand up there with me."

"Are you fucking serious?" He sniffed and wiped his nose. "Goddammit, Chase, you're making my eyes leak again. You really need to stop doing that. If we get caught like this, people are going to question our sexuality. They probably already do, by the way. Brynn and I look a lot alike. They're going to assume you're with her to alleviate your homoerotic fantasies about me."

"That's exactly why I'm with her. Although I don't know why I'm bothering. I could legally marry you in this state, so there's no need for the ruse. Oh wait, I don't like dick. Never mind."

"No shit. I like my own dick way too much to want another one in my life."

"Are we going to keep talking about dick, or are you going to say you'll be my best man?"

"Bro, I would be honored to be your best man. And you're a better guy than I am. I don't know if I'd ever talk to me again after the shit I put you through."

"That's okay, I'm banging your sister. Kinda makes up for it."

"Oh my god, shut the fuck up." He set his empty on the ground. "Seriously, never talk about my sister and sex. Ever. Damn it, why don't you have a hot sister, or a hot single mom? I'd so have revenge sex with one of them. Or maybe both of them."

I laughed. "Shut up, you would not."

"Yeah, you're right. Even I have limits."

"You know what you have to do now, though, don't you?"

"What?"

"You need to talk to Brynn."

He groaned. "Yeah, I know. Fuck."

I opened another beer for each of us and handed one to him. "You'll be fine. I'm pretty sure you're still her favorite."

"I doubt it, but I'll make it up to her."

We clinked our bottles together. "I know you will."

THE FLOWERS COOPER had planted outside my cottage were blooming. I paused outside and took a deep breath. It was a gorgeous day. The sun was warm and the lush scents of spring wafted through the air. I'd been over at the Big House to help my mom get ready for an afternoon wedding. Just being there, moving chairs and setting out floral centerpieces, had roused flutters of excitement in my tummy. In less than a month, we'd be getting ready for *my* wedding.

I went inside and nearly jumped out of my skin. Cooper was standing in the living room next to what looked like a pile of blankets.

"Oh my god, what are you doing here? You scared me."

"Sorry," he said. "I need to talk to you."

"What's that?" I pointed to the blankets.

"It's a blanket fort."

I blinked at him a few times, waiting for him to explain. But he didn't. "Um, okay. Why did you build a blanket fort in my living room?"

"I told you, I need to talk to you."

"What does talking to me have to do with a fort?"

He let out a breath, like he was getting impatient with me. "Really?"

"But why did you—"

"Just get in the fucking blanket fort, Brynncess."

He held the end of one blanket open while I ducked through. Inside was surprisingly spacious. He'd propped up couch cushions and used a few chairs to create the structure. Blankets draped over the top and sides. When we were kids, he used to make me blanket forts all the time. His had always stayed up so much better than mine.

Cooper got in and we both sat cross-legged on the floor. "I remember the day you were born."

That wasn't even close to what I'd expected him to say. "You do?"

"Yeah. Grandma and Grandpa took Roland and Leo to the hospital to see you, but I'd wandered off. Ben found me playing outside, so he took me. I remember Dad being mad because I was dirty, and Mom drinking water from this big cup with a straw. But mostly, I remember seeing you for the first time."

I wasn't sure why he was telling me this story, so I just nodded.

"You were so tiny. Just this little bundle with a pink hat. I wanted to hold you, but no one would let me. Mom did later, though, when Dad wasn't around."

"That's sweet."

He shifted, leaning back against the chair behind him. "Ben took me home and we went for a long walk in one of the vineyards. I remember because he kept me out past bedtime. He told me that having a sister was a really special thing. It was a big responsibility. It was going to be my job to watch out for you."

"Oh, Coop."

"I never forgot that. And when you got older, I realized how right Ben had been. Dad didn't do things right with you, and I think Ben had known he wouldn't. Dad never brought you flowers, or balloons on your birthday. He didn't make sure your clothes weren't slutty or tell you what to look out for when boys started noticing you.

"Roland and Leo didn't either. I don't blame them for that, though. Roland was doing his own thing, and he had Zoe. And Leo had to go join the fucking Army and get himself blown up. It left me with all the responsibility for you. But that was okay, because from the day you were born, and Ben had told me it was my job, I'd taken it seriously.

"Little girls need someone to look after them. They're soft and fragile, even the tough ones. I know you're tough, Brynncess, but you're soft on the inside. And you should be. I don't want anyone to take that away from you."

My eyes stung with tears and I sniffed hard, biting my lip to keep them from falling.

"I know I'm not your dad," he continued. "But the asshole we got stuck with wasn't good enough, so I tried to make up for it. Maybe I haven't always done a good job, but I'll tell you one thing, no one loves you like I do." He paused and looked down. "At least, no one did."

He met my eyes. I'd never seen Cooper look like this before. He almost looked like he was going to cry.

"I'm so sorry, Brynn," he said, his voice soft. "I went the wrong way with this. I assumed all the wrong things, and that was a shitty thing for me to do. I should have trusted you. Jesus, I should have trusted Chase. He's been my best friend since Kindergarten. I should have known he'd never hurt you."

I didn't think I could speak without crying, so I just nodded again.

"Chase is the best guy I know," he said. "Hell, if I was gay, I'd make him go gay so I could marry him."

"Oh my god, Cooper."

"I'm serious," he said. "But I'm not gay, and neither is he, which turns out is good news for you, because holy shit Brynn, Chase fucking loves you. If I could have picked a guy for you to be with, who else would I choose but him? He's the best. And yeah, maybe his track record with women is as bad as mine, but he's never been in love before. And he fell in love with *you*, and that's just about the coolest fucking thing I can even imagine. Frankly, I'm not sure why I didn't think of it sooner, because it's perfect."

"You're not taking credit for me and Chase getting together."

"You never would have met him if not for me," he said. "My friendship paved the way for you to be with the love of your life. See? I'm always looking out for you."

I laughed softly and shook my head. "Yeah, I know you are."

"Just promise me something."

"What?"

He looked me in the eyes, his expression serious. "Take good care of him for me."

That was it. I couldn't stop the tears from trailing down my cheeks. "I will. I promise. And Cooper, I didn't mean to take your best friend away."

"I know." He reached over and squeezed my hand. "But if someone had to, I'm really glad it was you."

TWENTY-SEVEN

BRYNN

"COME ON, Brynncess, the party bus is leaving," Cooper called from outside.

I slipped on a pair of flats and grabbed my purse. We had dress fittings today, and Cooper had declared himself our driver. I went out and piled into my mom's car with Grace, Mom, Zoe, and her increasingly large baby belly.

"Ready, ladies?" Cooper asked.

The dress shop wasn't far. When we arrived, Cooper got out to open doors for us, like he was a chauffeur, then hurried to open the front door as well.

"Thanks, Coop," I said as I went inside.

"Anything for the bride."

He'd done a complete one-eighty since his blanket fort apology. Now he was firmly on Team Wedding and jumped at the chance to help any time he could. He'd even called the bakery to make sure I hadn't actually ordered a carrot cake, since he knew Chase would hate it.

Jolene, the saleswoman I'd worked with to order the dresses, came out to greet us. She was a curvy brunette in her later forties who always wore shirts that showed several inches of cleavage. We said our hellos and she led us through displays of wedding gowns, bridesmaid and prom dresses, and other formal wear, to the fitting area. They had several couches facing a little podium surrounded by mirrors. I'd been here with my mom to choose my dress and look at bridesmaid dresses. Today our dresses were in, and we'd be getting our final measurements for alterations.

Cooper came back carrying a large grocery bag. He pulled out a bottle of champagne and a package of clear plastic cups.

"Jolene, I hope you don't mind my girls indulging in some bubbly," he said as he popped the cork. "And I'd be happy to pour you a glass if you'd like, sweetheart. Sorry Zoe, you don't get any, but I brought sparkling cider for you."

"Thanks, Coop," Zoe said.

Jolene smiled. "Please, have fun. I'll go see about your dresses."

Cooper passed out champagne and poured some cider for Zoe. "Does this mean I get to see the dress?"

"Yeah, I suppose you do," I said. "They'll need me to try it on again."

"Awesome." Cooper put the champagne down, pulled out his phone, and started typing.

"What are you doing?" Mom asked.

"Texting Chase to brag," he said. "I get to see Brynn's dress and he doesn't."

We sipped champagne and waited. A few other people wandered in and out of the store, but we had it mostly to ourselves. Cooper seemed to get restless. He alternated between sitting on the arm of one of the couches and walking through some of the nearby displays, looking at dresses. I wondered what was taking Jolene so long.

Grace chatted with my mom, which was so nice to see. The two of them got along well. It restored my faith in humanity a little bit. Despite the damage my dad had done, some really good things had come out of it all.

Cooper came over, holding up a blue sequined prom dress in front of himself. "This color would look great on me, don't you think?"

Grace laughed. "It does bring out your eyes. But I'm not sure if you're man enough to handle that much sparkle."

"Gracie, I would rock this sparkle. I'm all sparkle."

"That you are," she said.

Roland came into the shop, making a beeline for Zoe.

"What are you doing here?" Zoe asked.

"You left your ginger candies." He sat down next to her and handed her a small bag. "I was worried you'd get sick while you were out."

"This is so sweet," she said. "But I told you before I left, I'm having a good day."

"Still, it couldn't hurt to have these on hand."

Sometimes I felt like I barely recognized Roland. He'd changed so much from the grouchy workaholic who'd avoided us like the plague. Back then, I'd wondered what Zoe could have ever seen in him. But I hadn't known the real Roland. He was still serious—and sometimes too practical for his own good. But god, he loved Zoe. He treated her like a treasure. It made me so happy to see. Love looked good on my brother.

Zoe leaned over and kissed him. "Thanks for bringing these. I'll see you at home later."

"Are you throwing me out?" he asked.

"Well, it's kind of a girls' day," she said.

"Cooper's here."

I was about to say Cooper was just the driver when he

came waltzing over wearing a pink tulle skirt over his jeans, holding a satin wrap around his shoulders.

"I don't know why girl clothes are so fabulous and guy clothes are so boring." He stepped onto the platform and checked himself out in the mirrors. "Look at this. Why can't guys wear shit like this? It's not fair. I call sexism. Girls shouldn't have a monopoly on all the awesome shit. Seriously, what guy wouldn't want to wear a big frilly skirt?"

"Me," Roland said.

"You're missing out, bro." He turned and looked in the mirror over his shoulder. "It hides my sweet ass, though. That is a downside."

"Did I miss anything?" Chase came in, dressed in a crisp white t-shirt and dark jeans. His hair was damp, like he'd just showered.

"You're not supposed to be here." I stood and slipped my hands around his waist. He smelled fresh and clean. It made me want to forget the fitting and take him home to get naked. "This is for the girls."

"Cooper's here."

"Dude, what do you think?" Cooper said, turning in a circle. "Nice, right?"

"Yeah, bro, that's a good color on you," Chase said.

I looked up at him. "He's basically wearing a tutu."

Chase shrugged. "So? It's Cooper."

Which was basically the answer to any question about my brother.

"All right, ladies, sorry for the delay." Jolene returned, followed by another clerk, both of them carrying large garment bags. "Time for the dresses."

"Chase, you need to get out of here," Zoe said. "You can't see Brynn in her dress."

Chase glanced around at our little party, which now

included both Cooper and Roland. He sat on the couch and winked at me. "Yeah, I'm not going anywhere. I'll close my eyes."

"The more the merrier," Jolene said. She hung the dresses on a rolling garment rack and unzipped the first one. "We'll start with the bridesmaids. This one should be for Zoe."

Zoe and I glanced at each other in confusion as Jolene pulled out a bright pink dress. It was short, and strapless, and the most hideous shade of hot pink I'd ever seen in fabric form. It was *not* the dress we'd picked.

"I think there's been a mistake," Zoe said. "That dress doesn't have enough fabric to cover my boobs right now."

"Oh, maybe this is for Grace?" Jolene looked at the tags on the garment bag.

"No, that dress isn't for us," I said. "It's nothing like the dresses we chose."

"That's so odd," Jolene said. "I'm sorry, Brynn. This must have the wrong sales slip on it. Let's check the other one."

She opened the second garment bag, producing another dress identical to the first. Hot pink and hideous.

Cooper crossed his arms. "Damn it, I really want to comment on how good someone's boobs would look in those, but it's Zoe and Gracie wearing them."

Grace glanced at me and my mom, raising her eyebrows.

"You get used to him," I said.

"I don't even hear half of what he says anymore," Mom said. She glanced at Cooper, who looked at her in surprise. "I love you, honey."

"I'm sure these are just mislabeled," Jolene said while she and the other clerk put the two pink monstrosities back in the garment bags. "Let's take a look at the bride's dress. Then Cherise and I will go see about the others."

I moved around behind Chase and covered his eyes. "No peeking."

He rubbed his hand along my arm. "I won't."

Jolene opened the larger garment bag with a flourish. White tulle spilled out as soon as the zipper opened, as if the dress had been straining to break free from its vinyl prison.

It was the wrong dress.

I dropped my hands from Chase's eyes. "Um, that's not my dress."

"Heavens," Jolene said, placing a hand over her ample cleavage. "It's not?"

"No. Not even close."

"I'll go check in the back." Cherise scurried away.

"Like I said, they're probably mislabeled." Jolene set about trying to stuff all the tulle back into the bag, but it resisted her efforts.

I bit my lip, trying not to worry. Our dresses had to be in the back. We'd ordered them weeks ago and didn't have time to order new ones.

Jolene finally wrestled the dress into the bag and zipped it up, then whisked it away. We waited in tense silence for them to come back, hopefully laden with more bags containing the dresses we'd actually ordered. But when they both came out a few minutes later, they didn't have more dresses.

"There appears to have been a mix-up," Jolene said.

My heart sank. A mix-up? This close to the wedding? And of all things, it had to be my dress.

"Now, let's not panic," Jolene said. "I'm going to call the manufacturer right now and see what happened. Your dresses must be somewhere. As soon as we track them down, we'll call you in. And we'll make sure the alterations are done at no extra charge."

I took a deep breath. Everyone was looking at me, like they were expecting me to turn into a raging bride-monster. I wasn't going to freak out, but it was hard not to be worried. My dress was one of the things that really mattered to me.

"Okay, well, I guess we'll just have to wait until they come in."

Jolene sighed, her shoulders relaxing with obvious relief. "Good. I'm going to go call. I'll be in touch as soon as I have the dresses in hand."

"Thanks."

The dress situation took the wind out of my sails. Everyone else seemed to understand. Cooper drove Mom and Grace back to Salishan, and Roland took Zoe, leaving me with Chase.

"What kind of ice cream do you want?" he asked as we walked out to his truck.

I smiled. "Salted caramel?"

"Done." He picked up my hand and kissed the backs of my fingers. "Don't worry. Everything's going to be fine."

I leaned into him. "Thanks."

"Feel better yet?"

"A little."

"Ice cream," he said. "Then... a bath?"

"That sounds great."

"We've got this." He put his arm around me. "I'll make you feel better."

And the amazing thing was, he already had.

BRYNN'S PRESENCE at the desk behind me was pleasantly comforting. And slightly distracting. Not for the first time, I wondered if there was a better way to configure the furniture in here so we were closer. Could she run invoices if she was sitting in my lap? She'd probably say no, and to be fair, I'd probably just end up fucking her on the desk if I had her ass against my groin all the time. We wouldn't get a lot of work done.

But it had been at least five minutes since I'd touched her. I didn't care if we were working, that shit was ridiculous.

I swiveled my chair around and leaned into her neck, breathing in a lungful of her. Of Brynn. That soft, warm scent that lit up my brain like a drug.

"Mm." She hummed and tilted her head so I could kiss her neck. "I need to finish these invoices so you can get paid."

"Am I distracting you?"

"Yes."

I reached around to squeeze one of her soft tits. "I like distracting you."

She laughed softly, but she wasn't melting at my touch. Her body was tense, almost rigid.

"Are you okay?" I asked, pulling my hand away.

"Yeah." She turned her chair to face me. "I'm sorry. I'm just stressed."

I pulled her closer, the chair wheels squeaking on the concrete floor. "Come here. Talk to me. What's stressing you out?"

"It's just... the wedding, I guess. I don't want to be all bridezilla about it, but we don't have dresses. Cooper said the weather has been too cold, and depending on where the florist is sourcing her flowers, there might be issues. So many people haven't RSVPed that I don't know what to tell the caterer. Zoe keeps insisting it will all come together, but she can't go more than an hour without either puking or crying, so I don't know if I really trust her judgment right now. Plus her baby is due just a month after the wedding, and maybe we should have waited after all."

"Why would waiting help?"

Her lips parted, but she paused. "Well... we'd have more time to get things done. And I wouldn't be upstaging Zoe's baby with a wedding."

"Okay, first of all, are you really worried about upstaging Zoe? She's making a person. That isn't going to go unnoticed, regardless of when we get married. And it's Zoe. She's not the jealous-girl type."

"That's true."

I rubbed my hands up and down her thighs. "Second of all, what's the worst that will happen if nothing else goes right?"

"We run out of food because we didn't tell the caterer to

bring enough, we have no dresses to wear so I have to marry you in a t-shirt while holding a bouquet of dandelions because the flowers died."

"We'll order too much food and Cooper will Hoover the leftovers." I touched her cheek, my rough calloused hand sliding over her petal soft skin. "You are going to be the most beautiful bride, no matter what you wear. If they can't get your dress, we'll go find another one. We'll drive to every store in the state until we find one you love. And if you're holding dandelions when I marry you, then those will be my new favorite flower."

"Why are you so amazing?"

"Born that way," I said with a shrug. "You're just the lucky recipient of my amazingness."

She leaned in and brushed a kiss across my lips. "Okay, Mr. Genetically Amazing, I still need to get these invoices done."

"Fine, I'll let you work." My pout was only half-pretend. It would have been more fun to make out in the office, but she did have a point about getting paid. Especially because I was paying for most of our wedding. Shannon kept trying to argue with me about it, so I just paid for things behind her back so she didn't have to worry about it. But her mention of guests and RSVPs got me thinking. "Hey, speaking of RSVPs, did my parents respond yet?"

By the flash of worry that crossed her features, I knew the answer before she said a word. "No, I don't think they have. But I haven't checked the mail today, so maybe..."

"Yeah, maybe." Or probably not.

I'd called my parents shortly after I'd proposed to Brynn —the second time, that is, not after I blurted it out in the middle of an orgasm. Left a message. Hadn't heard back. I'd figured they'd at least send the little RSVP card to confirm they were coming.

They had to be coming. Maybe we weren't close, and they hadn't called me once since moving. But this was my *wedding*.

At this point, I just needed to call them and see what was up. I walked out into the empty shop and called their number.

Dad answered. "Chase."

"Hi Dad." I took off my baseball cap and scratched my head before putting it back. "How's the new place?"

"It's fine."

My dad hated small talk, so I didn't know why I was trying to engage him in pointless conversation. "So... did you and Mom get the invitation? We haven't heard back."

"Yes, we did."

I hesitated, waiting for him to say more. To say they were coming. "And?"

"Chase, what are you thinking?"

"Right this second, or in general? You're going to have to be more specific."

"Don't be a smart-ass. You're actually getting married?"

"Yeah, that's why we sent out invitations," I said, unable to keep the frustration from my voice.

"Did you get her pregnant?"

I closed my eyes and ground my teeth together to stop myself from losing my shit on him. "No, Dad, I did not get her pregnant."

He was silent for a moment and I got the feeling that he hadn't expected that. He'd been sure I was only marrying Brynn because I'd knocked her up.

Good to know you have so much faith in me, Dad.

He took a deep breath. "How long have you known this girl?"

"Did you read the invitation? She's Brynn Miles. I've known her since she was born."

"We didn't know you were dating anyone," he said. "This is very sudden."

"How would you know if I was dating someone, though? It's not like we do Sunday dinners and I could have brought her to meet the family."

I could hear my mom in the background, urging him to ask me questions.

"How long have you been dating this girl?" he asked.

The way he kept calling her *this girl* got my hackles up. "Since last fall."

"That's less than a year," he said.

"Yeah, I'm well aware of that."

"Chase, I dated your mother for two years before we even discussed the possibility of marriage. How could you marry a girl you've been dating for less than a year?"

"Because I love her."

He groaned. "Is that what you think marriage is? It's not that simple. Marriage is hard work. This is a lifelong commitment you're roping her into."

"Jesus, Dad, I'm not roping her into anything. I asked her to marry me. She said yes. It's not because she's pregnant, or because I conned her into it. We love each other. She's the most amazing woman I've ever known and it's a fucking privilege that I get to be with her."

"I just don't think you understand the level of responsibility involved."

"Why not?" I asked, trying not to raise my voice. "Why do you think I'm such a fuck-up? Because I didn't go to med school? Because I'm a mechanic? God forbid I not have a job where I have to put fucking certificates on the wall to show how important and smart I am."

"You've done nothing but squander your life," he said. "You run around with that man-child you call a roommate, partying, drinking, picking up women. Why do I think you're a fuck-up? Because you are. Because you've never done anything to prove otherwise."

His words stunned me into silence. I had no idea what to say to that.

"If you insist on going through with this, we'll come," Dad said.

"No," I said, my voice surprisingly even. "No, don't come. This is the most important day of my life and I'm going to spend it with the people who care about me. You don't need to be there."

I hung up without waiting for his reply.

Rage boiled hot, searing me from the inside. I felt like I was about to snap in half, and when I did, I'd spew fire. I needed to get out of here so I didn't take this out on Brynn.

The office door opened, and she peeked out. "Hey. Do you want to get some dinner soon? I'm almost done with these."

"No," I said, the word coming out harsher than I meant it to. I took a deep breath. "I just have to go deal with something."

"Oh, okay. Are you all right?"

"Yeah." I turned away because she'd know if she saw my face. I knew she had the power to make me feel better, but I needed a little time. Just to cool off. Think things through. "I'll text you later."

"Okay, if you're sure," she said. "I love you."

"I love you too, Brynn. So fucking much."

I left her in the shop, a knot of anger and shame settling

deep in my chest. Did *anyone* believe I was cut out for this? Every time we'd told anyone we were getting married, we were hit with the same reaction. Disbelief. Suspicion. Assumptions. Her family. My parents. The people who knew us—or should know us—best had questioned this from the start. Were they right?

Was I really just a fuck-up?

I drove out to the highway to get out of town. I had fucked up in the past. Probably a lot. And who knew, maybe I didn't deserve a girl like Brynn Miles. She was smart, and fun, and loyal. Beautiful. So goddamn beautiful, sometimes it hurt to look at her. Maybe I was on borrowed time with her, and any minute she was going to realize I wasn't good enough.

The highway curved through the jagged terrain, my headlights a pool of light in front of my truck. The hum of the engine and the feel of the pavement sliding beneath the tires helped calm me down. My heart wasn't beating quite so fast, and that knot of pain dulled.

I was far from perfect, but I hadn't messed up everything. I owned my own business. Made good money. It wasn't a fancy job that gave my parents bragging rights, but fuck them anyway. Nothing I'd ever done—no award, no achievement—had ever made them care. Nothing had ever been enough to make them love me.

Brynn loved me. That was fucking priceless. She loved me, and she needed me, and I didn't give a fuck who stood in our way. I was going to marry her and love the shit out of her forever. And everyone else could just fuck right off.

TWENTY-NINE
BRYNN

MY LAST GROUP left the tasting room, all smiles and with at least one bottle of wine each. They'd been a fun group—three couples who had been friends since college. They were all in their forties now, with kids approaching high school. They were first time guests, and they'd loved the wine selection. My job was a lot of fun when I had happy customers.

The hum of voices carried from one of the larger rooms, but my tasting room was empty. We'd be closing soon, and my feet were tired. A bath sounded nice. Or maybe Chase would give me a foot rub. He was at work today, too, on a job a couple of towns over. It probably meant he'd be working late, since he had to drive all the way back after he finished.

I hoped he was all right. He'd left the shop so abruptly yesterday. It had been obvious something was wrong. He'd texted later to say goodnight—it was late and he was going to sleep at his place, since he had to leave for work early in the morning. That wasn't a big deal, but I wondered what was going on.

A woman with long blond hair came in and sat at the other end of the bar while I was putting things away. She was dressed in a form fitting shirt that showed the swell of her very pregnant belly. Normally when someone sat at the bar, I assumed they were here for a tasting. But she was obviously pregnant. She couldn't be here to drink wine, could she?

"Are you Brynn Miles?" she asked.

That was odd. I didn't recognize her. How did she know my name? "Yes. Can I help you?"

"Possibly," she said. "You're with Chase Reilly?"

Every alarm in my brain and body went off at the way his name rolled off her tongue. There was a hint of poorly disguised venom in her voice and in an instant, I knew. She'd been with Chase. This was one of his exes. Whether she'd been a fling, or one of the few girls he'd actually dated before me, I didn't know. But she looked at me as if to say *I had him first.*

I stopped and rested my arms on the bar so my hands—and my ring—were visible. "Yes."

"I'm Shelly. There's something you need to know."

My heart hammered behind my ribs and nausea rolled through my tummy. I was already doing the math—counting the months backward. Chase and I got together in October. Seven months ago. That meant...

Shelly brushed her hair behind her shoulder. "The thing is, I'm having his baby."

It took every ounce of self-control I possessed to keep the storm of emotions that washed over me from showing. I kept my face as still as possible as I let her words sink in.

Having his baby. This woman. Pregnant with Chase's child.

Oh god.

I wasn't such an idiot as to take her word at face value. Chase hadn't said a thing to me about her, and he'd certainly never mentioned the possibility that he'd gotten someone pregnant.

"That's... interesting," I said. "I'm not sure why you think I'm supposed to believe you, though."

She shrugged, like she didn't care whether I believed her or not. "He's been trying to blow me off for months. Now I think he blocked my number. I just thought you should know what you're getting into."

Blocked number? Was this the girl who had been texting him? She was *pregnant*? Was this why he left last night?

Somehow I managed to keep my voice from shaking. "How do you know it's his?"

"Because it is," she said. "He had his fun with me and moved on, but he left me with a permanent reminder. I've been trying to get through to him, but like I said, he won't respond. I didn't want it to come to this, but I had to come to you. Someone has to convince him that he needs to do the right thing."

She rested her hand on her belly. Tears of shock and rage threatened to fill my eyes, but I swallowed them back. I wasn't going to let her see me cry. But I had no idea what to think. What to do. How to react. Had Chase really gotten some girl pregnant and not told me?

"What do you want from me?" My voice was shaking now, but there wasn't anything I could do about it.

"Like I said, I thought you should know, since he's apparently banging you now." She stood, and I couldn't help but stare at her belly. "And tell Chase to call me."

I swallowed hard as I watched her walk away. My hands shook so badly I didn't trust myself to put the rest of the wine glasses away. I'd probably break every single one.

What the hell had just happened?

Chase was having a baby? Had he really blown her off? That didn't seem like Chase. But I knew he'd blocked someone's number after he'd said she kept texting him. Only... had she been texting him because she was pregnant with his fucking baby?

I was so confused. This couldn't be happening. I was supposed to marry Chase in a few weeks. What had he planned to do, wait until we were married to drop this bomb on me? Did he think he needed to lock me down first? Or worse, was he trying to hide it from me entirely?

If my dad hadn't done exactly that more than twenty years ago when his then-mistress was pregnant with Grace, I never would have believed someone could hide a child from his spouse. But my dad had hidden two. Was Chase capable of such a thing?

I wanted to believe he wasn't, but she'd been right here in the tasting room, huge belly and all. What was I supposed to do with that?

Without paying attention to where I was going, I rushed through the kitchen and out the side door, dialing Chase's number as I went.

"Hey, baby," he answered. "I'm on my way back, but my reception is spotty out here. What's up?"

"I just talked to Shelly."

"What?"

"Shelly came to the winery."

"Ah, fuck. You've got to be kidding me."

My heart beat faster. "Chase, why didn't you tell me?"

"Tell you what?" he asked. "That I have a crazy ex-girl-friend? God, Brynn, she was barely my girlfriend. I went out with her for a little while, but it didn't even last that long."

"Crazy? This isn't about her being crazy."

"Then what are you talking about?" he asked. "She was trying to text me, but I blocked her number. You saw me do it. I don't know what she said to you, but I haven't seen her in months."

My breath came in gasps and I felt dizzy, tears obscuring my vision. "But you've been in touch with her?"

The note of panic in his voice was not reassuring. "Kind of. But I haven't seen her in... god, I don't even know how long."

I was shaking so badly, I could barely hold my phone. "Chase, I don't even know what to say to you right now. You should have told me what was going on."

"What? Baby, whatever she's doing, it doesn't have anything to do with us."

"How can you say that?"

"Because it's true. Where are you? Are you still at work?"

"She's having your baby, Chase, and you didn't think that was important information?"

"Baby, are you there? Brynn?"

"Yes, I'm here. Why didn't you tell me she was pregnant?"

"Brynn, I can't hear you. I'm—"

His call dropped.

I took a shuddering breath and slipped back into the kitchen, feeling panic start to overtake me. I didn't know if I wanted to scream, or cry, or crumple to the ground and disappear.

"Uh-oh," Zoe said from the doorway. "What's wrong?"

"Oh my god, Zoe."

I burst into tears and a second later, Zoe's arms were around me. I sobbed into her shirt while she hugged me. The feel of her belly pressing against me only made me cry harder.

"Brynn, honey, what happened?" She gently rubbed slow circles across my back. "What's going on?"

I couldn't calm down enough to speak. Every word I tried to get out came out as sobbing and blubbering.

"Okay, shh," she said. "Let's go. Come on, sweetie."

I let her lead me back outside, her arm around me. People might have been watching, but I had no room to care. Everything had just fallen apart, my entire life crumbling to pieces. I had no idea what this meant—for me, for Chase, for us. I'd defended him to my family, insisted he wasn't Dad. Had I been wrong?

Maybe this was just the way men were. You trusted them at your own peril. Look at everything my dad had done. My mom was an intelligent, capable woman. She was beautiful and smart, and she'd been with someone who'd spent most of their marriage cheating on her. If she could be taken in by a dishonest piece of shit, was I any different?

·Somehow, I made it over to my mom's house. Zoe took me to the living room, wrapped me in a blanket, and set me on the couch. Seconds later, a glass of ice water and a shot of something alcoholic were being shoved in my hands. I downed the shot without even wincing, then chased it with water. I heard other voices. My mom's. Maybe Roland's, or Leo's. I wasn't sure. Zoe quietly shooed everyone away, saying I needed space to calm down. My phone rang, and she asked me if I wanted to answer.

"It's Chase, but... is that the problem?" Zoe asked.

I nodded.

"Okay," she said, her voice soothing. She sank onto the

couch next to me. "You take your time, sweetie. When you're ready, you can tell me what's going on."

I settled back into the couch and shut my eyes. I just needed a minute—time to process what was happening. It felt too sudden, too chaotic. I couldn't stop thinking about Shelly, about that baby she was carrying. Chase's baby. A baby he'd been hiding from me.

THIRTY

CHASE

I BANGED on the door at Brynn's mom's house, but no one was answering. She had to be here. Lindsey had seen Zoe leading a sobbing Brynn to her mom's not long ago. Had they gone somewhere? Where had Zoe taken her?

I was fucking panicking. Brynn had said she'd talked to Shelly. I didn't know what Shelly had said to her but judging by the fact that Brynn wasn't taking my calls—and neither was Zoe, because I'd tried her too—it couldn't have been good.

I'd have time to be pissed at Shelly later. For now, I needed to get to Brynn so I could find out what the fuck was going on. It felt like my life had just exploded.

The door opened, and I tried to muscle my way in, but Roland blocked the door.

"Hang on there, buddy," Roland said, putting a hand on my chest. "Not yet."

"What the fuck is going on?"

"Outside," he said, his voice calm.

I stepped backward so he could come out onto the porch, and he closed the door behind him.

"Where's Brynn?"

"She's with Zoe," Roland said. "And I think you need to back off right now."

"What?" I was so close to losing it on Roland, but Leo came up the steps behind me, the two of them boxing me in. I was going out of my mind with worry, but not so much that I'd start shit with these two. "I seriously don't know what the fuck is happening right now."

"Everything okay?" Leo asked, eying me with suspicion.

"I don't know what's going on, but Brynn's pretty upset about something," Roland said.

"What the fuck did you do?" Leo asked, his voice low.

"I don't know. Brynn called me, freaking out because my ex was here."

Roland and Leo both looked like they were about two seconds from kicking my ass.

I put my hands up in a gesture of surrender. "I swear to you, I haven't even seen my ex since before Brynn. She was texting me for a while, but the girl's fucking crazy. I blocked her number. Brynn knew about that. I don't know what Shelly told her, but you guys, I would *never*."

Did Brynn think I'd cheated on her? Could she possibly believe that? What the fuck had Shelly told her?

Roland's expression softened. "Look, she's just upset right now. Zoe will calm her down, but I think you need to give her a little space."

"No, I need to talk to her." I went for the door again.

Roland put his arm across the door. "Trust me. She's not ready to talk to you yet. Just let her calm down."

I stepped back, feeling like my chest was going to cave in. Like I couldn't breathe. Whatever was happening, it had spiraled out of control so fast. Why had I been on the fucking road? Why had the stupid call dropped?

"I need to see her," I said, well aware that my voice sounded desperate. I didn't give a shit.

"I know, I get it," Roland said. "Just... give her an hour, man. We'll take care of her."

"Do you get it, though? She's so upset she won't talk to me. I don't know what's happening right now. This is my life, Roland. She's my life. I can't..."

Leo put his hand on my shoulder. "She'll calm down."

I staggered down the porch stairs, running my hands through my hair. I felt like I was going out of my mind. There was nothing but a door between me and Brynn, and I couldn't get to her. Not unless I wanted to make this exponentially worse by getting into shit with her brothers. Part of me wanted to say *fuck it* and go through them. But I was sane enough to know that letting it go to blows with Roland and Leo was a bad idea.

"Fuck." I stumbled backward a few more steps. I couldn't lose her. That wasn't an option. I had to fix this. I had to find a way.

In order to fix it, I needed to find out what had set her off in the first place.

"I'll be back. Don't let her go anywhere."

"Okay," Roland said. "We won't."

I went back to my truck and got in. If Brynn wouldn't talk to me, there was another way to find out what Shelly had said to her. I'd go talk to Shelly.

I DIDN'T BOTHER with texts or calls. I went straight to Shelly's apartment. Or what I hoped was still Shelly's apartment. She'd lived here last I'd seen her, but it had been a while. Luckily, she answered, saving me the trouble of wasting more time tracking her down.

"Hey, Chase," she said with a friendly smile. "It's so good to see you. Come in."

"No thanks." I kept my feet firmly planted a few feet from her door. I wasn't going anywhere near the inside of her apartment. Fuck that. "Did you go see Brynn Miles at Salishan a little while ago?"

She rested her hand on her pregnant belly. "Um, yeah, I talked to her."

"What the fuck did you say to her?"

She smoothed down a strand of hair. "Come in so we can sit down and talk."

"Not a chance."

"My feet hurt."

"Goddammit, Shelly, what the fuck did you do? She called me in tears and now she won't talk to me."

"This is your fault," she said, her smile quickly fading. "You're the one who won't answer my texts. Did you block my number?"

"Yes, I fucking blocked your number. We're not together, so there's no reason for you text me. I'm with Brynn, now. I'm getting married."

The color drained from her face and her mouth hung open. "Married?"

"Yes, I'm getting married. Or I was. Now I'm not so sure. You need to tell me what you said to her that has her so upset."

"Oh shit."

"Shelly," I said, feeling so exasperated I wanted to scream, "what did you say to Brynn?"

She rubbed her belly and took a deep breath. "I told her the baby is yours."

I stared at her, so shocked it took me a minute to reply. "You said *what*?"

"I told her I'm having your baby."

"Why the fuck would you tell her that?"

She opened her mouth like she was going to say something, then closed it again, glancing away. "It could be yours."

"No, it couldn't," I said through gritted teeth. "We both know it's not possible."

"But—"

"Shelly, for fuck's sake, I can do math. It's not physically possible."

Her shoulders slumped, and she let out a long breath. I stepped aside while she walked past me and sat on the top step. "It *should* be yours."

"Oh my god." I shook my head and lowered down onto the step next to her. "Who's the father? Please tell me you know."

"His name is Dalton," she said.

"And where is he now?"

She shrugged. "He's in the military, so I don't really know."

"Was he just passing through or something?"

"Kind of," she said. "He was on leave for a few months to recover from surgery, so he was staying with family here in town."

"Does he know?"

She shook her head.

I let out a long breath. Jesus. "So, what, you thought you'd pass the baby off as mine?"

"I don't know. I guess I thought if I could get rid of your latest flavor-of-the-month, maybe we could..."

"Seriously?".

She sighed. "I got scared. None of this seemed real until about a month ago when this belly popped out. I was barely showing for the longest time. I didn't feel much of anything, so it almost didn't seem like it was happening. And then the baby got so big and started moving and keeping me up at night. Dalton is off somewhere, and I never told him, and you're here, and you're a good guy."

"You really fucked things up for me," I said. "You lied to my fiancée and now she won't talk to me."

She sniffed. "I didn't realize. I thought she was just your latest hook-up. I didn't know you were engaged."

"The ring on her finger didn't tip you off?"

"I saw it, but I don't know, girls wear rings. I didn't bother to figure out which hand it was on."

I rested my forearms on my knees and shook my head.

"I'm sorry, Chase."

"Call the father, Shelly. He deserves to know. That's his child. You can't keep that from him."

She nodded slowly.

"What are you afraid of? Is he an asshole?"

"No, he's actually a really nice guy," she said. "Nice family. He's close to his parents. He has a good future ahead of him. I didn't want to mess that up."

"So you tried to mess up mine?"

"I..." She paused. "I um, I guess I wasn't thinking about it that way."

"I wish you would have. I'm sorry you're having a baby on your own but trying to rope some other guy into it isn't the solution. Especially when I know the baby isn't mine."

She didn't answer me, but I didn't really expect her to. There wasn't anything she could say to justify what she'd done, and I was glad she seemed to realize she'd been wrong. That wasn't the norm for her. At least, it hadn't been with me.

I stood and helped her up. "Call him. Do the right thing this time, okay? Promise me."

She nodded. "I will. I promise. Do you want me to go talk to Brynn? It'll be humiliating, but I guess I deserve that."

"No, stay away from my girl," I said. "You've done enough. I'll fix this when she'll finally talk to me again. Hopefully."

I walked down the steps, back to my truck, leaving her standing outside her apartment.

"Hey, Chase?"

"Yeah?" I glanced over my shoulder.

"You really are a good guy," she said. "And I'm sorry."

I just nodded. I didn't have anything else to say to her.

I drove straight back to Salishan. This was such a stupid misunderstanding. I couldn't stand the thought of Brynn believing another girl was having my baby. I didn't know how long it would take before Brynn would see me, but I was going to be there the second it happened. Even if it meant camping out on the porch at her mom's. They couldn't keep me from her forever.

In fact, they couldn't keep me from her much longer. If I had to break down the door to get to her, I would.

THIRTY-ONE
BRYNN

THE SHOT of whiskey Zoe had given me had calmed me down a little. She sat next to me on the couch, rubbing my arm, waiting for me to explain what was happening. I took a few more deep breaths. Things were coming into focus. My mom hovering nearby with a mug of tea, her forehead creased with worry. Zoe's gentle murmurs, telling me it would be okay.

"You ready to talk?" Zoe asked.

I nodded. "I'm sorry, I lost it there for a second."

"It's okay," Zoe said. "What happened?"

"Chase's ex-girlfriend came to the tasting room," I said. "She's pregnant."

Zoe's eyebrows lifted. "And by pregnant, you mean Chase is..."

"The father? I guess I don't know for sure. I tried to call Chase, but the call dropped. But yeah, it looks like he might be."

"Oh honey," my mom said.

Roland came in from outside, his brow furrowed with concern. Leo followed and shut the door behind him.

"Brynn, I don't know what's going on, but Chase was here. He looks like hell."

"What do you mean he *was* here?" Zoe asked.

"He left," Roland said.

"You let him leave?"

Roland stared at her. "You told me to keep him out."

"Yeah, just until Brynn could calm down. We need his ass here to fucking explain himself." Zoe glanced at my mom. "I'm sorry, Shannon, but I'm too pregnant to filter my language."

Before my mom could reply, Cooper burst inside.

"Whoa, hey family." He stopped, looking around at everyone. "What's going on? Mom, are you having a party and you didn't invite me?" His eyes landed on me and his smile faded. "What the shit? Brynncess, what happened?"

"Chase's ex-girlfriend is pregnant with his baby," Zoe said.

"What?" Cooper asked, his voice going shrill.

Roland and Leo looked just as shocked.

"No," Cooper said. "That's a terrible joke. Seriously, you guys, that's the worst. Don't mess with people like that, it's mean. Wait, why are you all looking at me like that? You're not kidding?"

"You don't know anything about this?" Zoe asked.

"No. What ex-girlfriend?"

"Shelly," I said.

Cooper's eyes widened. "That's not... No. Not possible. Really?"

I nodded. "She came to the tasting room to tell me. She's very pregnant."

"Where's Chase?" Cooper asked.

Roland gestured vaguely toward the front door. "He said he'd be back later."

"You really didn't know?" Zoe asked.

Cooper winced. "To be honest, I've been a little out of touch when it comes to Chasey."

"You mean you spent months not speaking to him because he started dating me," I said.

"Yeah, that."

"Okay, let's all calm down," Mom said. "We don't know the full story yet. Chase hasn't had a chance to explain, so let's not jump to conclusions."

"I've jumped to the conclusion that Chase has a hell of a lot of explaining to do," Leo grumbled.

"Exactly," Roland said. "Although... he did look pretty distraught."

"Well, maybe we'd be able to figure things out if you hadn't let him leave," Zoe said, her tone thick with annoyance.

Roland narrowed his eyes at her. "You're hungry, aren't you? I better get you some dinner. Are we still on miso soup?"

"All day, every day," Zoe said. "I can't eat anything else."

"Consider it done," Roland said. "I'll bring back food for everyone."

Leo gestured toward the door. "I'll make sure the Big House is locked up."

"Thanks, boys," Mom said. She glanced at Cooper, like she expected him to find a job to do.

"I'm not going anywhere." Cooper came over to the couch and squeezed himself between me and Zoe.

"God, Cooper," Zoe said. She pushed herself to the edge of the couch and slowly stood. It didn't look easy, with her belly getting so big. "I have to pee anyway."

My mom disappeared into the kitchen, leaving me alone with Cooper.

"What's this all about?" Cooper asked, his voice quiet. "Do you really think Chase got her pregnant?"

"She says it's his baby. I called him after I talked to her, but our call got cut off. And then I kind of freaked out. I'm calm now, but I'm still trying to make sense of everything. But I think it's possible. He and I have only been together for seven months. It could have been a month before me and the timing works."

He paused, tapping his hands on his legs. "Yeah, I don't know when he was with her last. I don't exactly keep that shit on my calendar."

"How could he not tell me something like this? Is this why he didn't want to wait to get married? He wanted to do it before I found out he had a kid? Was he even going to tell me? That's what Dad did, Coop. He had kids and he hid them."

"Chase isn't Dad."

"No, but I'm beginning to realize that people are capable of anything."

"Some people are genuinely shitty," Cooper said. "But Chase isn't one of them. I don't know what's going on with all this. I'll tell you one thing, though, Shelly is fucking nuts. I'd be skeptical about anything she tells you. That girl would do anything to get her claws back into Chase."

"Like get pregnant with his kid?"

"Or *say* she's pregnant with his kid."

"I saw her, Coop. She's very pregnant."

"Yeah, but maybe it's not his. You need to talk to him to find out. All this he-said, she-said bullshit? Listening to other people, but not talking to each other? This is how relationships get fucked up. If this is what's going on with

Chase, you need to talk to him. Not me, or Zoe, or Mom, or any of us. This is for you and Chase to figure out."

I leaned away and narrowed my eyes at him. "Wow."

"Wow what?"

"That was very wise advice," I said. "I didn't expect that from you."

"I'm wise as fuck, and I give great advice." He patted my leg. "Do you need me to go find him?"

"Sure."

Someone pounded on the front door. "Brynn?"

"God, I'm good," Cooper said, getting up to answer the door. "One Chase Reilly, as ordered."

I got up and wrapped the blanket tighter around my shoulders. Cooper opened the door and sure enough, it was Chase. His hair was disheveled, like he'd been messing it up with his hands. He ignored Cooper, looking straight at me.

"Brynn."

I put my hand up to stop him from speaking yet. I didn't want an audience for this, so I took him out to the porch and shut the door.

"Brynn, please listen."

"I will," I said. "But I need to say something first."

"Okay."

I'd been thinking about it while my family had been getting caught up, and I knew what I needed to say to him. "I'm not mad if you're having a baby with her."

"Brynn—"

"No, let me get this out, I need to say it. You were with her before me, right? Not after?"

"Yes, but—"

"If the baby is yours, I want you to know, I think I can make it work. It's not ideal, but we can figure something out with her, right? Alternate weeks or something?"

"Wait, what did you say?"

"I'm saying I know this changes a lot, but Chase, you can't push this under the rug. I'm not mad if you're having a baby. But you can't keep something like this from me. Did you think I couldn't handle it?"

"No—"

"Because I can. If my mom can welcome Grace with open arms, I can certainly welcome a child you conceived before we were together."

"Holy shit," he said, staring at me.

"What?"

"Just when I think I couldn't possibly love you more, .you do this."

"I'm not okay with everything," I said. "You need to explain to me why you were hiding this, because that part I can't understand."

"No, Brynn, I didn't hide anything."

"Yes, you did, you—"

He touched my lips with his fingertips. "No, I didn't. The baby isn't mine."

I wasn't sure I'd heard him correctly. "Wait, what did you say?"

"I didn't get Shelly pregnant. It's not possible. First of all, I always used a condom."

"Yeah, but condoms can fail," I said. "They can break."

"Maybe, if you buy shitty ones or they don't fit. I've never had one break on me. But even still, the timing doesn't work. It's been too long since I was with her. If I'd gotten her pregnant, she would have already had the baby. And she knows who the father is."

"Did you talk to her?"

"Yeah, I went over to see what the hell she'd done."

"Did you know she was pregnant?"

"I found out recently, but I had no idea she'd try to say it was mine. We both knew it wasn't possible. If I'd known she'd do this, I would have told you. But I didn't think it mattered if a girl I dated once was having a baby with another guy."

"Why would she do this?" I asked. "If she knows it's not yours, why would she lie to me?"

"She was trying to get rid of you. If you believed the baby was mine, she figured you'd bail. And in her messed-up head, that meant she might have a shot at getting back together with me."

"Oh my god." I stepped into his embrace, feeling relief wash over me as he wrapped me in his strong arms. "I'm so sorry. I just got so upset."

"No, you don't need to apologize. This is on me. I wish I'd never... there are a lot of things I wish I'd never done. I can't go back and change them now. But I can promise you, that's all in the past."

"I know."

"And I wouldn't have hidden that from you. Especially not after everything that happened with your dad. If there had even been a chance that baby was mine, I'd have told you as soon as I knew."

I let out a long breath. "God, that was terrifying. I shouldn't have believed her."

"That's actually true. She's completely untrustworthy," he said. "But you didn't know that. Like I said, this is on me. If I hadn't been such a fuck-up before you..."

"You weren't a fuck-up."

"No, I really was."

I laughed and ran my hands down his chest. "Was that why you left the shop last night? Did Shelly somehow get through?"

"No, that wasn't about her." He sank down onto a bench and ran his hands through his already messy hair. "I was talking to my dad. My parents aren't coming to the wedding."

"Oh my god. Why?"

"I told them not to."

I sat next to him and twined our hands together. Part of me was glad to hear that. I knew enough about his parents to dislike them intensely. "I'm sorry."

He squeezed my hands. "It's fine. They don't know who I am. So it doesn't matter what they think. Like I told them, our wedding is going to be the most important day of my life. I want to spend it with the people who care."

The front door opened, and my mom peeked out. "How's everything out here?"

"It's okay, Mom. False alarm. The baby isn't his."

She breathed out a sigh. "You're sure?"

Chase stood. "Yeah, I'm positive. I dated her last year, but there's no way it's possible, and she knows who the father is. She's... she has issues. I'm really sorry about all this."

"Oh honey, it's not your fault." She stepped in and wrapped him in a hug. "I'm relieved for both of you."

"We would have figured it out," I said.

"What's going on?" Cooper said, sticking his head through the partially open door. "Chase, please tell me this isn't happening, man."

"It's not happening."

"Oh my god, I was freaking out," Cooper said. "Like I would much rather you had knocked up my sister than crazy-Shelly, dude. Talk about disaster. That would have been an eighteen-year nightmare."

"Believe me, I know," Chase said. "I'm an idiot some-times, but not that big of an idiot."

"You're no such thing," Mom said, squeezing his arm. "You're ours. I know it doesn't work this way, but as far as I'm concerned, you're a Miles, Chase. You always have been."

"Shit, yeah," Cooper said.

Mom raised her eyebrows at his language, but I barely noticed. Chase lit up, like he was glowing from the inside. My mom was right. I'd be taking his name, but he was ours. He always would be.

COOPER HELD his hands over my eyes so I couldn't see. As he walked me forward, I felt gravel crunching beneath my feet. I was pretty sure we were at my mom's house when he told me to step up. The creak sounded like the stairs leading to her front porch.

"What are we doing?"

"Have patience, bride-to-be," Cooper said. "We're almost there."

I heard another squeak—probably her front door—and Cooper nudged me forward. I took a few more steps and he dropped his hands.

"Surprise!"

The first thing I saw were pearly white balloons. They were everywhere. Taped to the walls with strips of masking tape. Bouncing around on the floor. A banner that read *Bride To Be* hung across the entrance to the dining room and more decorations dangled from the ceiling.

My mom and Grace stood near the couch where Zoe lay with her feet up. Grace and Zoe wore pink plastic crowns that said *Bridesmaid*. Then I noticed Roland and Leo were here too. Leo sat in an armchair—was he glaring at Cooper?—and Roland sat with Zoe's feet in his lap.

"What's all this?"

"It's your bachelorette party," Cooper said, gesturing around with his arms. "I know you said you didn't want a big thing, but that's stupid. Zoe's too pregnant to plan one, and your college friends suck, so I decided to do it. Gracie helped."

"My friends suck?"

"Obviously. What's-her-face did you-know-what with that jackass you were dating. So she's clearly ostracized for the rest of history, but in the long run it was better because you needed to be with Chase anyway. And I guess I don't really know your other friends. Chase said they're mostly okay, but there's no one who's super awesome like we are."

I supposed that did sum up my friends at school. I was a lot closer to everyone in this room than I was with anyone I'd met in college.

As I stepped further inside, one of the dangling decorations brushed my hair. I grabbed it as it swung and realized it was a sparkly gold penis. "Are these penises?"

"Yep." Cooper grinned. "Some of them are dicks, but there are wedding ring ones and martini glass ones and high heel ones. They came in a pack. I ordered them online."

He looked so proud of himself, I couldn't help but laugh. "This is... really cute."

Leo stood. "Great, well, the decorations are done. Brynn is here. I'm going home."

Cooper stepped in front of the door. "Oh no. You're not going anywhere, buddy. The party just started."

"Why would I stay for my sister's bachelorette party?" Leo asked. "That's weird."

"If by weird, you mean awesome," Cooper said. "We have so much awesome shit planned. We're all staying, bros. Trust me. It's going to be legit."

"Just go with it," Roland said, and I noticed he was wearing what appeared to be a penis whistle around his neck.

"Dude, I made sure the whole party could be here, because, you know," Cooper said, widening his eyes at Leo. "And why'd you take off your dick necklace?"

Leo crossed his arms. "I'm not wearing a dick necklace."

"Pansy," Roland said. "I'm wearing a dick necklace."

"You are a dick necklace," Leo fired back.

"Boys," Mom said. "Do I really have to be the referee at Brynn's bachelorette party?"

Oh god. My mom was wearing a dick necklace.

Roland brought the little plastic penis to his lips and blew, producing a high-pitched whistle.

"Is it weird that I'm super turned on by that?" Zoe asked.

Roland winked at her and blew the whistle again.

Grace came over to put a white feather boa around my shoulders and a *Bride* tiara on my head. She leaned in to whisper. "I tried to help, but it got out of control pretty quickly. So just... have fun?"

This was going to be the weirdest bachelorette party ever.

Half an hour later, we were drinking mimosas—ginger ale for Zoe—and playing *pin the penis on the man*. There was music in the background—what Cooper called his *special bachelorette party playlist*, as if that were a normal thing for a guy to have—but I couldn't hear it because we were all laughing so hard.

Mom put the blindfold on Roland, spun him around,

and he wobbled toward a large cartoon man taped to the wall. There was already a dick stuck to the thing's belly button, one on his leg, and another on the wall about a foot away.

That one was mine. I was bad at this game.

Roland carried a paper penis in one hand and reached for the wall with the other. We all laughed harder as he felt around the poster, trying to place the dick in the right place. Zoe shouted encouragement—and bad directions. He stuck it on the guy's hand and pulled off his blindfold.

"Shit. Damn it, Zo."

I doubled over, I was laughing so hard, and Roland handed me the blindfold. "Okay, Mom, your turn."

Mom stood in front of me and I put the blindfold over her eyes. Cooper proudly handed her a paper dick.

"You've got this, Mom," he said.

As I spun my mom around, someone knocked on the door. Leo was closest to the front, like he was hoping for a chance to escape. He answered the door and a very startled-looking Ben came inside.

"Um, I'll come back," Ben said, looking around at the balloons and sparkly decorations.

"No, Benjamin, come in," Mom said as she felt her way toward the giant poster of a cartoon naked man, paper dick in her hand.

Ben's eyes widened.

"Nope." Leo patted him on the back. "You're stuck here now."

"We're having fun," Mom continued. "Have a drink. And we have cake."

"Oh god, Cooper did you get a penis cake?" Leo asked.

"No," Cooper said, and we all turned toward him. I think everyone was surprised. "I *baked* a penis cake."

Ben looked shell-shocked, but I just laughed. What else can you do when your crazy brother just announced he baked you a penis cake?

"Am I close?" Mom asked, still apparently focused on her game.

"Keep going, Shannon," Zoe called from the couch. "Straight ahead."

"You're almost there," Grace said.

Roland put his hands on his hips. "You can't help her."

"Hush, impregnator," Zoe said. "A little to your left, Shannon. There you go."

I couldn't help but glance at Ben. He watched my mom intently as she pinned the penis right in the center of the cartoon-guy's crotch.

The rest of us clapped and cheered as she took the blindfold off her face.

"Wow," Mom said. "Looks like I still got it."

Cooper groaned. "Oh my god, it was a huge mistake to let you play."

Ben looked a little red, so I caught his eye and nodded toward the kitchen. I met him there and got him a beer out of the fridge.

"Here, I think you'll need this."

He took the beer with a grateful smile. "Thanks, Sprout. Nice crown."

I touched the tiara. "Thanks. Grace got it for me. Did Cooper invite you, too, or were you unfortunate enough to stop by at the wrong time?"

"Wrong time, it seems."

"Sorry about that."

He shrugged. "Not the weirdest thing your brothers have ever done."

"I don't know. Did you see the decorations? And you

heard what he said about the cake. If you're not careful, Cooper will make you wear a penis whistle."

"He can try," Ben said with a wink.

I laughed. "I'm glad you're here. There's something I need to ask you."

He took a drink of his beer. "Sure."

"I was wondering if you'd walk me down the aisle?"

Ben froze, his beer bottle half lifted, his eyes locked on me. He stared at me for a long moment before answering. "You want me to do that?"

"Yeah, I do."

"Your father isn't coming?"

I took a deep breath. "We didn't invite him. I thought about it a lot, but I decided not to. He hasn't called me once since he left. He even went to see Grace's mom—or tried to. But me? Not a word. As far as I'm concerned, he gave up his walk-his-daughter-down-the-aisle privileges."

"Oh, Sprout." He stepped in and pulled me into a hug. "I don't think I deserve such an honor, but if it's what you want, of course I will."

"It's definitely what I want. There isn't anyone better."

He cleared his throat and took another drink just as my mom came into the kitchen.

"Sorry for the chaos," Mom said. "I see you already have a drink. Can I get you anything else?"

Ben smiled at her, his eyes crinkling at the corners. "No, I'm fine."

"Will you stay?" she asked. "Cooper did bake. At least, I think he baked. Hopefully he didn't try to cook it on the grill. I can't be sure."

"Should I run to the store for back-up dessert?" Ben asked.

It was Mom's turn to smile. "No. I have cupcakes hidden upstairs." She winked at me. "Don't tell your brother."

"Of course not." I nodded toward the other room. "I should get back to my party."

I ducked out of the kitchen, leaving my mom and Ben alone.

There was another knock on the door and Cooper went to answer it. "Awesome. I think the first of our entertainment is here."

"Entertainment?" I asked. *Oh god, please tell me he didn't get a stripper.* "What entertainment?"

"Oh, is this my thing?" Roland asked.

Now I was really confused. "Your thing? Zoe?"

Zoe shrugged. "He didn't tell me anything."

"Yep," Cooper said, then opened the door with a flourish.

Five women came in with big plastic totes and bags slung over their shoulders. I was pretty sure they weren't strippers. And if they were, they were the wrong kind.

"Pedicures," Roland said with a smile. He turned to Zoe. "This was my idea. Good, right?"

She leaned against him. "So good, baby. This is adorable."

Roland stood and came over to give me a squeeze around the shoulders. "I'm sorry I was kind of a jerk about you getting married. It's hard not to see you as the little girl you used to be. But Chase is a great guy. I'm happy for you."

"Thanks. This is all so sweet."

"Are you having fun? I know it's not a normal bachelorette party, but we did our best."

"I can't imagine anything better."

He smiled. "Good. Now go get your toenails done."

The ladies set up in the living room and we took turns getting pedicures. There were more drinks, and Mom and Grace brought out finger foods. A pizza delivery guy showed up and I'd never seen anyone look so confused. Of course, Leo had taped a paper penis to Cooper's forehead, which he'd happily decided not to take off, shortly before he answered the door.

Darkness fell, and after a few more silly games, Grace and Cooper announced that it was time to take the party outside. We were all a little tipsy, but our toenails looked fabulous. They led us out to an open area where they'd started a big bonfire. I was a little bit afraid they'd dragged my mattress out here, but it was just a normal fire.

Normal for us, at least. It was six feet high. Cooper took his bonfires seriously.

They'd set up a couple of folding tables with more food, stuff to mix drinks, and what I assumed was the cake Cooper had made.

I figured this was it, but a dark SUV pulled up and a bunch of guys piled out. They were all shirtless with firemen's pants and suspenders. I gaped at them as they sauntered over to the fire.

Oh god, they did hire strippers. And my mom and brothers are here.

"Hey guys," Grace said. "Thanks for coming."

My mom smiled. "Oh good, this should be fun!"

Leo looked like he wanted to disappear, and even Roland eyed them like this was pushing his limits. Ben stayed behind my mom and I was surprised he didn't put an arm around her to pull her away. I was pretty sure he wanted to.

"Um, Grace?" I asked.

She nudged me with her elbow. "Don't worry. They're actual firefighters, not strippers. They won't get more naked than this. Except maybe Logan." She pointed to a guy who looked about my age with an impressive set of abs—I was getting married, I wasn't dead—and thick dark hair. "He'll take his clothes off with very little encouragement."

"You must know them?"

"Yep, friends of mine. They're here to wait on you for the rest of the night."

Logan came over and stood in front of me, hands on his hips. "Damn it. Another one bites the dust. If you're having any doubts right now, baby, let me know, and we can run away together."

Cooper pointed at him. "Hey. Firefighter boy. Watch it."

Logan put his hands up and laughed. "I'm just saying."

"Okay, Logan," Grace said. "Why don't you get the bride a drink?"

He bowed. "Anything you want, beautiful."

The firefighters brought everyone drinks, paying special attention to me and Mom. Logan dropped to his knees in front of Zoe and gave her a foot rub. Roland kept trying to intervene, but Zoe waved him off, exclaiming how good it felt.

Mom sidled up next to me, a drink in her hand. "I hope it hasn't been too weird having your mom at your bachelorette party."

I leaned my head against her shoulder. "There are like half a dozen other things that are much weirder about this party. And actually, I'm really happy you're here."

"Me too. I know I was worried about you when you first said you were getting married. But honey, I couldn't be happier. I love Chase. I've always loved that boy like a son, ever since he was little. And he loves you so much. You two just keep on loving each other and you're going to have such a beautiful life."

"Mom, you're going to make me cry."

She hugged me tight and I squeezed my eyes shut to keep the tears from spilling.

Someone turned on music and the fire blazed, sending up little sparks that danced in the night sky. One of the firefighters grabbed me and spun me around. I almost tripped over my feet, but it turned into a dance. Then Roland was cutting in, so I danced with my brother around the bonfire. He twirled me the way he had when I was little, leading me through pirouettes and spins, leaving me dizzy and laughing.

Another set of strong hands gripped my waist and turned me. The next thing I knew, I was in Chase's arms, melting against his body. He wrapped one arm around me and took my hand in his, pressing me close so we could dance in the firelight.

"Hi, there," he said as we swayed to the music.

"Hey." I giggled, more than a little tipsy, but he held on, keeping me steady.

"Mind if I crash your party?"

"You must have heard there were shirtless firefighters."

He cracked a smile. "Actually, I heard there was cake."

"I don't know. Cooper said he baked it, so that could go either way."

"That is a risk. But getting to dance with you makes up for it. Are you having fun?"

"Yeah," I said, and he led me through a slow spin. "It's been amazing. I feel bad, though. Cooper spent all this time on my bachelorette party, but he's your best man. Are you guys doing something for you?"

"Nah. I've already done more than my fair share of partying. I had a few beers with your brothers and a few other guys last night. It was mellow. And perfect."

"Time for cake," Cooper shouted over the music.

We all gathered around one of the folding tables. Cooper pulled the foil off revealing a cake shaped like a penis. It was... quite anatomically correct, complete with chocolate sprinkles around the balls. Leo grimaced and shook his head, and Roland rolled his eyes. Everyone else laughed and clapped until Cooper held his hands up for quiet.

"Tonight, we celebrate my sister, Brynn. And Chase, who showed up when I wasn't looking. Hey, bro."

"Sup." Chase tipped his chin.

Cooper lifted a knife to cut a slice of cake.

"Wait," Mom said. "Let me take a picture first."

Mom stumbled—I think she was a little bit drunk—and Ben held her arm to steady her. She took a few pictures with her phone.

"Okay, let's eat," Cooper said, lifting the knife again. He hesitated, then moved the knife to a different angle. "Shit. I don't think I can slice a dick with a knife. Not even a dick made of cake."

Grace laughed and nudged him aside. "I've got this."

Cooper winced and turned away while Grace cut slices, and the firefighters passed them out. I had to give it to Coop, the cake was fantastic. Even Leo reluctantly took a piece.

As the night wore on, we danced around the fire, and polished off the cake. I switched to water—didn't want to drink too much. When people started to get tired, the party broke up. The firefighters were nice enough to stay and help Cooper and Grace clean up. Roland took a very tired Zoe home, and I noticed Ben making sure Mom got inside safely.

Chase put his arm around me as he led me back to the cottage. "You ready to get married in a few days?"

I stopped and slipped my arms around his waist while I looked up at him. "I can't wait to marry you, Chase."

THIRTY-THREE

CHASE

LOOKING IN THE MIRROR, I straightened my tie and adjusted my suit jacket. I was buzzing with so much adrenaline, I felt like I might start bouncing off the walls. Although who could blame me? I was about to get married.

"The only thing that sucks about this wedding is that I'm related to all the bridesmaids," Cooper said. He sat cross-legged on the table, his shirt open, his tie hanging loose around his neck. "What the hell, man? My pregnant sister-in-law and my half-sister? I put my chances of getting laid tonight at less than ten percent."

I glanced over my shoulder at him and grinned. "I'd put my chances at a hundred."

"Fuck. Right. Off." He pointed at me. "The fact that it's your wedding day does not justify sex jokes involving my baby sister."

"Trust me, Cooper," I said with a wink. "She's not a baby."

Groaning, he rolled his eyes and fell back on the table. "I fucking hate you."

"No, you don't."

"I should hate you, you prick," he said. "You're ruining my life."

"I hate you both, how about that?" Leo said. "And how is he ruining your life?"

"Numerous reasons." Cooper sat up and started ticking them off on his fingers. "He's leaving me for my sister. Also sleeping with my sister. Making me go to a wedding without hot single bridesmaids. And making me wear a suit. I just wore a suit for Roland's wedding."

"That was last year," Roland said. "Quit your bitching."

Cooper jumped down and glanced at himself in the full-length mirror. "I do make this look good."

"Isn't it exhausting to carry that ego around with you all the time?" Leo asked.

"Nope," Cooper said. "That's why I work out."

Roland shook his head and even Leo cracked a smile at that.

Ben poked his head in the door. He was dressed in a suit and tie, his beard neatly trimmed. "The photographer wants you guys outside for some pictures."

I checked myself in the mirror one last time—Cooper did look good, but fuck if I didn't look better—and followed Ben outside.

The photographer directed us to an open area on the side of the Big House. The weather was perfect—warm, but not too hot, the sun descending toward the mountain peaks that surrounded our little town.

All this waiting was starting to drive me crazy. I paced around the grass, shaking out my hands, trying to calm down. I wasn't nervous, I was excited, but the effect was more or less the same. My stomach was unsettled, and I couldn't stand still for more than about two seconds.

I wondered how the girls were doing. The dresses had

come at the last minute—the right ones, in the right sizes. Zoe was relieved she could actually fit into hers. I didn't know how that woman could still walk with that huge baby belly. Surprisingly, she was actually feeling better now—big as she was—than she had for most of her pregnancy. She wasn't throwing up all the time, and I hadn't seen her cry in at least a couple of weeks. That was a relief. Zoe was tough, so it was fucking weird when she cried. I still gave her M&Ms whenever I saw her, though.

In fact, there would be dishes of M&Ms out at the reception. Because we were awesome like that.

"Gentlemen, I'm going to run out to my car to get a different lens," the photographer said. He was a slim guy, probably in his thirties. "I'll be right back."

As he walked toward the front of the building, I had to do a double take. A man in his fifties with salt-and-pepper hair, wearing a button-down shirt and slacks, came striding across the lawn.

Lawrence fucking Miles.

He sauntered over like he still owned the place—which technically I guess he still did. A woman with bleached-out hair and bright lipstick clutched onto his arm. The sight of them made me want to puke. He brought his mistress here? On his daughter's fucking wedding day?

I must have lurched forward because Leo put a steadying hand on my shoulder. Roland's back had gone stiff and Leo glared at his dad, but it was Ben who looked closest to doing violence. At first glance, you might not have recognized it. Ben's apparently relaxed stance was anything but. The guy was a coiled spring.

Shit. This could get ugly.

"Fuck," Roland muttered under his breath. "Ben, can you go make sure the girls don't come out here?"

Leo did a subtle sidestep in front of Ben, blocking him from his father's view. "That's a good idea."

I could see what they were doing. We all knew Ben cared about Shannon—was maybe even in love with her. The Miles brothers didn't want their dad to know. Ben was one of the most chill guys I'd ever known, but all men have their limits. Lawrence Miles strutting around here with his fucking mistress was clearly going to be Ben's. We needed to get him out of here.

"Yeah, Ben, if you could make sure Brynn doesn't come out here right now, that would be awesome," I said. "I don't want her getting upset."

Ben cast a glare in Mr. Miles' direction, then went around the back of the Big House.

"Why the fuck did you guys invite him?" Cooper whispered.

"I don't think we did."

"Then how did he know?"

I shrugged. I had no idea.

"Roland, I'm glad I caught you," Mr. Miles said. "Where's your mother?"

"Unavailable at the moment." Roland crossed his arms.

Mr. Miles lifted a manila envelope and started to answer, but the photographer returned.

"Okay, gentlemen, we can get started."

"Yeah, just give us a second," I said.

"What's going on?" Mr. Miles asked. "Why are you dressed up?"

"You mean you're not here because of Brynn's wedding?" Roland asked.

Mr. Miles stiffened. "Since when is Brynn getting married?"

"Since she is," Cooper said. "You would have known if you hadn't fucking ghosted us."

"Is this some kind of joke?" Mr. Miles asked.

"No, Dad," Roland said, his voice even. "This isn't a joke."

"My daughter is not getting married," Mr. Miles said. "There's no way I'm allowing this."

His daughter? Oh hell no. I took a step forward. "What makes you think you get an opinion?"

His eyes moved to me and he blinked once, like he hadn't realized I was standing here. "Excuse me?"

"You bailed on your family. You haven't made a single attempt to see Brynn since you left. So I'll ask you again: What makes you think you get an opinion?"

"Why am I even speaking to you?" he asked, his voice dripping with disdain.

Oh, this was going to be good. Never in my life had I been more excited to utter these words. "Because I'm the guy she's marrying."

His face reddened and the vein in his neck bulged. There was a time when I'd been afraid of that look—of the deepening purple of his skin, that vein pulsing with rage. When we were kids, and Mr. Miles caught me and Cooper doing something we shouldn't—which was pretty often— we'd been able to tell at a glance how much trouble we were in by the degree of redness in his face. That vein? Always a bad sign.

But I wasn't afraid of this asshole anymore. Not even a little. I stood my ground, shoulders straight.

"You?" He spit the word at me as if it pained him to say it. "She's marrying *you*?"

I cocked a half smile. "Yep."

"Like hell she is."

"Lawrence, please." His mistress tugged on his arm, like she was trying to pull him away from us.

He shrugged his arm out of her grip. "Did you get her pregnant?"

I just rolled my eyes. Of course that was his first question. Dick. "No, she's not pregnant."

"I should have gotten rid of you a long time ago," he said. "You were always sniffing around my little girl."

"She's not *your* little girl," Cooper said.

Mr. Miles ignored Cooper, his eyes still on me. "I told Shannon not to feed the strays. You start feeding them and they never leave."

"You did not just call Chase a stray," Cooper said, lunging at him.

Roland and I caught Cooper before he reached his dad. His muscles strained against our grip, but we managed to hold him back—barely.

"You asshole," Cooper said. "You need to get the fuck out of here."

Mr. Miles didn't appear to be too concerned that his son was about to pummel his face into the grass. He should have been. Cooper had a mean right hook. I knew from experience.

"God, what a disappointment," Mr. Miles said. "Brynn had so much potential."

Now I was fucking over it. I let go of Cooper—Leo grabbed him before he could attack his dad—and got in Mr. Miles face. "Get the fuck out, you sack of rotten donkey dicks."

"Oh, the kid thinks he's a tough guy now?" he said.

"Lawrence," the woman said. "We didn't come here for this."

"Kristen, stay out of it," he snapped without looking at her.

"Awesome. I see you treat her just as shitty as you treated your wife." My eyes flicked to Kristen. "I hope you realize you're probably not the only woman he's fucking."

Mr. Miles slammed his hands into my chest, trying to shove me backward. I rocked on my heel and got back in his face. I didn't want to start an actual fight right before my wedding, but I wasn't taking his shit, either.

"Nice try, asshole."

"Fucking little punk," he said.

I stepped back, straightening my jacket. "At least I'm not a lying, cheating piece of trash. How stupid do you have to be to give up this family? You're the disappointment, you dumb fuck."

Mr. Miles glowered at me, his hand balling into a fist.

"Dad, you need to get the fuck out of here," Cooper growled. "Now."

I'd thought the angriest I'd ever seen Cooper was when he caught me with Brynn. But that had nothing on this moment. Cooper's eyes were wild, the cords in his neck standing out as he strained against his brothers.

"Come on, Coop," Leo said in a quiet voice, like he was trying to soothe a wild animal. "Let's not do this now."

"No, let's do this," Cooper said. "Right fucking now. He can't just show up when he wants to and fuck things up anymore. Especially not today."

"Keep your mouth shut, Cooper," Mr. Miles snapped.

Cooper jerked against Roland and Leo's grip. "I'd tell you to go fuck yourself, but not even you should have standards that low. You're not worth the dirt to bury you in."

Mr. Miles surged in and popped Cooper square in the face.

Kristen screamed, tripping over her heels as she backed up. I dove in, but Leo got to him first. Before I could even blink, Leo had his father on the ground, his arm pinned behind his back.

"Jesus, Leo, let me go," Mr. Miles said through gritted teeth.

Leo answered by pulling his arm harder and Mr. Miles groaned.

"I'm going to let you up," Leo said, his voice low. "Then I'm going to walk you to your car, and you're going to leave. Understood?"

The danger in Leo's tone sent a chill up my spine. I stared at him for half a second. He'd moved so *fast*. How the hell had he done that?

"Fine," Mr. Miles gritted out.

Leo started to let him up, so I grabbed Cooper and pushed so he had to take a few steps backward. Then I kept my arms around him in a bear-hug.

"It's okay, buddy," I said quietly. "Leo's getting him out of here. Stay with me, man."

I held him until his breathing normalized and he relaxed—at least enough that I felt like it was safe to let go. His eyes were on Leo and Roland, escorting their father to his car, his mistress trailing behind.

"That fucker," Cooper said. His eyes were still wild, but he didn't chase after them. "He's gone this long and he fucking shows up today, of all days."

"You hurt?" I pulled off my tie and handed it to him.

He wrinkled his nose and worked his jaw while he wiped the blood off his face, then turned and spat red. "I'd say he hits like a girl, but that would be a fucking insult to girls everywhere."

I glanced around, wondering if we'd had an audience. But we weren't in view of the front doors, and it didn't seem like anyone had been watching. I just hoped wherever Brynn was getting ready didn't have a window out on this part of the grounds. Obviously we'd have to tell her what had happened, but I really didn't want her to have seen that go down.

"Bro, I'm sorry," Cooper said. "Damn it, it's your wedding day."

"I don't accept your apology," I said, and he blinked at me. "You have nothing to be sorry for. That asshole doesn't have anything to do with you."

I almost couldn't believe that piece of crap had actually hit Cooper. His own son. Any shred of respect I'd had for him burned away to ash.

"You were never a stray," Cooper said, his voice vehement. "No one saw you that way. Actually, I think my mom liked you better than me because you always hung up your towels and you never left your dirty dishes out."

"That's true, I was a much better son. You still leave your towels everywhere, and you basically never clean up your dishes. You're a fucking disaster."

He smiled. "Fuck you."

"Fuck you, too."

We stepped in for another hug, holding each other tight, then doing the customary guy back-clap. Cooper moved, and I felt something against my hip. Something sort of... long and... stiff.

What the hell?

I pulled away. "Jesus, Cooper. Please tell me you have a banana in your pocket or something."

"Oh, yeah." He pulled an actual banana out of his pants pocket. "In case I got hungry later. Why, did you think I'd get a boner for you? You're a sexy beast, bro, but I don't swing that way. Sadly, you're going to have to make do with my sister. She's no Cooper Miles, but she's okay, I guess."

"Yeah, she's a little more than okay."

I realized the photographer was still here. He'd moved well away from us and now stood awkwardly watching.

"Sorry, man," I called over to him. "We can get back to pictures in a second."

He raised a hand to acknowledge he'd heard me. "Take your time."

Roland and Leo came back, Leo brushing dirt and grass off his suit.

"Dude, Leo, remind me not to get on your bad side," I said.

Leo straightened his jacket. "Just make her happy and we'll be cool."

I grinned at him. "Oh, I make her very happy."

Cooper groaned. "Chase, no."

"Too soon?" I asked.

"Yeah, always is too soon." He held up my tie. "Oh shit, this was your tie. I got blood all over it."

One of his eyes was already starting to blacken and Leo still had grass in his hair. My tie was bloodied, and our wedding was starting soon. I was in big fucking trouble.

"Oh my god, is everyone okay?"

I turned at the sound of Brynn's voice and suddenly nothing else mattered.

She was beautiful waking up in the morning, with messy hair, blinking the sleep from her eyes. Beautiful when she had her hair up in a ponytail and sat leaning over a book to study. Whether or not she wore makeup, no matter how she was dressed, my girl was always fucking beautiful.

But now? She was a vision.

Her hair drifted in curls around her face and a wispy veil bordered with lace hung down her back. And her dress. Fuck. Her strapless white gown hugged every curve before flaring just below her hips. The skirt was wide at the bottom, fluttering slightly in the breeze.

I stood, staring at her, utterly frozen. I'd never seen anything so beautiful in my entire life. My chest felt tight and the enormity of this moment hit me. Almost knocked me on my ass. This girl—sweet, wonderful Brynn Miles—was mine.

She could have done anything after I'd kissed her that day. Smacked me. Told me off. Avoided me. But she hadn't done any of those things. She'd chosen me. Moment after moment, day after day, no matter what had threatened to keep us apart, she'd chosen me.

I wasn't remotely worthy of her—of that kind of love and trust—but I was going to work my ass off for the rest of my life to try to be.

Cooper pushed past me. "Hold up, jackass, I get the first hug."

"What happened?" she asked. "You're hurt."

"Don't worry about it. It doesn't matter now." He gently hugged her, clearly being careful of her dress and hair. He said something quietly in her ear that I couldn't make out, but her eyes glistened with tears and she bit her lip.

"Stop it, jerk, I'm going to mess up my makeup." She laughed softly, dabbing her eyes.

There were probably other people around. I had the vague notion that the girls had come out with Brynn—Zoe, Grace, and Shannon. Maybe Ben was here, too. I didn't really notice. Brynn shone so bright, nothing else existed.

Just her. Just us.

I stepped closer, slowly, watching her like she was a

mythical creature, bound to disappear if I moved too fast. There were sparkles and lace and gauzy white. Bright blue eyes and red lips against porcelain skin. She was so beautiful, I could barely breathe.

"Hi," I said, completely awed.

"Hi," she said. "Ben told us Dad was here. Are you sure you're all right?"

"Yeah. He's gone. My tie, though. Cooper... I don't know. I kind of can't think right now because you're so stunning. I'm not even sure this is real."

Her lips parted in a smile and she rested her hand on my chest. "It's real."

"I love you." I couldn't think of anything else to say.

"I love you too." She slipped her hands around my waist and looked up at me. "You ready to get married?"

This really was happening. I was marrying Brynn.

"Yeah, baby. I'm ready."

THIRTY-FOUR

BRYNN

THE SMELL of bacon wafted out from Mom's kitchen, making my stomach rumble. I sipped my coffee and snuggled against Chase. He'd scooted my chair right next to his, like he didn't want there to be any space between us. His lips pressed to my head and I breathed in the moment. Sitting at my mom's dining table, surrounded by my family, my husband's arm around me. I was tired—we hadn't slept much last night—but I couldn't imagine a better start to our first full day as a married couple.

The amazing morning sex earlier hadn't been bad, either.

I hadn't realized getting married would change us as much as it already had. Everything felt different. I felt closer to him. The vows we'd exchanged yesterday had taken root deep inside me, binding me to Chase. It had been more than a contract—more than a ceremony. It had been a life-altering experience. One that I'd never forget.

We were leaving for our honeymoon tomorrow—a trip to Victoria, British Columbia. Neither of us had ever been, and we were excited to explore a new place together.

Although, the suite in our hotel had a huge bed and a jacuzzi tub—I honestly wasn't sure if we were going to leave our room all week.

"I think I can eat bacon," Zoe said, her voice bright. She sniffed a few times. "Yeah, it smells good. Oh my god, I haven't been able to eat bacon in months."

Roland rubbed her back. "You sure? I can run out and get soup if you want."

She rested her hand on her belly—which seemed to have grown overnight. "No, I think I can almost eat like a normal person again. Figures I'd have to be almost nine months pregnant before that happened."

"I'm so glad you're feeling better," I said. "You look amazing."

Zoe smiled. "I look vaguely like a beached whale, but thanks."

Roland gently touched her face. "Are you kidding me? You're a goddamn goddess."

"Yeah, one of those fertility goddesses," she said, rubbing her belly.

He was right—Zoe did look beautiful. And she'd looked incredible last night. After the almost-disaster that was our dresses, they'd come in, and Zoe's had fit perfectly.

In fact, everything about our wedding had gone perfectly. Even my dad's surprise appearance hadn't ruined it. The ceremony had been beautiful. Chase had teared up a little during our vows. So had Cooper, but I'd pretended not to notice.

The reception had been amazing. It had started off mellow, with appetizers and guests sipping wine. By midnight, everyone was tipsy, my mom and Ben were mixing cocktails like a couple of mad scientists, the music had been blaring, and inhibitions gone. Our family and friends had danced, drank, devoured what was left of the food and cake, and partied until we were all about to drop from exhaustion.

Chase and I had gone to our room over at the Lodge—the hotel adjacent to Salishan—and caught our second wind. If I'd thought sex with Chase had been amazing before, newlywed sex was on another level. He'd destroyed me last night—more than once. I was still achy and tired, but in all the best ways.

Mom had invited us all to brunch, but it was turning into lunch, given how tired we all were. It was well past noon. Even my mom had slept in this morning, which was unheard of for her.

Leo sat at the end of the table, his hair covering the scarred half of his face. He'd come in a few minutes ago and sat without saying a word to anyone. He hadn't been at the reception very long last night, but I hadn't expected him to stay. He didn't like being around large groups of people.

I was a little surprised he'd come to brunch. He looked as tired as the rest of us, even though he'd left the wedding early. I had the feeling that despite being kind of grouchy with people, he was lonely. It gave me a twinge of guilt for not trying harder to spend time with him. I could see that he was struggling, even if he always insisted he was fine.

Cooper leaned his back against Chase on his other side, sandwiching Chase between us. He had his hat pulled down over his eyes, like he was taking a nap at the table. Chase didn't seem to mind; he understood Cooper better than anyone, so a random guy cuddle at the table was probably normal to him. Things were going to be different for the three of us, now that Chase and I were married. But I hoped they both knew there was still plenty of room for their friendship.

Someone knocked on the door. I glanced up from my coffee, but Roland answered it. A second later, Ben came in. You'd never have guessed he was up late partying with us last night. He always looked a little rugged—that was just him—but he appeared perfectly rested, his eyes bright.

"Hey, Ben," I said.

He smiled, and if he'd been wearing a hat, I think he would have tipped it. "Morning, Sprout. Boys. Zoe."

My mom appeared in the kitchen doorway wearing a pink apron with cupcakes all over it. Her hair was pulled back and she was drying her hands on a white towel. "Oh good, I'm glad you came by. Brunch is almost ready. Although I guess it's lunch now. I think we're all dragging a little today."

Ben smiled at her and I don't think any of us missed the look in his eyes. "Are you sure there's enough for one more? I don't want to impose."

"Don't be silly," she said, waving her hand. "I don't know how to cook for less than a dozen. And I told you last night you should come. I meant it."

"At least let me come help." He followed her into the kitchen.

I heard her insisting that she had everything under control—the same thing she'd told each and every one of us when we got here and tried to help—but Ben wasn't swayed by her protests. A few minutes later, they brought out food on large platters, setting it all in the middle of the table.

"Thank you so much, Mom," I said. "This is amazing."

"I'm glad you two came over," she said. "I wasn't sure if you'd want to get out of bed today."

Chase coughed, covering his mouth, and I felt my cheeks warm.

Cooper sat up, groaning. "Mom. No."

"What?" Mom asked. "We were all up so late last night. They must be exhausted."

"Yeah, I'm sure that's why they'd be in bed." Cooper adjusted his hat. "Gross."

Mom smiled and rolled her eyes. "Okay, there's that too. But they are newlyweds. What's wrong with—"

"Stop talking now Mom please oh my god I can't with this right now I'm kind of hung over and this is way too much can we just eat in peace without references to anything my baby sister does in bed thank you very much."

"Don't forget to breathe, honey," Mom said.

We piled our plates with food. Mom had outdone herself. Crepes, sliced fruit, eggs, toast, bacon. She offered mimosas, but none of us were in the mood for more alcohol yet.

Chase's leg rested against mine and every so often, he leaned over to kiss my temple. I felt all warm and gooey inside and I couldn't stop smiling.

After being completely silent since the moment he walked in, Leo finally spoke up. "Are we going to keep pretending it didn't happen, or are we going to talk about it?"

Chase squeezed my thigh under the table—a silent gesture of reassurance.

Mom put her fork down and wiped her hands on a cloth napkin. "No, we do need to talk about it. I let it go yesterday because of the wedding. But I need to know why he was here."

"Hang on." Roland got up and came back to the table with a manila envelope. "He brought this."

"What is it?" Mom asked.

"It's a counter to your divorce settlement offer," Roland said. "And it isn't good."

Mom let out a long breath. "What does he want?"

"The winery," Roland said.

The table erupted with voices. Cooper flew out of his seat, shouting obscenities. Leo stared at Roland, his mouth open. Chase gripped my leg and Ben pressed his hands into the table, his eyes cold steel.

"Okay, okay," Mom said over the din, gesturing for everyone to quiet down. She waited, casting a glare at Cooper until he stopped ranting. "What are my options?"

"Our options," Leo said. "You're not in this by yourself."

She tipped her head to him. "Our options, then. What do we do?"

"I already sent copies to the lawyers, so they'll be able to advise us," Roland said. "I don't know if he has any chance of getting what he wants, but that's not the biggest problem. The first thing the court will do is order mediation. If Dad doesn't bend on this, we'll have to go to trial. That's going to be both expensive and exhausting."

Mom straightened her shoulders. "Is there a chance the court would give him what he's asking for?"

"I want to say no, but he was Salishan's CEO for a long time," he said. "The documents make the argument that if you could have taken over the business from your parents, they wouldn't have put him in charge. He basically says you weren't capable of running it then, and aren't capable now. And he claims years of hardship and missed opportunities because he spent his entire career here, which he only did so you could pursue your passion. It's basically the same argument people make when one spouse works while the other goes to college. They gave up opportunities to support the other in their career, and are therefore entitled to more of the assets."

"That asshole," Mom muttered. "He hated this place. Why is he trying to take it?"

"This is bullshit," Cooper said. His black eye seemed more noticeable now, considering it was Dad who'd given it to him. "He can't do this. No fucking way am I letting him take our land. I'll fucking gut that son of a bitch."

"Calm your ass down, Cooper," Leo said. "You're not helping."

"I thought for sure he'd take our offer," Roland said. "But given what he did yesterday, I guess I shouldn't be surprised."

"He doesn't just want the money," Mom said. "He wants to hurt me. That's the only explanation."

Cooper had retreated away from the table. He stood with his arms crossed, a look of pure hatred on his face. The only person in the room whose rage might have rivaled Coop's was Ben. He stayed quiet, but anger poured off him in waves.

"Where is he getting the money for all this?" Mom asked. "His lawyer can't be free. I'm surprised he's not trying harder to settle. Like you said, going to court will cost us both a fortune."

"She has a lot of assets," Leo said, and there was no mistaking by his tone who he meant by *she*. Dad's mistress. "I think we can assume she's bankrolling this."

"But why?" Mom asked.

"This land is worth a lot of money," Roland said. "If someone subdivided it, they could make a killing. He's probably promising her they'll retire off the money he makes."

"But he can't possibly take *everything*," Mom said.

"No, but if he takes this to trial, he can convince the court the property is worth more than we're saying it is in our settlement offer," Roland said. "Then we'd be forced to sell and divide up the proceeds according to the court's instructions. He wants this to go to trial because he thinks he'll wind up with more money that way."

I listened to Roland's explanation with a growing sense of horror in the pit of my stomach. How could my dad do this to us? My great-grandparents had built this place. My mom had grown up here. They'd raised the four of us in this very house. How could someone be so horrible?

Chase put his arm around my shoulders and pulled me closer. I hated being so helpless, but his steady presence helped.

"Listen, I'll talk to the lawyers in the morning," Roland said, adopting his take-charge voice. "This isn't ideal, but we'll figure it out."

"We're not selling the fucking land," Cooper said from the other room.

Leo caught my eye. He looked like he was about to panic. Oh god. If we had to sell, it would mean Leo would have to leave. And he hadn't left Salishan property in years.

Without another word, Leo got up and walked out the front door.

"Oh no," Mom said.

"I'll go talk to him," Ben said, standing.

Mom reached out and touched Ben's arm. "Thank you."

"He'll be fine," Ben said, his tone soft and soothing. "Don't worry."

Ben left, and a tense silence settled over the table.

"Sorry, Brynn," Roland said. "I didn't mean to ruin brunch."

"It's not your fault. This is all on Dad. I don't know why I let the things he does surprise me at this point."

Cooper came back to the table and piled his plate with

more food. "Seriously, screw that guy. He's not ruining my breakfast."

We went back to our meal, although I was too full to eat any more. The food was making me sleepy and I found myself leaning against Chase's arm, almost nodding off. Everyone else chatted over the last of their brunch and coffee. Mom turned the conversation to the impending arrival of her first grandbaby and the mood in the room improved significantly.

After a while, everyone finished and got up to go their separate ways. Chase and I had already checked out of our hotel, so we went to the Blackberry cottage. We still had to pack for our honeymoon, but all I wanted to do was crawl back in bed and take a nap.

So that's exactly what we did.

We took our clothes off, just to feel each other's skin, and settled in bed beneath the soft sheets and fluffy comforter. I knew this mess with my dad was likely to get worse before it got better, and the idea of losing the winery was horrifying. But tangled up in Chase's arms, feeling the rise and fall of his chest as he breathed, I let it go.

Chase and I were embarking on a new life together. It had been a bit of a whirlwind since that first time he'd kissed me. But I had no doubts. I'd found love young, but that didn't make it wrong, or less real. I felt nothing but gratitude that we'd not only found each other, but had the courage to stick together, even when things were tough.

Life was going to throw more challenges our way. That was just the way it worked. But together, Chase and I could face anything. I loved him with everything I had, and the miracle of it all was, he loved me just as much.

And there was nothing better, or more important, than that.

EPILOGUE

CHASE

IT DIDN'T MATTER how often I kissed my wife, I never got enough. I traced my lips along hers, enjoying their softness. My tongue darted out and brushed the velvety tip of hers. She tasted sweet and minty and delicious.

I nudged her onto her back and she giggled into my mouth. Our new couch was bigger than the old one—softer, too. Cooper was still pouting about getting rid of the old one, but I'd been on Brynn's side. The old couch was kinda gross. This one was much more comfortable, and it was still great for making out.

"God, why?" Cooper asked.

I heard the fridge open and he let out a dramatic groan. Brynn and I both laughed.

"Stop making out on the new furniture," he said from the kitchen. "Or anywhere I might see you. It's disgusting. I'm having regrets about our living arrangements."

"You're full of shit."

"Of course I am, but do you have to be grinding into my sister every time I come out of my bedroom?"

I moved off Brynn and helped her sit up. Instead of

living in one of the cottages over at Salishan—Brynn's mom had offered—we'd decided to room with Cooper for a while. It had been Brynn's idea. She was worried her brother would be lonely without me.

She had a theory about why he'd gone so crazy over the two of us dating. He'd been hurting at the thought of losing his best friend and needed some help making the transition from being one of two single dudes partying it up all the time, to being the friend of a married man.

She'd definitely been onto something. We'd brought up the idea with Cooper after we got back from our honeymoon and he'd lit up like a Christmas tree. He whined about having to see us make out all the time, but beneath his complaints, I could tell he was glad we were still here.

And overall, it worked. We had enough space for three. Plus, we were all busy. Cooper and I both worked full time, and sometimes on weekends. Brynn wasn't in school again until fall, but she was busy working the tasting room at Salishan and helping with events. Zoe was so close to having her baby, she needed the extra help.

Plus, Brynn worked part-time in my shop. She was a freaking genius at accounting and kept everything well organized. I loved having her there. In fact, I'd started trying to arrange my schedule so I'd be in the shop on the afternoons she was there, rather than working in the field. Any excuse to be close to her.

She leaned against me and tucked her legs up on the couch. I wrapped my arm around her and pulled her close. God, I loved this woman. Being married to her was the greatest thing ever. It had only been a few weeks, but I woke up every morning so fucking grateful that she was mine.

Cooper wandered out of the kitchen, shirtless in a pair

of gray sweats. His hair was a mess and I caught sight of something along his ribcage.

"Dude, what happened to you?"

"What?"

I pointed to his side. "You have a bandage or something. Did you get hurt? That looks serious."

"I do?" He raised his arm and tried to look at his ribs. "What the hell?"

"You don't know what that is?"

"No." He tugged on it and winced. "I got a little drunk last night, but I don't remember getting hurt. This does kind of burn, though."

"Here, let me get it."

I got up to help. The bandage was roughly square with tape along all four sides. I figured the best thing to do was rip it off fast, so I pulled one edge free and yanked hard.

"Ow! Fuck!"

"Holy shit," Brynn said.

I stared at Cooper. "Dude, is that real?"

"Is what real?" He lifted his arm, trying to look.

He had a tattoo along his rib cage, beneath his arm. A tattoo of a unicorn.

"Did you get a tattoo?" I asked.

"Did I?" He kept his arm up and turned, trying to get a better view. But the result was a lot like a dog chasing its tail. He kept turning in circles. "Holy shit, I did."

I tried not to laugh, but it was pretty fucking funny. He'd gotten a white unicorn with a multicolored mane and tail—mostly turquoise, pink, and purple.

"Oh my god, you got so drunk you got a unicorn tattoo?" Brynn asked.

"Now I remember," he said. "Yeah, I met this girl and

she was a tattoo artist. She told me she wanted to do some ink, so I let her."

Brynn stared at him, open-mouthed. "You asked for a unicorn?"

I couldn't tell if Cooper was about to freak out or not. He kept lifting his arm, trying to get a good look at it. Finally, we went into the bathroom.

"Dude!" He came out a second later, a huge smile on his face. "This is fucking awesome. This is the best tattoo I've ever seen. She wasn't entirely sober either, and she did an amazing job. Do you see the shading in the tail?"

I moved to take a closer look. "Yeah bro, it's actually really good."

"It's a unicorn," Brynn said. "With a lot of pink."

"I know," Cooper said, his eyes huge. "Fucking sweet."

She shook her head and laughed. "Only you could pull that off, Coop."

"I know, right?"

Her phone dinged, so she picked it up off the table and swiped the screen. "Ooh, our wedding pictures!"

"I wanna see." Cooper practically jumped onto the couch. "Fuck, ouch. I need to be careful of this thing. It's tender."

I sat down next to her and watched as she swiped through the online gallery. I couldn't keep the enormous grin off my face. Our wedding day had been the best day of my life. Or one of them, at least. It was hard to choose. The first time I'd kissed Brynn was up there. So was the first time we'd slept together. Getting engaged. Our trip to Victoria. Basically every day with Brynn was the best. But our wedding had been amazing.

I touched her hand so she'd pause on one of her, standing in the garden, her veil fluttering in the breeze. "I want this one for my desk at the shop. Look at you. So beautiful."

She nudged me with her arm. "Thanks."

Cooper bounced his leg, shaking the whole floor. "Keep going."

The pictures were gorgeous. Not that it was hard when the photographer had such a beautiful subject. And I'd looked pretty great, too.

She got to one of us with her brothers. We were all outside with the Big House in the background. It was impossible to ignore Cooper's blackening eye, and Leo still had some grass in his hair from wrestling their dad to the ground. I was wearing Cooper's tie, since I'd handed him mine to wipe up the blood.

"Jesus, we were a mess," I said.

Brynn tilted her head. "I know, but I think this picture is my favorite."

"Why?"

"Because of what it means. You stood up to him for me, and for Mom. And my brothers stood up for you. So yeah, Cooper and Leo look a little rumpled, your tie is crooked, and Roland kind of looks like he wants to strangle someone. But what I'll always remember about this moment is how good I felt, knowing that even though my dad was an epic asshole, the rest of you were amazing—for me, and for each other."

"Damn it, Brynn." Cooper stood, sniffing. "I'm not tearing up, you are."

I was feeling a little choked up, too. She was right. The way her brothers had stood up for me, and allowed me to stand with them, meant everything to me.

How many times had I wished I was a Miles? Now I

was one. It might not be my last name, but I was one of them just the same.

Of course, maybe I always had been. I just hadn't realized it.

"What are you guys doing today?" Cooper asked. He was back in the kitchen, poking through the fridge again.

Brynn winked at me. "I plan to climb Chase like a tree all day."

He poked his head out long enough to roll his eyes. "Whatever. Zoe's coming over, so take it to the bedroom. Pregnant lady gets dibs on the couch."

"Why is Zoe coming over?" I asked.

"She's pregnant, dumbass."

"I know she's pregnant, dick. What does that have to do with anything?"

He came out again, eating straight from a to-go container of fried rice. "Roland has to go help Gracie with something out in Tilikum. So I'm Zoe-sitting."

"Dude, don't say that where she can hear you," I said. "She'll murder your face."

Cooper grinned. "Yeah, probably. But Roland doesn't want her to be alone, so I'm hanging out with her today. Which is fucking sweet because Zoe-bowie is my girl."

"Why doesn't she go to Mom's?" Brynn asked.

Cooper stuck his fork into what was left of the fried rice and scowled at her. "What are you implying? That I can't Zoe-sit a pregnant woman? That Mom has superior skills in this area? I think not."

"No, I didn't mean that. I just wondered—"

"Silence, little demon-sister. I'm going to take excellent care of Zoe today."

"I'm sure you will," Brynn said. "But she's so close to

having the baby, and obviously Roland doesn't want her alone in case she goes into labor. So—"

"I have it covered," he said. "Trust me. I've been watching tons of YouTube videos."

"Videos about what?" Brynn asked. "God, Cooper, she'll have the baby in a hospital, even if she goes into labor while Roland is gone."

"I know I'm not *delivering* the baby," Cooper said. "But I know all about being a labor support person and stuff. Lamaze breathing. Meditation and visualization. Timing contractions. Cervical dilation. Potential medical interventions and their pros and cons. I've got this shit on lockdown."

"Bro, if I was having a baby, I'd totally want you as my labor support person," I said.

Cooper smiled and went back to his rice. "Thanks, man."

Brynn looked back and forth between the two of us.

"What?" I asked.

"Nothing."

"Actually, as much as I'd love to be here to hang with Zoe, I have something else planned for us today."

"Can't, dude, I already told you I'm chillin' with Z-Miles," Cooper said.

"I meant planned for me and Brynn," I said. "That thing we talked about?"

Cooper's eyes widened. "Oh, right. Awesome. Don't worry, dude, I haven't said a word."

"Thanks, bro."

Brynn slid her hand into mine. "What do you have planned?"

I winked at her. "You'll see."

AN HOUR LATER, we were dressed and on the road. Brynn didn't ask questions when I went straight to Salishan. I drove out past the Big House and the guest cottages, then kept going down a side road that wound along a creek that cut through the property.

I parked on the edge of an open expanse of land that they didn't use for anything. Yet.

"What are we doing out here?" she asked.

"Looking at our house."

"Our house? I don't understand."

The field was level, but behind it, the land rose in a sharp incline up the side of the closest peak. Tall pine trees covered the hill, with just a few spots of exposed gray rock. The higher mountains beyond rose into the clear blue sky. It was beautiful out here.

"I talked to your mom after we got home from Victoria. Long story short, she offered us a parcel of Salishan land to build a house of our own."

She gasped, covering her mouth. "Oh, Chase. Are you serious?"

"Yeah. Although if we decide to do it, we'll have to wait until her divorce is finalized. Considering the shit your dad is trying to pull, this might not end up happening. But she wanted us to know that if it's in her power to make this work, and if it's what we want, we can build here."

"This is what you want? You want to live here?"

"Shit yeah, I want to live here," I said. "Are you kidding? I grew up on this land. Maybe it wasn't mine the way it was yours, but I love this place. I can't imagine anywhere else I'd rather be. But if you want some space, or want to go live somewhere else, I won't hold you back. I'll follow you anywhere, if that's what you want."

She took a shaky breath and swiped beneath her eyes. "This is my dream, Chase. This was what I was dreaming about when I wrote *Brynn Reilly* in my diary. I used to imagine that we lived here, at Salishan. We were married and built our own house and got a dog."

I put my arm around her shoulders and hugged her close. "Awesome. What kind of dog should we get?"

"How about a sweet rescue dog who needs love," she said.

"I love our dog already."

She laughed, leaning into me. "Why are you so amazing?"

"I don't know." I shrugged. "I'm not, really. I just love you."

"You keep making all my dreams come true."

I kissed her head. "Do any of those dreams involve me going down on you in my truck? Because I'd be more than happy to make that dream come true right now."

Grabbing my hand, she laughed, tugging me toward my truck. "It's what I've always wanted."

She was what I'd always wanted. I hadn't always known it. She'd been right there in front of me for most of my life. But once I'd opened my eyes and truly saw her for the amazing, beautiful woman she was, I'd been hooked. She'd taken my heart, but I never wanted it back. It was hers. And I was going to spend the rest of my life cherishing her. Loving her. Taking care of her and making her happy in any way I could. Because she was my family. My love. My life.

Because she was mine.

AFTERWORD

Dear Reader,

Whether you went into this book knowing Chase was the hero, or you found out when you opened to chapter one, I sure hope it met your expectations.

I knew that Chase would fall head over heels for Brynn way back when I started planning the series. They've known each other their whole lives, but Chase always kept Brynn off his radar. She'd crushed on him for years, and really, who could blame her.

And when they finally did come together, it was fireworks and magic and all sorts of awesome things.

This was an interesting book to write because the conflict was more external than internal. Once Chase realized he wanted to be with Brynn, there was no hesitation. Even with his history of keeping relationships short and casual, Brynn changed everything. And she'd spent her entire life loving him from afar. It didn't take much for the two of them to realize they were made for each other.

So it wasn't a case of either character pushing back, or

needing time, or living in denial. They fit together like two pieces of a puzzle, and they both knew it.

Brynn's family, however, wasn't quite so excited. Especially Cooper. And there we have the source of most of the conflict and tension.

What I loved about writing this book was incorporating not just a romance, but Chase and Cooper's bromance. Their friendship faces its first big test in this book. Up to this point, they've always gotten along fine. They were living their lives, both happy with things as they were.

Enter Brynn, and not only does Cooper have to cope with his BFF having a very serious girlfriend, that girl is his baby sister.

It's no wonder Coop had a rough time. He was struggling with a lot of change, coming at him from multiple directions.

But in the end, love, and bromance, wins the day. And now we have the goofball boys finding a new path for their friendship. One that includes Brynn in an entirely new way.

I hope you enjoyed Brynn and Chase's story! There is definitely more to come from the Miles Family. Cooper's story is up next!

Thanks for reading!

CK

ACKNOWLEDGMENTS

Reviews are a great way to help other readers discover new books and authors. Thanks to everyone who's read and reviewed **Forbidden Miles**. I appreciate it so much!

Thank you so much to everyone on Team CK. Elayne for cleaning up the manuscript and making sure it's all polished and shiny. To Cassy for creating another gorgeous cover.

To my beta readers, Nikki and Jodi, for helping me make this book the best it can be. Your feedback was amazing as usual.

A special shout out to Nikki for pushing me to write the book the way I did. Yes, you were right. I'll admit it.

To David for your ideas, support, and love. And for inspiring you know who.

To my author friends for being amazing and always having my back. I love your faces!

Last, but most definitely not least, to my readers for continuing to read my books and support this crazy thing I do. I love you all so much.

ALSO BY CLAIRE KINGSLEY

For a full and up-to-date listing of Claire Kingsley books visit www.clairekingsleybooks.com/books/

For comprehensive reading order, visit www. clairekingsleybooks.com/reading-order/

How the Grump Saved Christmas (Elias and Isabelle)

A stand-alone, small-town Christmas romance

The Bailey Brothers

Steamy, small-town family series. Five unruly brothers. Epic pranks. A quirky, feuding town. Big HEAs. (Best read in order)

Protecting You (Asher and Grace part 1)

Fighting for Us (Asher and Grace part 2)

Unraveling Him (Evan and Fiona)

Rushing In (Gavin and Skylar)

Chasing Her Fire (Logan and Cara)

Rewriting the Stars (Levi and Annika)

The Miles Family

Sexy, sweet, funny, and heartfelt family series. Messy family.
Epic bromance. Super romantic. (Best read in order)

Broken Miles (Roland and Zoe)

Forbidden Miles (Brynn and Chase)

Reckless Miles (Cooper and Amelia)

Hidden Miles (Leo and Hannah)

Gaining Miles: A Miles Family Novella (Ben and Shannon)

Dirty Martini Running Club

Sexy, fun stand-alone romantic comedies with huge... hearts.

Everly Dalton's Dating Disasters (Everly, Hazel, and Nora)

Faking Ms. Right (Everly and Shepherd)

Falling for My Enemy (Hazel and Corban)

Marrying Mr. Wrong (Sophie and Cox)

Flirting with Forever (Nora and Dex)

Bluewater Billionaires

Hot, stand-alone romantic comedies. Lady billionaire BFFs and
the badass heroes who love them.

The Mogul and the Muscle (Cameron and Jude)

The Price of Scandal, Wild Open Hearts, and Crazy for
Loving You

More Bluewater Billionaire shared-world stand-alone romantic
comedies by Lucy Score, Kathryn Nolan, and Pippa Grant

Bootleg Springs

by Claire Kingsley and Lucy Score

Hot and hilarious small-town romcom series with a dash of mystery and suspense. (Best read in order)

Whiskey Chaser (Scarlett and Devlin)

Sidecar Crush (Jameson and Leah Mae)

Moonshine Kiss (Bowie and Cassidy)

Bourbon Bliss (June and George)

Gin Fling (Jonah and Shelby)

Highball Rush (Gibson and I can't tell you)

Book Boyfriends

Hot, stand-alone romcoms that will make you laugh and make you swoon.

Book Boyfriend (Alex and Mia)

Cocky Roommate (Weston and Kendra)

Hot Single Dad (Caleb and Linnea)

Finding Ivy (William and Ivy)

A unique contemporary romance with a hint of mystery.

His Heart (Sebastian and Brooke)

A poignant and emotionally intense story about grief, loss, and the transcendent power of love.

The Always Series

Smoking hot, dirty talking bad boys with some angsty intensity.

Always Have (Braxton and Kylie)

Always Will (Selene and Ronan)

Always Ever After (Braxton and Kylie)

The Jetty Beach Series

Sexy small-town romance series with swoony heroes, romantic HEAs, and lots of big feels.

Behind His Eyes (Ryan and Nicole)

One Crazy Week (Melissa and Jackson)

Messy Perfect Love (Cody and Clover)

Operation Get Her Back (Hunter and Emma)

Weekend Fling (Finn and Juliet)

Good Girl Next Door (Lucas and Becca)

The Path to You (Gabriel and Sadie)

ABOUT THE AUTHOR

Claire Kingsley is a #1 Amazon bestselling author of sexy, heartfelt contemporary romance and romantic comedies. She writes sassy, quirky heroines, swoony heroes who love their women hard, panty-melting sexytimes, romantic happily ever afters, and all the big feels.

She can't imagine life without coffee, her Kindle, and the sexy heroes who inhabit her imagination. She lives in the inland Pacific Northwest with her three kids.

www.clairekingsleybooks.com

Made in the USA
Las Vegas, NV
12 October 2023

78984275R00194